MURDER In TAHOE
(CASINO STYLE)

David Hannuksela

Mystery Book Publishers Inc.
Bellevue, Washington

Visit our Web Site at . . .
www.murder-mystery.com/books

Mystery Book Publishers Inc.
P.O. Box 52761
Bellevue, WA. 98015-2761

Printed in the United States of America

*Dedicated to my mother.
Her strength and character has
provided me an example my entire life.*

Acknowledgments

For additional insights into the Gaming industry...
Neil Brooks (Controller, Hyatt Lake Tahoe),
the real Steve Berkich (Chief of Security, Hyatt Lake Tahoe, Retired)
& Paul Marazzo (Casino Manager, Hyatt Lake Tahoe, Retired)

For insights into the world of a Medical Examiner... Kim Duddy

For converting my scribblings back to standard English...
Don Soreng, Sydney Ranney & Mary Enges-Maas

For literary advise... Karen Lowe & Mike Reed

For a great job of final editing... Nora Steen.

For technical support... Don Soreng (Database) & Brad Decker (Web Page).

For being there when all this came together...
Rob Mayo, Wally Chin & Derrick Eng.

Cast of Notable Characters

Paul Mannerheim
Controller and watchdog of Aaron Davenport's successful hotel/casino, located at Lake Tahoe, Nevada.

Sam Logan
Casino Manager with power to grant his own dreams and willing to run over anyone in his way.

Susie Parsons
Personnel Director with an appetite for power and wealth. Good looks were merely an asset to be used.

Aaron Davenport
Owner of one of the more profitable casinos in Nevada. Too old, too tired, and looking to settle up the loose ends of his life.

Thomas Elliott
Attorney with drive, ability and financing needed to fulfill his ambition to take control of Aaroní's empire.

Steve Berkich
Chief of Security, ex-cop. Renewed by a sense of the chase, but worried about the knife he may find in his back.

Matt Hamilton
Private Investigator hired by Paul Mannerheim to find answers to unanswered questions.

Vic Welles
Casino Host and Southern playboy. Beneath a friendly image lies a hidden agenda.

Scott Sherman
Con artist and opportunist looking for a career change in the changes coming out of the casino.

Randall Yarbrough
Wealthy wheeler dealer looking for opportunities.

Carl Desmond
President of company, and son-in-law of Aaron Davenport. Enjoys the trappings, office and title that came with marriage.

Robert Danbury
Lieutenant with Douglas County Sheriff's Department. A hunter on the trail of his most difficult opponent.

Willie Grant
The victim. Missed by no one.

CHAPTER 1

Thursday, November 24
Thanksgiving Day
Lake Tahoe, Nevada side
4:15 p.m.

Willie stopped his car at a wide bend along State Highway 28, running along the Nevada side of Lake Tahoe, ten miles south of Incline Village. Not wanting to keep his more important partners waiting, Willie arrived fifteen minutes early. As an unintended benefit, this also provided him with extra time to enjoy the evening's sunset. Willie seldom bothered to take the time to notice the beauty of the area, mainly because he was not usually awake during daylight hours. Now that he was almost forced to observe it, the beauty amazed him.

As happened during this time of the year, the weather was a mixture of rain and snow. At night it snowed, during the day it mostly rained. Soon it would be solid snow. The local ski resorts, unhappy with the light layer of snow, were proclaiming a dismal season. They wanted to be in full operation by the Thanksgiving weekend. However, the temperatures at night were dipping a little below freezing, which encouraged the ski resorts stay open with the help of artificial snow-making machines. After the rain this afternoon, there were just crusty patches of snow huddled in the shadows beneath the trees.

Most of the trees in the area were evergreens and reached up well past one hundred feet. The once golden aspens now stood stark and bare. Since last month, Nevada had switched back from daylight-savings time and the nights seemed to arrive very quickly, accompanied by the cool evening air. Like a child, Willie forced his warm breath out in short bursts to observe how it mixed with the crisp mountain air.

Willie gazed down at the pristine magnificence of Lake Tahoe. The lake was one of the largest and cleanest alpine lakes in the world. It was twelve miles at its widest point, and twenty-two miles long. The so-called experts estimated the average depth at almost a thousand feet. Willie could only appreciate the top few feet, but that was enough for him. It was clear and beautiful. The basin originated from glacier activity, and even now, the always chilly water temperature convinced many swimmers little had changed since the last Ice Age.

The panoramic vista matched Willie's outlook, both were filled with clear and bright details. Willie Grant was an unassuming little man, only because his life reflected his achievements. Even among his criminal peers, he was considered a bit player. A ninth-grade dropout, he mentally "tuned out" of the system several grades before that. From then on, his numerous, but minor contacts with the law, consisting mainly of impulse crimes involving little if any planning. He engaged in burglaries and picked a few pockets when things were going well; vagrancy and panhandling when things were not. Purse snatching might have been included in the official files — if not for the fact that he was fast on his feet. That agility did not extend to his mental capacity. The many bosses he encountered during his short-lived spans of employment only represented unreasonable restrictions on his freedom. Discipline was definitely not part of his vocabulary. His long-term vision of the future only extended to his outlook on the next roll of the dice. Willie was single and always had been. While Willie never chose to roll the marriage dice, it did not keep him from fathering two children during his life, but they were as unaware of him as he was of them.

A poet once expressed the thought that sometime in each person's life one manages to stand in the sun and enjoy, briefly, what fortune might have granted from the beginning. Andy Warhol expressed it as every individual's "fifteen minutes of fame." Whatever it was called, Willie's time was at hand. How appropriate that today was Thanksgiving, for he was indeed grateful. "Finally, life would be different." In Willie's world, money was the cure all other shortcomings. Now he was involved with people who could bring him all the money he needed to be among the "respected and admired". The work was easy, and rewards were vast. Another few weeks and he would be enjoying the best the world had to offer! Like a snake shedding his skin, Willie's life would start anew... leaving the old Willie Grant behind in a crumpled heap.

Tonight, like several other nights in the past, he waited for an update from his partners regarding the next phase of the plan. Most of Willie's time was spent scrambling for enough money to buy his next beer, cover his next run at the crap table or pay just enough of the back rent on his trailer to persuade the owner from throwing him out. But now the future looked bright. He used this new-found opportunity to pay some of his more immediate irritations. For Willie, life looked as awe inspiring as the sunset hanging over the rim of the California side of the basin, casting a glow on the upper tree line and its mirrored reflection on the lake. After almost two years of living here, Willie wondered why he had never noticed nature's beauty. He was touched by her gentle embrace.

It was one of the few moments in Willie's life when he felt at peace with man and nature. The moment was short-lived. Suddenly, Willie felt something in the center of his back. The dirt on Willie's grubby overcoat failed to slow the speed of the projectile as it moved through his body. Within a fraction of a second it became an enormous pressure, followed by extreme pain exploding out from his whole body. Willie's confusion ended abruptly, as he started to fall forward, staring at the muddy ground. Before his face hit the muck, the last of his brain activity stopped and Willie Grant went to face a God who would hopefully be more merciful toward him than his fellow man. Brief as it was, life rewarded Willie one last image of the most peaceful and picturesque view he had ever witnessed. He was spared the sight of his murderer.

*

Friday, November 25
11:50 a.m.

Danbury was one of two lieutenants employed by the Douglas Country Sheriff's Department. Above him were a younger captain and an even-younger Sheriff. While he had no desire to rise above his current position, it was not from lack of ambition, but more a case of an abundance of sanity. Sheriff was an elected position, and that came with too much baggage for normal people to endure. He had also seen too many captains come and go, depending on the temperament of the various sheriffs. Danbury felt high up enough in the department to enjoy a certain amount of independence, but not too high to worry about losing his head once every four years. Each night, he went home to his wife and four children with a combination of job security and job enjoyment. To be exact, only one of his children still lived at home, and in another two years she would be off to college. Danbury felt he enjoyed the best of both worlds; a secure position in the Sheriff's department and a stable family life in the best part of the USA. He did not relish the idea of his mandatory retirement in another seven years.

Lt. Danbury felt a little out of his element. According to the Douglas County Sheriff's Department duty roster, Lt. Robert Danbury was assigned the role of departmental detective. A position he felt ill suited for when it came to this type of murder case. Douglas County was basically a rural area. Besides the normal family disputes, almost all its serious crime involved acts of passion or petty greed. Crimes that involved little if any intricate planning. Only impulsive anger, a second of satisfaction, followed by months or years of consequences. But this case was different. Not a crime of panic here;. It was clearly premeditated.

3

Lt. Danbury went over the facts as he knew them.

The killer apparently lured the victim to this quiet location, shot him at close range in the back and buried the body under some mud, rocks and leaves. He or she then took the time to drive Willie's car into Reno, and leave the vehicle at an airport garage. The killer believed the car would be towed to the impound lot and labeled as abandoned. The owner of the vehicle, ignored by the police on the assumption he just took a flight out of town and left his worthless car behind. Six months later, the car would be sold for a hundred dollars at public auction. But, the perfect crime always centered on "ifs".

If an early morning hiker had left his dog at home, the body might never had been discovered. Even at that, it was a thousand-to-one shot that the body was discovered so soon after the murder. If the killer's plan had gone as scheduled, the warm temperatures that arrive with summer would have accelerated the decomposition of the body. Leaving behind only a pile of decaying bones; yielding not much more than teeth and hair samples, assuming it was ever found at all. It was a better plan than just dumping the body in Lake Tahoe, where it might have been preserved indefinitely in the frigid waters.

The crime scene yielded little in the way of clues. Due to a light amount of early morning rain, and a few degrees of higher-than-normal temperature, the ground was slightly soft. Fortunately, the ground was still hard enough to make digging a deeper grave a very difficult chore for the murderer. If the crime had been committed one week later, a layer of new snow would have blanketed the area until late spring. Lt. Danbury had dental stone casts made of the twelve different shoe prints found near the body. Eight of the prints were made by backpacker boots, and the remaining four by street shoes. Despite some basic training on how to behave at a crime scene, it was already obvious that the vast majority of prints were made by his own curious deputies. The body was found thirty feet down the slope from one of the many scenic turn-offs used by tourists as they stopped to enjoy the view of the lake without causing major accidents. The recently paved wide spot in the road yielded no tire markings and little more than some candy wrappers and other road-side litter.

An extensive search failed to locate the shell casing. If the murder weapon was a revolver, the shell casing remained in the weapon and departed with the murderer. The more likely scenario... the weapon was an automatic, which was more widely used, and ejected the empty casing. It occurred to Danbury that one of his deputies might have stepped on it, unintentionally burying it under a half inch of mud. He would have a deputy go over the area with a metal detector, but in all likelihood, the shell casing left with the murderer.

After the photographs were taken, the body was transported down to the Washoe County morgue for an autopsy. The first step in Danbury's investigation was to send an impression of the victim's fingerprints down the mountain to the new Automated Fingerprint Identification System, recently purchased by the Reno Police Department. Within an hour of their arrival, the prints were compared to the million of fingerprints that made up the computer's massive database, leading to a matching computerized image appearing on the monitor. The victim turned out to be a local. His name was William, a.k.a. Willie, Grant. The name generated a quick cross-reference of motor vehicle registration records which provided the needed information that ended in the successful search for the victim's vehicle. The airport and bus station were always the obvious and first locations checked by the Reno police.

For Danbury, the case's single saving grace was the victim. Even an initial background check revealed no one would create a stir if this case was ever solved. A cursory page-two comment in the local papers, with no follow-up, would suffice for what seemed a minor murder case. It should have been on page one but that would have been bad for tourism. No one would pressure him for a daily progress report. The easy route for him was to rationalize this loss of life as a long-term saving to society, but he was not in the habit of walking away from a challenge. And he was not about to start with this crime.

There were more knowledgeable policemen serving their communities, but Lt. Danbury did have his share of advantages. He had a strong sense of curiosity balanced by tenacity. If this murder went unsolved, it would not be for lack of effort on his part. If aware, Willie would have been flattered by the concern for him after his death. By dying, he achieved what he lacked in life - notoriety.

Even though Reno was located in Washoe County, Danbury had already contacted the Reno Police Department and asked for their assistance. Lt. Danbury was now on his way to their lab to see what secrets Willie's car might reveal to him about its registered owner, or last occupant. As Danbury's car negotiated the winding road down the mountains, he thought to himself, "The desk sergeant could handle the missing-hiker reports."

CHAPTER 2

Six weeks earlier.
Thursday, October 13
1:45 p.m.

Every now and again Paul Mannerheim pondered his unique environment. The casino business was not only uncommon, but sometimes unbelievable. It was the only business, besides oil, where you could make money despite a lack of constant striving for a better "product." The right setting and a more pleasing environment were the keys to its success. The setting was especially pivotal. As any real estate agent can tell you, it boiled down to... *"location, location, location!"*. Throw in a little marketing and a whole lot of money, and you are in business. Most of the management never bothered obtaining some kind of higher education. Understanding the human weakness for greed was the primary requirement for steady employment. It was like a drug dealer understanding his clients' physical needs. Casinos totally understand their clients' psychological needs and just offer the opportunity to fulfill them.

It was the standard Thursday luncheon for the management team of one of the largest hotel/casinos in the Tahoe basin, owned by Aaron Davenport. Twelve individuals were seated comfortably around the mahogany table, enjoying a lunch that, for most, would also carry them though the evening without the need for dinner. Paul Mannerheim enjoyed the meal, but considered the time spent to be more political than informative. The trivial was usually elevated to the centerpiece of controversy. This particular day they were discussing the color of the carpet in the hotel lobby. Last week they debated the closing hours of one of the restaurants. About the only time they ever examined anything relating to a normal company was during the review of the monthly financial statements. If it was a good month, the casino executives managed to take credit for some small point they claimed caused the increase. If it was a bad month, they managed to blame to weather.

Sometimes there was cause to blame the weather. Tahoe was a haven of beauty. But for that beauty - the mountains and its skiing, the lake and its boating - you paid a price. Lake level was a consistent 6,225 feet above sea level, and at that elevation the weather was a lot more unforgiving than most tourists are willing to accept. Every year some visiting Boy Scout troop, dressed in shorts, would go hiking in late September and get caught in an unexpected snow storm.

Mannerheim always carried an overnight bag in the trunk of his car in case he had to spend a few snowy nights at the hotel. He did not mind. Even though he got tired of eating hotel food, it was better than his home-styled condo cooking.

As Controller, Paul Mannerheim was one of the three people around the table who was not related to the owner by blood, marriage or a background of thirty years. His training as a CPA equipped him well to be responsible for the financial aspects of the company. His experience in Vietnam shrewdly equipped him well to deal with the back stabbing environment of casino life, but he still carried a few mental scars from his introduction into this "industry."

The other two outsiders were Susie Parsons, the Personnel Director, and Thomas Elliott, the corporate attorney. Technically, Tom was not part of the company. Aaron brought Elliott in last summer to negotiate with Tahoe's one and only food servers' union. The union agreement was settled almost two months ago, yet he still seemed to find cause to walk the halls and stay on retainer.

As usual, Aaron was absent from the management luncheon. Mannerheim did not blame him. Paul felt if he owned this place, he would not inflict this boredom on himself either. Not when there were places like Palm Springs for golf in the winter, Alaska for fishing during the fall and Hawaii for the other times of the year. Aaron probably knew the place ran better in his absence anyway.

Financially, Aaron Davenport had lead a truly blessed life. He bought a magnificent piece of property in south Lake Tahoe when land prices were not much higher than the value of the timber growing on it. Davenport started a small truck stop with ten slot machines and a lone twenty-one table. Twenty years later, he had to beat the tourists away with a stick. Another twenty years later, he was still amazed when he thought about his two thousand employees and his fourteen-story hotel/casino. For obvious reason, no casino in the world had ever built a thirteen-floor building, for obvious reasons. Every year, he was still surprised when Mannerheim informed him of the year-end net income. More or less, the place netted a cool ten million a year, after taxes. Aaron had the option to employ five hundred less people, adopt some twentieth-century management practices, and net an additional ten million, but he never exercised that option. Mannerheim went to the wall enough on the inefficiency question to know that Aaron was comfortable with this pace of progress. Besides, any increase in the bottom line would not increase the quality of wine on Aaron's dinner table. Mannerheim resigned himself to the fact that it was Aaron's toy; let him play with it the way he wanted to. Besides, any substantial increase to the bottom line would not be reflected in Mannerheim's annual salary. For Paul, it was better to sit back, enjoy less pressure, a cleaner desk and more leisure time. Besides, efficiency was not all it was cracked up to be, the only thing that mattered was the bottom line. Barring relocating the casino to Death Valley, Mannerheim saw no dark clouds on the financial horizon. The property was debt-free. In fact, Mannerheim's main financial problem was investing all of Aaron's surplus funds.

The major difference between Aaron Davenport's hotel/casino and the vast majority of Nevada's other casinos was Aaron himself. One of the last of an old breed of individual owners. Bill Harrah, Pappy Smith and all the other gaming pioneers were long gone from Northern Nevada. Even if their heirs desired to pick up the torch and carry on their tradition, it was not to be. They were all forced to sell out in order to pay the huge amounts of inheritance taxes. The heirs were replaced by faceless corporate structures, Harvard business school graduates, computer printouts and efficiency experts. And so it would be when Aaron dies. As long as he could still draw a breath, Aaron would run his hotel/casino based on his own instincts, desires, loyalties and dreams. He was a dinosaur. One of the last of an old breed of individual owners.

More efficient casinos operated in Nevada, but few had as favorable a location. As Las Vegas was consuming larger tracts of desert for ever more massive hotel/casinos, Tahoe's casinos were restricted to the area they currently occupied. The militant environmentalists worked tirelessly to assure no additional casinos were built and those already built, remained at their present sizes. Ironically, in addition to the environmentalists, the other big winners were the handful of already existing casinos. With no threat of additional competition, they prospered all the way to the bank. And there laid Aaron's key advantage. It overcame many of Aaron's mistakes in judgments. Above all, the bottom line hides a multitude of sins.

Mannerheim maintained a corporate philosophy. This evolved into a set of survival rules. Rule # 3 was one of the most important, and stated, *"Always work for a profitable company, as opposed to one that is losing money."* Mannerheim realized that if you worked for an unprofitable company you have a lot of heat focused on you all the time. You end up working twice as hard and end up looking half as good, as compared to a profitable company. Aaron's casino was tailor-made for Rule #3. Mannerheim seldom worked past five o'clock.

Unfortunately, Aaron's private life had offset his public life. Two years earlier, his wife and only daughter died in an auto accident. Rumor was... that the daughter was driving and had consumed a little too much toddy for the body. The local paper took a page from the casino script and blamed black ice. Now, the only family left for Aaron, in his old age, was Carl Desmond, a son-in-law he never really cared for, and a brat of a grandson named Adam. Mannerheim always thought if Adam were not fifteen, he would qualify as the poster child for Planned Parenthood. It was commonly agreed that they would need divine assistance when the kid got old enough to play in his grandfather's sandbox. Carl Desmond, Adam and a minor bunch of impatient heirs were just waiting to fulfill their greed. They eyed each of Aaron's birthdays with the same enthusiasm a Republican President eyed the next birthday of an 84 year-old liberal on the Supreme Court.

Carl Desmond, as the President and ceremonial head of the company, was in charge if Aaron Davenport, the Chairman of the Board was absence. If Carl could have arrange it, he would not have been there either. He was far more comfortable at the head of the table of the local Rotary, or the Limit Growth Action Committee, or any one of a dozen other groups where he could show off his expensive suits and flash his title. Being the "President" of the area's largest employer granted him a large degree of importance around town. Mannerheim was told at the outset it was a good idea not to try to out-dress Carl. Desmond was a vain fifty, and still kept a close eye on the cocktail waitresses. In order to keep peace in the "family," the Food and Beverage Director, Len Goodrich, knowing the lay of the land, made sure there were always several willing gold diggers employed on his beverage staff. During every Thursday's luncheon, Carl felt uncomfortable because he was under the assumption everyone was expecting him to lead the discussion (an assumption not shared by anyone else around the table).

Susie Parsons was in the middle of her presentation on problems relating to sexual harassment. While quoting some personnel magazine about the need for group role playing in order to bring this problem into focus, she made the mistake of pausing to emphasize a point. Suddenly Sam Logan spoke up.

"Are we about done?"

The real power present had spoken. Sometimes Mannerheim thought Sam Logan, the Casino Manager, only tolerated the rest of them because he needed the food and rooms for "his" casino. Whenever possible, he managed to keep direct discussion down to a bare minimum. Logan did not considered himself part of the management team sitting around the table. His view of management was rather a narrow pyramid, with himself and Aaron sharing the upper elevation and the remaining hirelings jockeying for the lesser positions. Because he did not want to engage in much discussion with the IRS and Nevada's Gaming Control Board agents, Logan tolerated Mannerheim in order to keep those necessary evils under control.

Sam Logan was in his late fifties. As it was once described to Mannerheim, Logan's ancestry was part-English, part-Norwegian and part-Rottweiler. Mannerheim initially thought Logan had only three suits... all dark, all three-piece. Later, he figured out Logan's closet was full of well-tailored suits but they were all just limited to basic drab. Logan had also been in the casino industry for over thirty years. Mannerheim willingly acknowledge Sam's savvy in the casino business. Logan managed to survive, even thrive, in a cut-throat business. Over the years, his enemies tried but failed to pull the "old goat" from his throne. But, with the complete loyalty of Aaron, nobody even tried anymore.

Logan also made no attempt to hide his dislike for lawyers or Personnel Directors. As far as the former was concerned, Mannerheim was in basic agreement, but for the latter, he had seen other Personnel Directors and found no problem with Susie. She knew her job, was less pushy than most, and the fact that she was easy to look at did not hurt the mix. Unfortunately for Susie, the fact that women now had something approaching "equal rights" was news to the majority of males working in most Nevada casinos. If a survey was taken, the concept would doubtless be lacking in the preponderance of the world's casinos. It was a real old boy's club, and the women they harass were not the type to file a grievance.

Like clockwork, Carl Desmond responded, "I agree. That will about wrap things up for this week. I want to thank Lenny and his department for providing the great meal we all enjoyed today." Mannerheim always assumed it would be a great meal when it constituted in ninety percent of your job-approval rating. Len smiled and thanked Desmond. Mannerheim was just happy nobody reviewed his debits and credits like they reviewed Len's wines and deserts. When it came to food, *everyone's* an expert.

CHAPTER 3

Mannerheim was impatient to get moving. As usual, the Thursday meeting took its normal two-and-a-half hours, and the Gaming Control Board auditors were waiting down the hall from his office. By now, they probably had a few questions about somebody's unreadable initials on a long-forgotten fill slip. Mannerheim kept a small sign on his office wall with the quote, "*Auditors come in after the battle and kill the wounded.*" But, despite their bother, Mannerheim actually enjoyed their biannual visits. They allowed him the opportunity for normal conversation. It was also a chance to have someone competent - and someone interested enough - to appreciate his work.

Besides Gaming Control Board auditors, Mannerheim had to deal with IRS auditors, room tax auditors, sales tax auditors, internal auditors, independent outside auditors... just to name a few. Two months ago, he went through an IRS audit. During the review, their main focus centered on the casino dealers and the food and beverage revenue.

Back in the mid-seventies all casino dealers had a good thing going. They worked for minimum wage, but that just provided them pocket money. Their real income came from superstitious players who lavished numerous tips, or in casino jargon, "tokes," upon the dealers. All in the vain hope that it could somehow influence the outcome of the next hand. These attempts to alter destiny provided the average dealer with at least a hundred dollars in tokes per shift. None of these "tokes" ever found their way onto any 1040s as declared income.

All would have continued unchanged had it not been for one little requirement by the casino. If they let each dealer pocket his or her own tokes, then nobody would want to work the graveyard shift, due to the low activity and the resulting low tokes generated from the wee hours of the morning. Nor would any dealer want to work roulette, or that old carnival game, The Big Wheel, due to the older-grandma clientele who played those games. However, every dealer lusted after the high-roller, high-limit crap game and, preferably, on a busy-weekend swing shift, which would generate the maximum amount of tokes for the individual dealer. In order to maintain some control over their dealers' work schedule, the casinos were forced to require all tokes be collected, pooled and divided equally among the dealers on a weekly basis. A rotating team of dealers collected, counted and divided the take. In this way, nobody cared what shift or what game they were assigned, or when their vacation was taken, or how friendly they were, because they would all receive an equal share of the take at the end of the week. A unique form of communism flourished within the casino.

The IRS was somehow notified and arrived at the doorstep of the casinos. They quickly came to the conclusion that it was a great system. After the IRS subpoenaed the dealers' toke sheets they were especially happy to see how the system was so well-documented. Based upon the IRS's findings, each dealer was hit with a bill for back taxes, plus interest and penalties. The dealers were then introduced to the nation's revenue laws, and collectively threw up. They even hired lawyers to fight it. The lawyers were elated to take the dealer's money, even though they knew it was a hopeless case.

Meanwhile, based upon their delight with finding all this new found tax revenue, the IRS applied the same principal to the tips of the nation's waitresses and bartenders. With them, tax revenue was based on a percentage of the total sales generated. This forced all companies serving food and drinks to keep track of all sales by individual server, creating a massive bookkeeping chore in order to provide this source of revenue for the government. As usual, the IRS's new procedure neglected to compensate the various businesses involved for this service.

And, once again, the food server analysis, and a review of the dealers toke sheets, were the main purposes of the IRS's recent visit. Mannerheim was relieved to see the departure of the IRS auditors and, by comparison, almost happy to see the arrival of the Gaming Control Board auditors. The Gaming Control Board auditors were less combative and not as obnoxious by IRS standards.

*

The field workers of the Gaming Control Board were composed more of accountants than bureaucrats. They reminded Mannerheim of his days in public accounting. Their main purpose was to insure the image of gangsters running the casinos was not rooted in fact. The Gaming Control Board not only audited casinos, but was responsible for granting gaming licenses to people who wanted to own a casino. Before granting approval, they would investigate the background and money of the individual to insure both were legitimate. Besides owners, the Board licensed all casino management. Mannerheim even had to be investigated and licensed. And what the state giveth, the state can taketh away. In order to determine if they wanted to taketh away, they came in and audited the place for anything not conforming to their numerous rules and regulations.

In the early history of Vegas the underworld did build and generally control the state. But nowadays, there was too much public disclosure to suit their taste. Major corporations discovered the huge profits that were possible from legalized sin. Now, MGM, Hyatt, Hilton, Holiday Inn, among many others, all own casinos. Despite this reality, some of Mannerheim's old college roommates still thought he must know half the mob. After the fourth time of trying to explain to them that even they could go out and buy shares of stock in most of the companies owning casinos in Nevada, he gave up and decided to play on their illusion. It made him a colorful character whenever they all got together for a reunion. These reunions initially took place when they each married. Now as each appeared to be on his second time around, the future seemed to guarantee a steady round of reunions.

Jeff Meyers was the "in-charge" of the three-man audit team from the Gaming Control Board. Typically, they would spend anywhere from two to three months auditing a major casino. During this period, they reviewed the internal control procedures, flowcharted the accounting systems, as well as their usual checks for fraud. They were in Week Three, Day Two of their review.

"Good afternoon, Jeff.", announced Mannerheim, as he turned the corner to one of the two offices he arranged for them to occupy during their stay. Paper and boxes were scattered around the floor without regard for the poor clerks who had to put everything back together again when the audit came to an end. Mannerheim could already visualize the requests for overtime.

"Good afternoon, yourself. What's the matter, bored with your little meetings? Decide you want to engage in a little work for a change?"

"Unfair! Playing corporate politics is more work, and more risk, than you government employees can imagine."

Joking aside, Mannerheim was right in that regard. Corporate politics were a basic part of his job survival. Because most casino operations were built on individual loyalty they incurred a high rate of turnover depending on who's in charge from day to day. Mannerheim knew that one day or another he would be on the wrong side of Sam Logan, or someone like him. The odds that he would receive a gold watch in twenty years from this, or any other, casino were remote. He did not dwell on the topic because he knew his resume would be marketable when the time came.

"Got any questions or complaints, or should I go retreat to my own office?"

"Of course. As always, we have both. First, your gal didn't drop off that box of marker payments we wanted."

Paul sighed. The problem solver in him enjoyed the analytical aspect of accounting, but disliked the clerical aspect, which was one of the most bothersome features of accounting. Fortunately he was now in the position to delegate that chore, at least as long as the delegated employee did their job.

"We have a couple of people out with the flu this week. But it's no problem. We just finished the monthly financials. I can spring someone loose to help Florence gather them up for you. Got anything more *technical?*"

"Yes. We've noticed a significant increase in your Marker Receivables. Up 156% as compared to this quarter last year. Got anything I could put in my notes to explain the upswing?"

A "marker," in casino jargon, represented an IOU signed by the player and served as evidence of credit extended by the casino. Any player may apply for credit, much as anyone would with a credit card company or a bank. The player's creditworthiness was evidenced by his prior experience with that or other casinos around the state. The player must also provide enough details to confirm a favorable financial status. The word "receivable" was an accounting term and just indicated the credit was not yet been paid back.

Paul paused a moment before answering. Auditors are under the gun from their superiors to complete their work within certain time restraints. That being the case, they usually accept most plausible answers to their questions, but it still had to be plausible.

"Just the fact that we have had some rotten players in recently."
Mannerheim just drew that observation out of the air. He knew Meyers could not determine the validity of the statement, and it had the benefit of sounding reasonable.

"So instead of them taking *our* money with them when they leave, they have been leaving *their* markers with us instead. That's one reason we manage to make a profit, which in turn lets us pay those nice gaming revenue taxes, which in turn allows the State of Nevada to pay your salaries, which in turn provides you the opportunity to ask those questions."

"The house must have had a rotten run of luck last year in order to look so good this year." Meyers uttered the remark as he scribbled the comment into his notes, silent evidence that he accepted the logic of the explanation.

"That's why they call it gambling. It does have its ups and downs."

*

Walking back to his office, Mannerheim reflected on the answer he had just given Meyers. Even though the state could analyze the total activity, reflected in the drop box count, and compare it to the net hold (win), they had no way of knowing how any individual player might have done. Even the casino personnel could only give the Casino Shift Manager an approximate estimate of how any specific player fared. You needed someone to follow a player around, look over his shoulder, figure out how much he passes off to his wife or girlfriend, or just tokes the dealer, before you could determine an exact win/loss figure to the house. All that aside, Mannerheim knew of no major players in the place over the last several months. There were no junkets by the Casino Host either. To run up the marker balance to that extent, there should have been one or another. It was a slow time of year, as usual. The weather was too cold for swimming or other lake activities, and the snowfall was too light for skiers to hit the slopes. Meyers was right. He better get back to attending to business between all these useless meetings.

Mannerheim's afternoon was more productive than his morning. He checked in with his office manager, Dorothy. She informed him there were no real fires to be put out. A brief discussion with Richard Fitzgerald, his Chief Accountant, revealed no technical problems confusing the bookkeepers that he, or the other two accountants could not straighten out. Fitz did his usual complaining about all the time it took to answer those silly questions from the Gaming Control Board auditors.

Mannerheim managed well over a hundred employees throughout various departments. He spent most of his time dealing with the accounting department, but also managed data processing, credit collection, timekeepers, the "cage" on the casino floor, as well as the "soft" and "hard" count teams. "Soft count" referred to the team which counted the currency from the drop boxes attached to the casino tables. Those boxes were collected after every shift from each of the fifty-six table games on the casino floor. "Hard count" referred to the team which counted coins from the six hundred and forty-five slot machines, which were emptied during the early mornings each Monday, Wednesday and Saturday. Those were his primary responsibilities, but not his principal activities. Due to the time consumed with "corporate politics," he had to put his trust in Dorothy, Fitz and his various department heads to keep the day-to-day problems under control.

Telephone calls were down to a level slightly less than normal. As always, calls came from people who had a problem, caused a problem, or just needed

17

something. At 4:45 a friendly call came in, passed along by Paul's' new secretary, through the intercom.

"Mr. Mannerheim, it's Steve Berkich on line two."

As with most new secretaries, Betty was still formal with her boss. Despite his previous comments, it would take more time to get Betty to drop the Mister title.

"Thanks Betty." As he reached for the phone.

"Steve, how's our local crime fighter doing?"

"Paul, how many times do I have to tell you? Being Chief of Security is more public relations than crime."

Steve Berkich was an ex-cop, now in charge of the Security Department. Despite his detective background, he recognized the change in occupation was more than a change in just his title. Most of the time his department dealt with people who were drunk and obnoxious, but they mostly were customers and not criminals. And when you dealt with customers you can-not be "badge-heavy." For that reason, Berkich learned over the years to hire non-cops who were trainable, instead of ex-cops who were too pushy, set in their ways and overly concerned with being in control.

Mannerheim developed his own unique brand of humor. Unfortunately it was not totally appreciated by most people. Berkich was one of the few that actually enjoyed Paul's humor, even when he was the willing target, for he knew Paul expected him to respond with his own jabs.

"I heard a report that someone was going to steal the casino carpet, but your security people were sleeping on it."

"Anymore talk like that, and you're going to be the one to buy the beer."

In fact, neither needed to worry about who bought the drinks. Mannerheim's ability to sign for complimentary drinks, food and even hotel rooms far exceeded those of the Chief of Security, but both had "comp" privileges to spare.

Paul was quick to accept the hint.

"I could use a beer. See you in the Lakeview Room in about half an hour."

Mannerheim was a man with few roots. His youth was spent moving around six Western states, as required by his father's work in construction. That, plus a three-year stint in the Army, resulted in Mannerheim inability to establish a stable trend of consistent residency in any one place. For the next four-year period after the Army his movements decreased, only because of the time it took to complete college. College was followed by his public accounting experience, and its required sixty-hour work weeks, which consumed another few years.

These achievements made for much activity but not much of a social life. In the end, his family solely consisted of a younger brother who lived in Arizona. Both parents had passed away.

Mannerheim had a couple of previous employers in the Tahoe Basin, while building his resume as a Controller, and managed a collective total of seven years in the same residence, which was a personal best. Each passing day increased that record. Mannerheim now enjoyed the idea of settling down, working less on his career and more on the enjoyable aspects of life. Hotel/ casinos were well suited to the goal of enjoyment. This was the main reason he migrated to Tahoe, instead of an accounting position with IBM or Ford.

Aside from some college roommates and some CPAs Mannerheim worked with in his past, hotel/casinos also served him as a setting for building friendships. Steve Berkich was one of the better examples.

CHAPTER 4

At 5:15 Mannerheim stepped out of the elevator on the top floor of the hotel and headed for the Lakeview Room. "Room" being another name for bar. The lounge shared one-third of the floor's available space, while the remaining area housed one of their gourmet restaurants. Steve Berkich was already seated at one of the window tables. Mannerheim and Berkich were friends based on the fact they shared several common traits, not the least of which was punctuality. Both also held a common dislike for the political nature of upper levels of management. Even though Mannerheim was more involved in that aspect, Berkich did not associate Mannerheim with most of the political animals in the company. He respected Paul mainly because he never saw Mannerheim compromise his position, no matter who he was dealing with. That trait, Mannerheim acknowledged, was certain to result in his being employed at a variety of establishments over his ensuing career. Mannerheim thought Berkich led a far more interesting life than his own daily menu of meetings and paperwork. Their bond of friendship was strengthened even further by their common military serve in Vietnam, and the fact their ages where only a year apart.

Steve was enjoying the last bit of daylight as the sun's rays bounced off the lake. Mannerheim approached the table while Berkich used his reflection from the window to comb his thinning hair. Not missing the chance to throw another jab, Paul was the first to comment.

"I don't understand why you waste your money buying a comb with so many extra teeth."

"A real comedian, but I suggest you don't give up your day job to try out as a lounge act. Knowing what an impatient drunk you are, I ordered your usual. The gal should be back anytime."

"I appreciate that."

Even though Berkich was grateful his position usually insulated him from the cut throat environment that dominated the corporate structure, he was still curious about current events in management's continuing soap opera.

"How's things on the second floor? Aaron show up for the weekly lunch?"

"No, he's in Alaska this week. Kodiak Island, to be exact. Probably chasing some poor bear around the woods. He should be checking in again sometime next month."

Based upon Aaron's prior history, Berkich's surprise might have been greater if the old boy was around.

"He should just try to talk the bear into a friendly game of craps for its coat. Besides, he's getting too old to do something as crazy as beating the brush for a new rug."

"I'll be sure to tell him about your concern for his old age and poor health. Sure be glad when he does check in. I want him to call this pest from New Orleans and tell him he's still not interested in selling the place."

Mannerheim's remark was in reference to a wheeler-dealer from New Orleans named Randall Yarbrough. For the last two months, Yarbrough's sole purpose was to pressure Aaron into selling the operation to his consortium. Initially, he called Aaron's high-paid, low-worked secretary. She, however, quickly passed the call off to Mannerheim after hearing Yarbrough mention he wanted to make a "financial" proposal. She figured it had something to do with money, so in Aaron's absence, it was the Controller's responsibility to take care of it. Mannerheim informed him it was a family-run operation and the family probably was not interested in selling. This fact was confirmed by Aaron while he was still in Palm Springs. Not willing to accept a little sales resistance, the guy just would not take "no" for an answer. Believing money can buy anything, he kept coming up with different offers every couple weeks.

"At least you have to admire his tenacity."

"I guess. Wish I had what he spends on phone calls."

Hoping to get a rise out of Paul, Berkich suddenly changed the subject.

"Say, how's the beautiful Susie Parsons. Did she monopolize your attention during the noon banquet?"

"Oh, she was there in all her splendor."

Berkich continued his pursuit.

"I'm at a loss as to your reluctance in making a serious move on her."

"The problem lies in her goals. The curse of ambition to be exact. It has made her mind too conniving to waste on thoughts of romance, her beauty too much of an asset to waste on idle pursuits of love and her vision too narrow to waste on me."

Berkich was not totally sympathetic with the obstacles standing in the way of the desired goal. "There goes the poet in you, confusing sex with romance."

"Yeah, Steve, spoken like a man with two divorces in his past. But, if you must know, I made a move on her last winter when I took her to the bathtub races on the slopes over at Incline Village. She was polite, formal, friendly, but firm when she informed me that her priorities centered around a future corner office and a *high* six-digit income. Dirty dishes, dirty diapers and in-laws are not part of that vision. Any serious relationship would be an impediment to her career. Her ambition burns within her and provides all the warmth she needs."

Berkich became philosophical.

"If that's the case, she sure picked the wrong industry. Doesn't she know the casino industry is not like any other? The Neanderthals in the pit will eventually be her undoing."

"Oh, she knows how the terrain is arranged down there. She's convinced that even casinos will catch up to the twentieth century and embrace equality and the women's movement. She wants to be the one waiting in the wings when it arrives."

"That's like waiting for the next ice age. So this is what it has come down to, you two are just *friends?*"

"Even being her friend is like playing craps. She counts her friends like a banker counts his assets. To be used when the time comes. It's like a pilot fish swimming next to the mouth of a shark. A good team today, maybe lunch tomorrow."

Berkich took a sip from his drink before he replied.

"I get so choked up over these tender love stories."

"Say, to change the subject, how's the trial going? You get our ex-dealer convicted yet?"

Berkich pondered a moment, figuring out the best way to express his problem.

"Not yet. The legal system is like watching a glacier move. Which is mighty slow going. It may take forever to get that snake convicted. The judge announced today he's going on vacation for the next two weeks. I've made three trips to that courthouse and ended up just warming a seat in the gallery. The defense attorney is a new kid, fresh out of law school and is approaching the case like it's going to make or break his career. Reminds me of some of the reasons I gave up being a cop."

"Steve, I thought it would be open and shut. You've got the video tape from the "eye-in-the-sky." That should be enough right there."

Berkich shook his head.

"You'd think so. But his lawyer is claiming his client was just an *innocent* victim of a clever card mechanic, and not his partner in crime. Even though the tape clearly shows the player sitting at the dealer's table, sitting at the *first* seat to the dealer's left. The District Attorney explained the dealer simply waited for an ace to be dealt to his partner's hand. As we know, that's the position where the dealer deals his first card out. He palmed it and threw it back to him as the first card of the next round of play. Because it's also the *last* hand he collects at the end of the round, he had it available to toss back each and every time. The tape does show the player getting that *same* ace hand after hand. The District Attorney explained all that to the jury."

Paul was mystified. "So what's the problem?"

"It's plural, there are problems. First, he explained to the jury the advantage this ace provides the player. That, if the player could count on an ace in each hand, he would get twenty-one over *thirty* percent of the time when it's matched with a ten, jack, queen or king. If he gets an eight or a nine he's got a nineteen or twenty. So almost half the time he's got a pat hand. Even if he gets a rotten card, like a four or five he could still take two additional cards before exceeding twenty-one and going bust. The district attorney even had to explain to half the jury an ace counts as *either* a one or an eleven toward twenty-one. You'd think a jury in Nevada would know that. Schools better start teaching math again. But in the end, we could not state, with any amount of certainty, how much the dealer and his missing partner cost us with their sham."

Paul had to agree, even though it seemed like a minor complication.

"True, we can't document the exact amount. We think it was in the thousands, but we know it was several hundred dollars, so doesn't that automatically make it a felony? So what difference does the exact amount make?"

Based on Berkich's previous experience as policeman, he understood legal procedures, even if he did not appreciate the system. He went on to explain the system to his friend, who valued common sense above legal technicalities.

"Only to the jury. The defense attorney claims it was a one-shot scam by the player, who acted solo and ripped us off for just a few hands, and a minor amount. Claims the player was the one who switched cards during the hands. The defense attorney is trying to convince the jury the missing player was some kind of magician. It didn't help the damn tape wasn't in *perfect* focus. All in all, it appears to be leaving some doubt in the minds of the jurors."

Before continuing, Berkich took another gulp of beer.

"Oh, I wish we managed to catch the player, the dealer's partner. The guy bolted through the crowds as soon as he saw us coming. The only thing I've got is a printout from the surveillance tape to recognize the guy. If we could turn him, it could make the case solid against the dealer."

There was still a question in Paul's mind to what he considered the obvious.

"I'm confused. You had an eye witness sitting at the table. Didn't Helen's

24

testimony count for anything?"

"Yeah, Helen was great, but the defense attorney harped on the fact she is old, gray and hard of hearing. I almost came out of my chair."

Berkich was referring to Helen Enges, a seventy-four-year-old retired bookkeeper. Her social security did not quite make ends meet, so she took her numbers ability and went into semi-retirement as a card counter on the blackjack tables. Roughly, twenty years ago someone first published a book on "card counting" while playing twenty-one. If you managed to keep track of the cards already played, then you had an advantage in determining the probability of the remaining cards appearing. If there was a large number of low cards left in the deck, it was safe to take a "hit," or another card. The reverse was true when a large number of high-count cards remained in the deck. This author's work spawned ten similar books. Each author claimed to be forbidden from playing in every casino in the State of Nevada due to his great ability at card counting. Many clubs in the state panicked and started shuffling the cards after every deal. Finally, they realized that only one in every hundred counters had the ability to keep track of the deck with any degree of accuracy to make any money. The other ninety-nine were going broke trying to recoup the price of the book. The clubs figured out they were losing a fortune... Not because of the card counters, but because shuffling all the time slowed down the game and their resulting revenue. As an alternative, casinos went to a card container called a "shoe" that held six decks, instead of the single deck, in order to give the counters more to think about.

Helen was one out of a hundred blessed with the ability to keep track of the previously played cards in order to determine the mix remaining in the shoe and altered her bets accordingly. But she was not greedy and just worked the tables to supplement her social security. Because her bets were relatively small in comparison with high-rollers, she also did not draw much attention from the pit bosses.

One night three months ago, she was playing the tables and noticed the same ace repeatedly ending up in the hands of the adjacent player. She reported it to a security guard, who introduced her to Berkich. Normally the "eye in the sky" should have caught it, but in this casino the human "eye" behind the lens looks through his camera to the floor below and dwells on dealers' procedures. Procedures like... how many times the dealers shuffle the cards (acceptable number is 3 to 5 times), or if they talked too much with a friendly player. Those easy-to-find procedural errors seemed to come before concern for dealer honesty.

That, and the fact that they were independent of security, always irritated Berkich. The resulting arrest of the dealer made security look good, the pit look bad and the "eye in the sky" personnel look like clowns. Ever since the incident Berkich had befriended Helen by giving her meals, compliments of the Security Department, and turning a blind eye to her abilities as a card counter.

"So what's your next step?" Paul asked.

"According to the District Attorney, we... make that me... has to try and locate the missing player and get him to implicate the dealer as his partner. It's either that or the miserable little slimeball will probably walk, free-and-clear."

Paul wanted to finish the topic with some encouragement.

"Well, I trust you will save the day. Say, maybe you can even save my day. I've got a question for you. Between your many breaks, you spend a fair amount of time walking the casino floor down there. Have you noticed a lot of high rollers walking in off the street over the last few months?"

Steve gave it some thought before replying.

"Nothing that would draw a crowd. Why do you ask?"

"Oh, just the Gaming Control Board auditor commented about a sharp increase in recent marker activity. And to be honest, I don't remember any big players or high-roller junkets coming in that could explain the increase."

Berkich was quick to give a nod of agreement.

"There hasn't been. But wait a minute! That reminds me. Helen did mention something I was going to tell you about."

Paul grinned at his friend.

"You ought to put her on your payroll. She will discover more sitting at a blackjack table during a couple hours than half your security department does all year just walking around. So what's new with Helen?"

"She reported something strange. She claims she saw a player receive a large marker, play a single hand, move to another table and get another marker, and then just leave. Claims she witnessed this several times on several different nights."

Paul's focus zeroed in on that observation.

"Why would the pit issue markers with no action?"

"You're the Controller, you tell me."

Paul replied as he stared into the darkening sky.

"I don't know, but I'll look into it tomorrow."

CHAPTER 5

Friday, October 14
7:35 a.m.

Mannerheim turned his car over to valet parking and made his way toward the second floor. As usual, he stopped for his morning cup of coffee at a small bar located just off the casino floor. One of Lenny's better bartenders prepared a substantially better cup of coffee than what came out of the pot in the accounting department.

The bartender saw Mannerheim nearing and started pouring the coffee. Max Gray, Logan's Slot Manager was sitting at the bar, staring into his own cup. His usual cheery face was replaced by that of an unhappy basset hound.

Since Max did not seem to be very talkative, Paul started the conversation.

"Morning, Max. What's the matter, they change the coffee recipe?"

Max moved his eyes in the direction of Mannerheim, while managing to keep his head over his coffee cup.

"No. Somebody won another plane last night."

What started out as an outstanding PR promotion about three months ago was turning into a bad joke. Max installed a circular bank of twelve slot machines, with a four-seat Mooney airplane in the center of the circle. It looked magnificent, with a wingspan of over 36 feet, a length of 27 feet, a large, three-bladed prop, all hanging over the slot section at the west end of the casino. Mounting it was no easy task. The fuselage barely managed to squeeze though the double doors of the casino. It took a full day for two mechanics and three helpers to reassemble the wings back on the plane. A large assembly of pulleys, tackle, steel cables and other assorted equipment was used to suspend all 2,225 pounds of the plane midway between the ceiling and the floor. The finished display drew considerable attention and was featured on the front page of the local paper. If a slot player managed to line up three 7s on any of the twelve machines, he or she instantly won the plane. On one occasion the lucky customer was a pilot and received an identical plane. The remaining winners received a cash equivalent. Regardless, nobody wanted to install another plane.

Paul was astonished.

"Another plane! Correct me if I'm wrong, but doesn't that make four planes you've given away."

"Five!" Voiced with complete morose.

The promotion was starting to exceed the principals of basic mathematical probabilities. The Controller in Mannerheim was starting to come out as he continued his inquiry.

"I thought the slot manufacturer claimed that bank of machines should only give away one plane every six *months*, based upon standard usage. You're giving them away at the rate of one every two or three *weeks*."

Max sheepishly glanced at Paul.

"That's right. If you think you're surprised, you should have seen Logan's reaction. It was not a pretty picture. At a cost of well over one hundred and fifty thousand apiece, this is getting expensive."

"Max, based upon my knowledge of slot machines, each reel has 76 stops. So in order for each of the three reels to line up their 7s means the odds are 76 times 76 times 76. Roughly, that's odds of almost a half-million to one."

The Slot Manager's stare returned to his coffee.

"A little less, but a lot higher than what's been going on. I had Bally's people in last week to check their computer chips in the machines. They still claim they're 76-stop chips. The way it's been going, I thought they must be 42-stop chips, but who can tell by looking at a stupid little computer chip. I hate this computer age."

In the old days, when casinos used mechanical instead of electronic slot machines, they could physically only squeeze 36 symbols on each reel. With the arrival of the electronic age, they replaced the old reels with computer monitors that could randomly displayed any number of symbol stops, still represented by cherries, plums or bars. That raised the odds against winning any big jackpot by at least tenfold. This enabled casinos to establish higher jackpots, which resulted in higher levels of play from their customers.

In order to further stimulate the dreams of slot players, a slot machine manufacturer (IGT) established a network of over six hundred machines in different casinos across the entire state. The system was tied to dedicated phone lines for accountability of the progressive jackpots, and dedicated surveillance cameras for security. That afforded even small clubs the opportunity to offer their customers slot machines that gave them a choice of two multi-million-dollar payoffs, one jackpot for quarters (Quartermania) and another for dollar machines (Megabucks). Like an annuity, the jackpot was paid to a winner over a twenty year period. The flashing lights above the machines advertised everything except the sixteen-million-to-one odds it took to win the prize.

Paul tried to reassure his friend.

"Don't worry Max. Despite this little setback, you're still the biggest revenue producing department in the place. Millions ahead of the pit."

"I know, I know. But this is getting to be embarrassing. That airplane was my pet idea. Now it appears I've got the only bank of slot machines in the entire state of Nevada where the odds seem to favor the players."

"Well, cheer up Max. Maybe the worst is behind you and nobody will hit it again until sometime next year. Odds *always* prevail during the long run. Give it a little time and your numbers will come around."

Max barely raised an eyebrow with that encouragement. "We can only hope."

Max Gray and Mannerheim often crossed paths, but seldom swords. Even though the slot department reported directly to Sam Logan, the Casino Manager, it generated more profit to the bottom line than did the casino. It consistently pumped out its nickels, dimes and quarters without the glamour, or ego that was attached to the pit. That lack of ego was reflected in their department head, Max Gray, who was normally very easy-going, and even had a sense of humor, which Mannerheim appreciated. Even when the high-rollers were absent, all those buses kept arriving with customers itching to shake hands with the "one-armed bandits". This huge revenue required constant attention and internal review by Mannerheim.

The coin counting room may have weighed and counted slot revenue, but it reported to Mannerheim, in keeping with "separation of duties" required by the auditors. Mannerheim's count-team employees, teamed up with some of Gray's slot employees to move small wagons around the casino floor three nights each week. They paused in front of each slot machine, unlocked the cabinet door below the machine, pulled out bucket holding the excess coins that fell from the machine's hopper, and replaced it with an empty bucket. A slip of paper, indicating the machine number was placed in the bucket. When the rounds were completed, they transported the wagon down to the basement and into the coin count room. The revenue from the machines, as identified by the machine's number on the slips of paper, was reflected on a computer run later that day. Any machine that was not producing its estimated revenue was reviewed and examined. At least on paper, that was the established procedure.

Once the buckets were in the coin count room, their contents would be weighed, dumped onto a moving conveyer belt, and finally funneled into a coin-counting machine. The accumulated "wrap" was compared to the "weigh", and noted for any differences. New coins were less worn and therefore weighed more, which caused a variation. Mannerheim always considered the comparison useless, but acknowledged that it provided a possible psychological benefit. It *could* discourage employees who considered pocketing some loose coins. In actuality, a minor difference was just attributed to a "new coin" variation. Only if the theft was done on a substantial scale would a variation demand an investigation. Based upon that possibility, Mannerheim accepted the procedure. Besides, it was an established industry practice that did not require Mannerheim's approval. He put more faith in the three overhead cameras suspended from the ceiling in the count room, and monitored by the surveillance department.

Mannerheim personally reviewed the coin count surveillance tapes at least once a month. A notable theft in another hotel/casino had left a strong impression to oversee the accuracy of his own operation. The *entire* staff in the count room of one Vegas operation was in collusion. They managed to remove the seals from their weight scale and fix it to record only half of its true amount. Another example of man's ingenuity on how, when a control procedure is established, a way is always found to circumvent it. In this particular case, the crooked staff then wrapped the total amount of coins. The half that corresponded to the measured weight went to the owners, and the other half went to the employees. Sort of an accelerated retirement plan. Mannerheim wondered how, on a daily basis, the employees managed to push fifteen-thousand dollars worth of nickels out the back door. It was finally revealed that they loaded the rolls of coin back on the wagons, and pushed them up to the casino floor. Then they went over to the change booths, which were used to provide customers with rolled coin, and replaced the newly rolled coin for currency, thus keeping the fixed amount of the booth in balance. Their final step was to walk out of the casino with a lot of currency in their lunch bags.

The only thing about the scam that really amazed Mannerheim was how twenty-eight people could all keep their mouths shut over a five-year period. One finally let something slip to a girlfriend who later turned them in. Estimated figures put the loss to the casino at well over twenty million. Their management just looked at "total revenue trends", instead of looking at the individual machine revenue, and comparing it to industry averages. As long as the trend rose they were ignorant, but happy. In the end, their Controller was terminated for letting it happen, and the outside auditors were sued for failing to notice the poor performances of the individual machines. After hearing this story, Mannerheim added two more cameras in the coin count room. The last thing he wanted was to face any similar disaster on his watch.

*

9:17 a.m.

Fitz brought the marker update in to Mannerheim the next morning, and it was worse than the quarterly numbers Meyers had asked about. Since the end of the quarter, the marker-receivable total was up another million, three hundred thousand dollars. The grand total current marker balance equaled four million, six hundred and fifty-three thousand dollars.

Fitz then provided even more news.

"I've got the detail of the marker receivables you asked for yesterday."

"Thanks."

Mannerheim studied it for several minutes before commenting.

"Most of these names are new to me. Run the players with a balance of over fifty thousand dollars through Central Credit. I want to see their histories."

Central Credit was a computerized clearing house that kept track of players. All player activity in Nevada was recorded by Central Credit and available to any other casino. If a player was overextended, other clubs declined to take the risk and provide him with even more marker credit. Or if a good player had an established record, as documented by Central Credit, he could walk into any other club in the state and be granted credit with a minimum of additional scrutiny.

"Can do, but its going to take some time with this list." Said Fitz, waving the lengthy printout

"Do the best you can, as fast as you can."

As Fitz walked out of Mannerheim's office, Betty, his secretary, was walking in. "Susie Parsons called. Wants to remind you, you're meeting her for lunch."

Betty mentioned Susie's name with a grin. Betty, in her mid-sixties, was a grandmother and felt everyone over the age of twenty should be married and busy having children. Her oldest child was just a little younger than Mannerheim. She mentally took it on herself to remedy Paul's situation. After the third time of telling Mannerheim about the merits of Susie, Mannerheim got the drift of her message. He figured she must be in partnership with Berkich. Betty continued.

"After that you have a one o'clock meeting with the Hotel Manager to discuss procedures for handling travel agent discounts."

*

Mannerheim found Susie already holding down a booth at one of the coffee shops, located just off the casino floor.

Susie was in her late-thirties, as opposed to Mannerheim's mid-forties, but still an age in his drop zone. She still managed to maintain a figure of a woman in her mid-twenties, helped by the fact she never pushed it out of shape by having children. Mannerheim was told by one of her personal clerks that her boss was married once, when she was very young. The whole experience lasted just a few months. Once, Mannerheim tried to confirm her marital history, but Susie made it clear she never wanted to discuss it. Recognizing a deep scar when he saw one, he never brought the subject up again.

"Sorry to see Logan step on your presentation yesterday."

Mannerheim always knew how to open a conversation with a non-offensive remark.

"That overbearing Nazi. If there was ever grounds for abortion, Logan and his casino clowns are living proof."

"Don't be timid. If you don't like the man, just come right out and say so."

"Let's change the subject."

"Okay. Tell me, why is Tom Elliott still hanging around. You two settled that little union dispute over two months ago, but I'm still getting billings from his Reno office for 'services rendered,' and each one of them have been pre-approved by Aaron."

"Its been too long since we've had lunch together. Elliott has been bending Aaron's ear in Palm Springs before he took off for Alaska. I know for certain he has made two flights down there for some kind of meeting."

"What for?"

"My guess is he's trying to convince Aaron he needs to prepare his estate."

"You mean he's going down there just to revise his will?"

"There's more to it than that. I worked with Tom closely over the three months it took us to resolve our labor dispute. He's a conniver, and he saw enough of the operation to know the potential of this place under new ownership. I think he's trying to talk Aaron into selling, or at the very least, a reorganization with him in key control."

"Aaron would never go for that."

"You're forgetting about Aaron's bypass surgery last year. It got him to face his mortality. Think about his grab-bag bunch of relatives. It's much easier in the end if they divide up a pile of money instead of a lot of brick and mortar."

"Assuming you're right, and Aaron really wanted to sell. He had plenty of opportunity. He could easily sellout to that New Orleans buyer, Yarbrough."

"There's a problem with Yarbrough. A sale to him would provide the cash, but it wouldn't protect the future job security for all of Aaron's old drinking buddies who work here. Yarbrough is looking for a quick turnover. He would buy the place and look for a quick profit on the resale. He wouldn't care about Aaron's old friends. You know most of them couldn't find a job that pays what Aaron pays. Besides, they are all geared to working at half-speed. Aaron can't put all of them in his will. My bet is Elliott has been working on a solution that settles the estate, and provides some written protection for half these brain-dead employees."

"But Elliott is an attorney. A labor attorney at that. He hasn't any background for running a hotel/casino operation."

"He has a knack for organization. All you need to hire top talent is money. Besides, being a lawyer, he's a good talker. He also knows all the money brokers in Reno who can put together a leveraged buyout."

"This can't be just speculation on your part. How do you know all this?"

"I worked with him for three months. He asked the right questions, and dropped enough hints. I can see the handwriting on the wall. And it may not be all that bad if he pulls this off. Despite what he tells Aaron, he'd have to replace the casino people in order to turn this place around and make the kind of money it would take to afford a leveraged buyout. Either that, or he'd make their lives so miserable that he'd drive them out. The only people around here who he would find workable are the two of us."

All of a sudden the fog cleared for Mannerheim. Susie was already in Elliott's camp. This was her opportunity to wipe out Logan and his casino "clowns." It would also give her a solid right seat to the new power base. It was also the obvious reason they were having lunch. In Mannerheim's position as Controller, Elliott would need to win him over, or replace him. Knowing both, Susie was for winning Mannerheim over. Elliott probably did not care one way or another.

"Susie, buyouts, especially leveraged buyouts, are accompanied with a lot of casualties, usually a big chunk of their employees. In order to support the new debt load, management would have to *cut* expenses, and the *biggest* line item in their Income & Expense Statement relates to salaries."

"Paul, I know you think this place can function with five hundred less employees, but you're in management. You're safe."

"Safe! It was before your time, and mine too, but have you heard what happened when Bill Harrah died? He left behind two of the best hotel/casinos in

Nevada, along with a massive inheritance tax bill. The operation was forced into a sale to Holiday Inn. After the purchase three Holiday Inn executives showed up at Harrah's management meeting. They looked down Harrah's meeting table and counted over twenty vice-presidents. They went into shock. Told them they managed over twenty-five *hundred* hotels with less management than Harrah had for two locations. They assured those vice presidents that Holiday Inn had no experience in running casinos operations, and they intended to keep everything as Bill Harrah built it."

"Let me guess. Every one of those vice presidents was history within a year."

"Try six months. They guaranteed everything would remain the same. Nothing remained the same. Even the quality of the food took a dump."

"If and when the time comes, I think Elliott would entertain the possibility of a solid employment agreement for both of us."

"That sounds more promising than any verbal commitment, but Elliott has got a long way to go before it's time to discuss that possibility. In the meantime, can you keep me advised if you see any more handwriting on the wall?"

"My pleasure."

*

Mannerheim returned to his office. As he walked by his secretary's desk, Betty asked,

"How was lunch?"

"Adequate...adequate." Mannerheim then slowed his step in order to be available for a response he was sure would come.

"*Try* to contain your enthusiasm."

Mannerheim enjoyed throwing Betty unexpected responses. Her last three bosses were all sales types, and she still did not know how to handle an accountant. Mannerheim enjoyed playing with her learning curve.

As Mannerheim sat at his desk and pondered his conversation with Susie, Fitz walked in. "Don't tell me you have something to show me already?"

"Turned out there wasn't much to do, and not much to show you. Not one of those new players, who have a marker balance over one hundred thousand, has a record of *any* kind with Central Credit."

"That's impossible!"

"Sad but true. I even checked their credit applications on file in the Cage.

Aside from a name and address, it's bare bones. We have players on file with just a five thousand dollar credit limit with more info than these new players."

Mannerheim picked up the phone. "Betty, track down Vic Welles for me."

*

Vic Welles was one of the more interesting characters in a place that was full of characters. He played professional football somewhere in the South until eventually all the drugs, girls and parties between games took their toll. He retired at the ripe old age of twenty-eight. Deciding he still liked the girls, drugs and parties, he looked around for an occupation that would provide it. Legal options with those particular job benefits were slim, until a rich fan, who was also a rich gambler, introduced him to a casino owner. Vic then found a home, and his true calling in life, as a Casino "Host."

A Casino Host was a "good old boy" who made sure the top players were happy during their stay at the casino. He handled anything that would result in a player being unhappy. He made sure the wife and children were given the royal treatment. He made sure the ski resorts gave them preferential priority on the runs. Or had snowmobiles available, if that was their taste. Or provided a fast boat for the kids to water-ski during the summer. Or shopping trips to exclusive stores. Or anything that entertained the wife while her husband was busy at the tables losing their inheritance. If there were no wife or kids, so much the better. Vic had a short list of female companions available for a good player. Mannerheim's accounts payable clerk knew better than to question certain "travel and entertainment" expenditures from Vic's department. Even the various auditors knew what made a player happy, and did not question certain expenditures that may not stand up to much scrutiny. Auditors were there to determine proper business expenditures, not the moral aspects of these payments.

Mannerheim irritation with Vic rose to the surface on more than one occasion in regards to his loose concern for paperwork. Instead of going though the Purchasing department, he would just call and authorize something, or scribble his signature on an overpriced invoice. Then a surprise billing would arrive on Mannerheim's desk for several thousand dollars. However, Vic was such a likable guy, it was hard for anyone not to let him get away with almost anything. The mark of a true Casino Host.

There often comes a time when casinos find they created a monster in their Casino Hosts. They develop such a close bond with the "high-rollers" that when the Casino Host changes employers, he will take half the best players with him to his new casino. Consequently, many casinos do not use Casino Hosts, which puts more pressure on the pit management to be a little more friendly and follow-up on the players' whims themselves. So if a Casino Host was used, it became very difficult to terminate them and run the risk of losing good players. Any experienced Casino Host knew the leverage he had, and took full advantage of the situation. It was like a spoiled kid who knows how to work his parents. They can get away with almost anything, and usually did.

"Hi Vic. Its almost two in the afternoon. This must be early for you."

"It is, but anything for my favorite number cruncher. What's the matter, can't your accounts payable girl read my crayon?"

"Oh she's getting better at it, but she did want me to ask you to use another color besides orange. She has trouble reading it."

"Sorry, but that's all that's left in the box."

"I'll send over a fresh box."

"You're all right for a Yankee."

"Besides that, I've got some routine questions from the Gaming Control Board auditors you may be able to help me with."

Mannerheim always knew what would get the attention of someone too loose with procedures and regulations.

"Well, we have to keep our local bureaucrats happy. What's their problem?"

"They are concerned with the sharp increase in marker receivables. Have you seen the recent aging detail listing?"

Normally, Mannerheim assumed the casino executives scanned their computer terminals in order to be updated on all recent and historical activity, but Vic was different. While he had a computer terminal in his office, but he would not use it. Once when Mannerheim gave him a computer briefing, Vic looked at the monitor with a blank expression, and muttered something to the effect, *"This is where hi-tech and low-life collide."* After that, and several other failed attempts, Mannerheim gave up and made sure his staff just sent Vic daily "hardcopies" of everything that pertained to him.

"Sure have, but I can't help you partner. As you know, it's off season for most of my players. My last gig was that golfer junket last month. All this current action is due to players the casino managed to bring in, not me. I'm even taking a few days of vacation time till things pick up."

"I'm curious. You spend most of your time around here partying with players till four in the morning. You eat the best meals on the face of the earth. You have more girls around you than most of the royal family of Saudi Arabia. What do you do while you're on vacation, that you can't do when you *work*."

"I go up into the mountains, where I just fish and listen to the peace and quiet. You Yankees have some pretty little hills around here."

The closest Mannerheim ever came to visiting the south was a trip to Texas and was surprised at the state's flat terrain. The powers-to-be decided anything that rose fifty feet above the normal landscape was enough justification to label it a "mountain." Mannerheim imagined Vic must have gone into shock the first time he glimpsed the Sierra Nevada Mountains. That observation, among several others, did not leave Mannerheim with a favorable impression of Texas. Considering he was in the army at the time may have clouded his objective viewpoint. Not withstanding the circumstances, Mannerheim shared General Sheridan's observation of Texas. Seems the old boy came down after the Civil War, looked around and announced, *"If I owned Texas and Hell, I'd rent out Texas and live in Hell."* It was a quote Mannerheim never shared with Vic.

"Of course. So you don't know any of our recent players?"

"Sorry old buddy, better check with the pit."

Vic was right. Mannerheim had checked all the other bases. He knew the next player in the process was Logan.

CHAPTER 6

Saturday, October 15
9:22 p.m.

As parties go, this was one of the best. Catered by the best. Attended by the rich and famous, at least in their own minds. The gathering of the elite was being housed in a home of one of their own. If you can call something that has an extra four thousand square feet of space over and above what the three occupants would otherwise normally need, a home. It was more a testimonial to the occupant's financial success than just a need for adequate shelter. Including the master bathroom, each room was built with concern for a panoramic view of Lake Tahoe. With that requirement in mind, the outside of the house looked like it was put together by random selection. The house served its purpose. As you walked through the door; you smelled money. And like casinos, the image of success was almost as important as success itself.

Scott Sherman's last thirty years were spent with these types of people. People he seldom liked, and never trusted. He viewed them with contempt. To him, they were a useless species. But with years of practice, he learned how to hide that contempt. He looked around at people whose only concern was their image. Most in the room never even earned the money they were so proud of. Even the ones who made their own money, were seldom by means that did not serve anyone's higher interest than their own. And if fortune, or their own inabilities, turned too much against them and they lost their personal finances, this pack of vultures would turn against them on a moment's notice. Friendship would vanish. Memories would fade. They would no longer be acceptable. As for Scott, he was not here to be accepted, but rather because his alternative choices were so unacceptable.

Scott was born and raised in Oklahoma in the early '40s. His father destroyed his health, his body and finally his spirit trying to make something grow in ground that would only yielded scorn for his efforts. Scott squandered the joy of his youth for his family's efforts. But out of the ashes of the failing farm a determination was born deep within Scott. He vowed to succeed. No matter the method. No matter the cost. He was determined to succeed.

Schooling was more of a legal requirement than a necessity, due to the time the farm required, but it did not mean Scott was ignorant. He had two teachers, Machiavelli and an old high school coach who recognized a natural athlete when he saw one. The coach introduced the boy to tennis. A game where ability and determination were focused down to one individual against another. No team dependency. Just one-on-one street fighting. At least that was how Scott looked at it. It was a game the younger Scott utilized to crawl out of his poverty. A game that could generate money. Money to help him take his family out of the fields. What he made from hustling the young, arrogant rich kids soon paled compared to what he made in local tournaments. He also saw the need to reinvest his dividends back into better instructors. By the early 1960s Scott's career peaked with a singles win at the US Open. It was his claim to fame, and a footnote in history that forever made him socially acceptable. The money back then was minimal compared to the money made in professional tennis today, but it was enough. Unfortunately the money came too late for his parents. It only served to make them a little more comfortable prior to their departure.

Professional tennis has always been a game for youth. After the spring in his step slowed a notch below competitive standards, Scott evolved into a career of his own. He returned to the rich. He hustled them as adults, as he hustled them while they were children back in Oklahoma. He discovered the willingness of the rich to search for ways to spend their money. People tend not to value something they did not earn, and if they do not value it, they will risk it. Scott went after this unearned money. He took their money while he fed on their banquets.

The Oklahoma drawl was long gone. He also overcame his slow start in school. Thanks to a huge interest in reading, his knowledge expanded to the point where he did not embarrass himself in any company. Even though Scott was "socially accepted," he never felt himself to be one of society's elite. He was an outsider. His roots were too deep and too different. By using his skills, Scott's lifestyle developed into a good living. Those skills centered on his natural, if aging, athletic ability and a determined mind. A mind like a shark. Always hungry, always moving, never resting.

Scott eyed his mark. Tailor-made to his own specifications. Bruce Reed was fourth generation old money. The generation who gave no thought to the pain of working. The world was built to entertain them. Reed was on his third marriage. His father, as did his father before him, taught him to work on his marriage as well as he taught him to work in the world, which was not at all. Scott wondered if his ego exceeded his belly, but soon only cared if his wallet exceeded both. He knew all three were more than ample for his requirements. According to his background check, annual trust income of over two million, and total assets of just over ten million. Most of the assets were composed of expensive homes scattered around the globe. Somehow this guy managed to dispose of a huge amount of his annual income. Scott was here this evening to offer him a means of assistance in this endeavor.

Scott stood by the bar. He was on his fifth vodka. He spent the afternoon playing tennis with Reed. Showing him some basic court strategies that would help an older player cover the majority of the court, while managing to play the bulk of the shots. Knowing when to let some shots go, and when it was worth your energy in going for the pursuit. A little like life.

"Bruce, I must admit, you didn't do too badly out there. Considering someone of your age."

"My age! I may have a couple more pounds on me than you do, but you're older than I am."

"True, but age is more a state of mind, and my mind is still in its prime. You on the other hand, should consider contributing some of your wealth toward all available medical advances in that area."

"Fine talk for someone engaged in preserving your brain in alcohol."

"I can still do things you can only dream about."

"An empty boast by an over-the-hill tennis player."

"Empty is it? Care to put a wager on a test of our related abilities?"

"How much, old man?"

"Say...fifty thousand dollars."

"Scott old man, I don't want to ruin your retirement. How about the cost of lunch tomorrow?"

"Don't worry about my bank account. I can afford to take fifty thousand off you. But let's be fair. Let's test our skills on something off the tennis court. Got any ideas how I could embarrass you?"

"Okay, old man. How about a little two-on-one basketball. With you against me and Joe's teenage kid over there."

"Is that the extent of your imagination? Can you not conceive of anything more demanding than a game of basketball? Let me help you expand your limits. I propose that I can take that basketball and dribble it up a flight of stairs. I could even do it blindfolded."

"That's impossible. Let's forget it. I don't want to be known as someone who takes advantage of an old drunk."

"No guts, no glory."

"Very well. You're on, old man."

41

   Within a few minutes a basketball was located and Scott Sherman moved it up the flight of stairs with the proficiency of a Magic Johnson. A confused Bruce Reed found himself writing out a check minutes later.

   His work completed, Scott quickly found a reason to make an early departure, and call it a night. As he disappeared into the night he took the reward for over two months of practice. He left wondering how five vodkas affected the potted plant.

CHAPTER 7

Tuesday, October 18
3:52 p.m.

Betty checked with Logan's secretary and set up a four o'clock meeting in Logan's office. Near the appointed time Mannerheim left his office and passed by clusters of his employees working to reconcile food, beverage, hotel, table or slot revenue reports. Calculators and computer monitors filled desk space not occupied with various piles of paper. It looked like any other busy accounting office across the country. As Mannerheim turned into the hallway he noticed the new earth-tone carpet recently installed. In another fifty feet he turned again, through a security-locked door and headed down the stairs to the casino floor. Immediately the color of the carpet changed to a subdued color of red. As he descended down the stairs the tone intensified until it was bright red.

Even if someone was only attending a convention or just a hotel guest, it was hard for them to avoid the casino. If they were walking from the hotel lobby to the elevator, and needed to use a restroom, they found the only available restrooms were placed in locations on the floor that forced you to walk through the entire casino in order to get to them.

The slot machine trays were all made of tin, because they make the most noise when the coins, or tokens fell into them. On top of the slot machines were flashing lights, along with built-in sound effects, that went off every time a jackpot was paid. The walls and ceilings of the casino were paneled with dark, reflective glass. Neon lighting helped establish an endless, depthless feel to the room. As with the color of the carpet, everything was designed to generate a higher level of tension and excitement. All working to draw the players into the activity.

Once on the casino floor, Mannerheim maneuvered his way through the crowds. He always made it a point to look at the faces as he weaved in and out of the people. It reminded him of the throngs of people moving through an airport terminal. In both locations, the crowds seemed to be in a rush to get to unknown destinations. In the case of casinos, it was as if they were rushing to a specific slot machine that was just waiting a certain five-minute period for the exact person to arrive and play, so it could pay off its precious jackpot. Every face carried the expression of anxiety and greed. Unfortunately for most, it would go the other way, and they only rushed to lose their money. As Mannerheim walked the length of the casino, he noticed a higher-than-normal number of slot machine players. *The buses must be in with another tour*. The casino gave them coupons for a free roll of nickels and a free breakfast. Especially in casinos, there was no such thing as a free lunch, or even a breakfast. Almost all would go home far poorer, but few would admit it once back on the bus.

In order to help lubricate their wallets, all players who wanted a "free" drink quickly were handed one. The minimal beverage cost to the casino was more than recovered in higher table activity. It all helped to cloud reality and added to the fantasy environment. Time was nonexistent, which was why you never see a clock on any casino wall. Keeping with the fantasy theme is the main reason casinos substitute chips for cash on the table. If the players were playing for cash they would consider it money. Chips made it similar to playing monopoly. It was just "play money," not all that important at the time.

Glancing around the tables he noticed the familiar regulars. Even though Mannerheim did not work in the pit area, he did walk through the casino floor enough to recognize those faces. The same locals came back day-after-day, as if they were reporting to work. Others arrived not long after their money. For those the pit called the "third-of-the-month club," meaning senior citizen gamblers who flocked to the casino as soon as their Social Security checks arrived in the mail.

Mannerheim passed pit number four, containing twelve twenty-one tables, a like number of dealers and two pit bosses. Mannerheim glanced at the pit bosses. He knew both, but their names eluded his memory. It did not really matter. Both looked like clones of their leader. They were dressed in well-tailored dark suits. They, and all like them, always looked like they were going to their mothers funeral. Mannerheim once collectively referred to them as pallbearers, but because there were usually only two to a pit instead of six, he recently changed his description to "the Brothers Grimm."

During his first few years in the casino industry, Mannerheim held a resentment over the pit bosses salaries. Despite the fact few obtained any education beyond the twelfth grade, or performed any massive job responsibilities, they were *very* well paid. It was based on the *hope* that if they were overpaid then they would not be tempted to steal from their employer. Only in the last four or five years did Mannerheim's salary exceed that of the average pit boss. Mannerheim did not begrudge anyone making a good income, but he preferred they earned it. Their major level of stress appeared to be falling arches. They stood and monitored the activity of the six twenty-one games assigned to each of them, and observed the law of probabilities, which in reality was out of their control. It always amused Mannerheim when they made "management decisions." If the player's luck was running against the house, the pit would rush to change dealers, change the deck or the dice, or even change the green felt on the table, and sometimes even replace the entire table. Rumor was they even took a really unlucky table out back and set it afire. All this on the hope of regaining control of their turf.

As Mannerheim was passing the twenty-one tables he saw a friendly face, Sarge. Sarge worked as the part-time maintenance man for the condo association were Mannerheim lived. In fact, Sarge worked for several condo associations in that capacity. Mannerheim did not even know his real name. "Sarge" was a hangover from his military service. After he left the army, he and his wife moved up to Tahoe and started a small appliance repair shop. All went well until Sarge discovered gambling. After their savings, home equity and business disappeared toward gambling debts, his wife also disappeared. Now he "lived" more in casinos than his one-room apartment. His attendance was based on the timing of his Army retirement check, and small amounts of sporadic income from his various part-time employers.

Mannerheim went over to Sarge's table.

"Hello Sarge. How are things going?"

Sarge had a couple hundred dollars in chips piled on the table in front of him.

"Great. I'm on a roll. After I win this place I'll give you a raise."

"Sounds good. In anticipation of that, I'll go upgrade my next vacation."

Sarge could get a drink anytime he wanted one from a passing cocktail waitress that patrolled the pit area. Mannerheim was more interested in when he last ate.

"Need anything? How about if I arrange dinner for you at the coffee shop?"

"Thanks kid, but I'm fine."

Mannerheim could never figure out if Sarge called him "kid" because he looked younger than his forty-some years, or he could not remember Paul's name.

"Okay Sarge. Look me up if you need anything."

With that Mannerheim headed back toward Logan's office.

Sarge always reminded Mannerheim of his once-favorite uncle. Mannerheim still remembered when his uncle visited his parent's home. Always dressed in his clean, blue Navy uniform, chest full of campaign ribbons from adventures in World War II. He always gave his nephew a small gift from some distant part of the world. After his retirement he established a pattern that Sarge would later follow. The only difference was the method. Mannerheim's uncle's path of self-destruction was not gambling, but alcohol. What once was a model of a man, turned into an empty shell. His uncle only cared about his next drink, while Sarge only cared about his next bet. Both lost all it took a career to build. Long ago Mannerheim realized alcoholics and gamblers were incapable of trust. They lied, cheated or robbed to feed their addictions. They had only one priority, one loyalty left in life. Yet some fond memories of his uncle lingered for Mannerheim, which were reflected in his view of Sarge.

Once past the twenty-one tables, Mannerheim arrived where the real action took place, the crap tables. Of the few "professionals" who managed to make their living from gambling, nine out of ten were crap players. The image of card counting aside, even Mannerheim noticed good players waited for the dice to run a certain direction. Then, like a surfer with a good wave, they stayed on the crest, riding it for all it was worth. Bet management was the key to their success. If anybody always bet the same on each hand, the law of probability resulted in their demise. The odds *always* favored the house. The games were designed that way. Being casinos were not philanthropic organizations, they did not sponsor even money bets. They would not stay in business if they did. Somebody had to pay for their payroll, overhead and profit.

Mannerheim arrived at Logan's office exactly at four o'clock even though he already knew the scenario. He was accustomed to Logan's little games. Logan would be away from his office, then finally appearing after a twenty minute delay. It helped set the tone of whose time was more important. It always reminded Mannerheim of Truman and McArthur both circling the field, sparring to make the grand entrance. But in this case, Mannerheim gladly acknowledged who held the bigger title, and the bigger ego, in order to save the wasted time.

Instead of being located on the second floor like the rest of the executive offices, Logan's office was just off the casino floor. It was not much larger than Mannerheim's but it was paneled in rich, dark wood. Its atmosphere set a tone for any visitor that they were on the holy ground of someone really powerful and important, not somebody's workplace. It was also the only office that did not have a computer terminal. Mannerheim felt it also needed some brighter lighting. He admitted to himself that he was impressed with the richer feel of the office, but still he would not give up his window for it.

True to form, Logan made his entrance according to his own gameplan.

"Paul, I'm sorry I'm late, but these players call the tune around here. Got to keep them happy so you can count their loses."

Just to remind Mannerheim of who made the profits around the place.

"No problem Sam, but you should replace some of these magazines every now and again."

"I'll have someone look into that. So what can I do for you? The message I got concerned some inquiry from the Gaming Control Board auditors."

"Yes, at first I thought it would be more convenient if they talked to you directly, but then figured we could save some of your time if we cleared it up instead."

"I appreciate that. You know how much I enjoy talking to those smart-mouth little college kids." An intended indirect reference that Logan was not impressed with Mannerheim's college education either.

"It's no big problem. They just had a question on the rise in our marker balance. Seems we have incurred a significant increase over the prior year, and they just need to write something down to document the reason."

"Well, that's easily explained. We've had some special players in from Hong Kong. Fortunately their luck was bad and ours was good."

"From Hong Kong! Was this to the credit of Vic?"

"No, they've been players I've known for years. You know where the big players with *real* money comes from. It was before your time, but a few years back, they came from the oil rich Arab countries. After that the high-rollers briefly came out of Mexico when they found a little oil. Unfortunately their good fortune was mixed with bad timing, and the price of oil took a dump just as the Mexicans were looking promising. For the last decade or more, Orientals have been our best players. They just love to gamble. It certainly has never been Americans."

"True, not with our tax laws. It does diminish one's ability to earn a few after-tax million in order to just drop it on a crap table."

Mannerheim knew the history lesson. He once saw a player from Hong Kong waste twelve hours on a Baccarat table. A game Mannerheim considered snobbish, and not the least bit interesting. The player left behind markers amounting to one point three million U.S. dollars. Within thirty days the markers were paid in full. Despite the fact that anyone from Hong Kong had easy access to the Macau gambling casinos, the Portuguese province a short boat ride away, they seemed to enjoy traveling across the big pond in order to take their chances in Nevada. But those days appeared to be diminishing for Nevada's casinos. Since the Tiananmen Square massacre in '89, Mannerheim noted even Hong

Kong players turned very conservative as they started to move their money to Canada or Singapore in anticipation of the Chinese takeover of Hong Kong in '97. They got very nervous, very fast.

"Vic tells me he didn't have anything to do with your recent list of players. Curious they didn't want to party. Who took care of their wants and wishes while they were not playing the tables?"

"Vic wasn't needed. They left their wives and kids in San Francisco to shop. As you can see, we have a little shortage of snow to make skiing enjoyable. They came alone and just wanted to gamble. The pit managed to cater to their little needs without the benefit of Vic. Anything else?"

"Yes, just one more little point to clear up. In an attempt to comply with their request, we checked them out through Central Credit. We were surprised to find there wasn't any history on them."

"Again, that's easily explained. They do their main gambling in Hong Kong and not in the states. The only reason they come over here was because they know me, and accepted my invitation to be my guests. They also don't like Reno or Vegas, but seem to find our mountain air different than their sea air. Being they don't wander over to any other casinos, it's not surprising nobody else has a record on them. So don't you worry about it. They're my players. I'll handle them. Thanks for your concern."

The audience was over.

That went as predicted. It was his turf, his business, his decision. Sam was polite, but did not really tell Mannerheim much of anything. In fact, for Logan, he was almost too polite. In the past he hit the roof if questioned about his credit granting practices. In front of players he charmed the rings right off their fingers, but with employees he did not put up with much questioning.

As Mannerheim turned the corner to enter his own office he announced,

"Betty, locate Berkich for me."

CHAPTER 8

Wednesday, October 19
8:33 a.m.

Mannerheim arrived at his office and started his day by reviewing the activity report from his Cage Shift Supervisor. It indicated the normally boring activity figures. The pit netted just seventy-three thousand, with a lower than normal amount of marker activity. It was a slow day, but reasonable when taken into account the time of the year. The slots were emptied during the night and were currently being weighed, wrapped and counted. The results would appear on tomorrow's activity report, but in today's memo section Mannerheim was amused to find another slot player managed to line up three more sevens, which resulted in the loss of another Mooney airplane. Mannerheim immediately reached for his phone and hit Max Gray's three digit extension. Not having a secretary, Max picked up the receiver himself.

"Good Morning Max, Paul here."

"Good has nothing to do with this morning."

"I see by the activity report you have one less airplane this morning. I hope you at least got some good pictures of your new winner."

"Yeah, but they're losing their value. It's beginning to be old news. I'm thinking of papering my office wall with photos of all the winners of those airplanes."

The major benefit of giving away large jackpots was the free advertising it provided. It was good for business for potential customers to see an example of their gambling goals. When someone won a large amount of money their smiling picture was plastered on the front page of the local papers. The newspapers were willing accomplices in this marketing effort. There were two reasons for this. First, Tahoe had a severe shortage of local news items. Aside from the weather, environmental and minor crime stories, casino activities were the primary source of what was happening within the basin. The second reason, and more important... it was good for business, everyone's business. Never had a picture of a big loser made the front page. For if local casinos did *not* prosper, then thousands of local businesses would soon feel the ripple effects of a local recession. Several of those local businesses were, of course, newspapers.

"Max, I just thought you might be interested in a little fact concerning you."

"Which is?"

"I figured out that if you give away just one more airplane, you will have generated an air force larger than sixty-four third-world countries."

"Paul, anyone recently tell you that you have a warped sense of humor?"

Click.

At that moment Fitz walked into Mannerheim's office.

"You know Fitz, some people don't seem to have any sense of humor."

"Yeah, I've been meaning to talk to you about that."

*

11:12 a.m.

Even though Mannerheim was six foot two himself, Matt Hamilton was at least an inch taller, and a good twenty pounds heavier, which made him at least thirty pounds overweight. In Berkich's opinion, he was a first rate private investigator. Steve relationship with Matt spanned more than fifteen years. Both served in the Reno Police Department as detectives. Hamilton served in that capacity for over half of his twenty years. He took an early retirement at forty-five even though his police retirement did not kick in till he turned fifty-five. For the last three-years, since leaving the RPD, he worked to develop his private investigation business. The first year he matched his police salary. This year, he was well on his way to doubling it.

Prior to Hamilton's meeting with Mannerheim, Berkich warned him the case involved the *possibility* of internal theft. Therefore, as a standard precaution, he checked Paul's office for any listening devices. He found none.

"Steve indicated you have a very confidential project for me. I'm curious, it's well known that you people use the firm of Haskins & Perkins for your investigative work. Why call me?"

"Haskins & Perkins have ties too close to the casino, and this investigation involves the casino."

Mannerheim then spent the next few minutes updating Hamilton about the sharp rise in marker activity, the lack of Central Credit information, the observations of Helen and Logan's explanation of it. He then opened it up for questions.

"Mr. Logan's story sounds reasonable. Why do you doubt it?"

"Two reasons. First is the fact that Vic Welles, our Casino Host, was not included in the loop. *All* players want to be catered to. They want free hotel rooms, free meals, free drinks and the best seats in the showroom. Most of the time what's important to the player is not the freebies themselves, it is feeling "important" in front of their family and friends. It's the ego aspect of the industry, and the casino is more than willing to provide these freebies and feed that ego. Win or lose, they will receive their freebies. Gambling is, in large part, ego. The bigger the player, the bigger the ego. For a handful of players to run up this high a volume of markers means that they are the type of players that Vic would get involved with. If somebody like Vic doesn't humor their demands then the pit has to, and there's a real shortage of baby-sitters down there."

"And the second reason."

"It's what Helen Enges told Berkich. These *players* received their markers and just walked out. They didn't play. Casinos only give credit, or markers, because they expect the players to 'play'. With enough 'play', there will always be enough 'win', or 'hold' for the casino. However, there is a little game a lot of players try. They want all that comes with being a player without running the risk of losing thousands of dollars on the tables. Therefore, players think of ways to build the illusion that they are playing more than they actually are. They get a marker, but instead of gambling with the funds they start to pass chips off to their wife or girlfriend, as they play as little, and bet as little, as they can possibly get away with. After awhile, they claim they lost everything and need a new marker. Later they meet the wife, who has already exchanged the chips for cash, and go off to their free meal in the gourmet restaurant at the expense of the casino. Many even go home with the money and take their time paying off their markers. Sort of an interest-free loan from Aaron Davenport. The casino people know this game. That is why they closely monitor the activity of a player. If they pass off their chips, or do not play at all, then they do not give them their little freebies. Certainly they would never give them any more markers. At least that is how the system was supposed to work. The fact that it didn't seem to follow that standard routine is cause for suspicion."

"So all you have now is suspicion?"

Mannerheim felt confident concerning Hamilton, even if he did not have much charm. The investigator reminded him of Sergeant Joe Friday - just the facts and a face void of much humor.

"It's either based on a combination of these unique circumstances, or it could just be my overly suspicious imagination, nurtured by the fact that in the bottom of my heart, I just don't trust Logan and his pit. They operate in a world of their own down there. I have to be sure and that's why you're here."

"So you think the Casino Manager, Logan, established some bogus players. Then these players walked out with your chips, and left behind markers that were never intend to be paid off. Where do all those chips go from there? It's hard to buy groceries with a hundred-dollar casino chip."

"Our chips are like legal tender in the state of Nevada. Any casino in the state will gladly take them in and exchange them for their own chips, or even cash them in for currency. For the amount of chips that could be involved, it would take some time. Recently I've noticed a sizable increase in the amount of our chips being returned in the chip exchange program with other casinos. We've had to buy back some from as far away as Vegas. Even so, lately we've been consistently running low on hundred dollar chips in circulation on the casino floor. My Cage Manager notified me she has had to pull some from our reserve inventory of chips."

"I see. Another question... why don't you just reassure yourself of their identity, their addresses and their balances by requesting a written confirmation of their marker activity? I understand that's a common audit procedure. You could have your outside auditors, or the Gaming Control Board auditors confirm the balances, then do a follow-up investigation if you're worried they may be bogus players."

"That would be common procedure in a common industry, but the casino business isn't common. Even our auditors don't send written confirmations of markers receivables to our players. Think about it. If you lost twenty thousand dollars to a Nevada casino, how would you feel if we sent a confirmation of that fact to your home, and your wife saw it. After the divorce, we would never see that player again, and probably not see our money either. Even if we sent the confirmation to their office, a big-mouth secretary could spread the word and ruin a business career. Some people still maintain the idea that gambling is a character flaw."

"So you don't *ever* confirm your receivables?"

For the first time some emotion managed to creep into his comments.

"That's right. Until recently, markers were *not* even legally enforceable in our own state of Nevada, not to mention the rest of the country. That has changed. We can now go after our customers if it's obvious we have no other options. However, most courts still look at us like we're a bookie trying to collect an IOU from a poor soul we took advantage of. Remember, aside from New Jersey and some Indian reservations, casino gaming is basically illegal in the rest of the nation."

"From what I hear, your industry is spreading like cancer."

"I wouldn't phase it like that, but you're right. Legalized gambling is increasing rapidly as more and more states approve full or limited gambling operations. Anything from huge casinos to riverboats are under consideration or under construction. I'm sure we'll tighten the collection process as more states get on board. But for now, our best tool to collect our markers is to not issue that player any more new markers until he pays off those old ones."

"Unique business you have here."

"Matt, why do I get the feeling you don't know all that much about casinos? I was under the impression you've lived here for years."

"True, but I don't even go into casinos unless the job requires it. Don't think much of gambling. In almost any other state I'd arrest the whole bunch of you for gambling. If you want the truth, I'd take more pleasure in busting you than working for you."

"Being I don't have to maintain my standard polite board room dialog with you, I'll drop the businessman's front and get right to the point. I can't put an ad in the newspapers looking for a private investigator. Berkich tells me you're one of the few competent ones around. So I may be struck with you, but I'll call this whole thing off if I can't rely on your loyalty."

"Loyalty!... you ask too much. But I'll promise you this... I will never let my personal opinions interfere with my professional obligations."

"Okay, I'll settle for that. Am I paying extra for that chip on your shoulder, or do you just throw it in as part of your hourly rate?"

"Comes with the package."

"I hope you aren't too disappointed if Logan turns out to be clean."

"In truth, I would be. It's just that I view gambling similar to drugs or booze. My father squandered a good hulk of his weekly salary on the tables while I was growing up. When it came to gambling, my mother looks at casinos and considers them coming straight from the pit of Hell. I made a pact with her never to use my abilities to help casinos. Steve told me this job would not violate that pact. That was the only reason I even showed up to meet with you. I can see now where he was coming from. In fact, this could be a pleasure."

"At this point, I'm for anything that makes you happy."

For the first time Hamilton revealed a small smile.

"I will never understand why people continue to throw away their hard earned money on something that destroys themselves and their family."

"Matt, never underestimate anyone's capacity for self-destruction."

53

"Maybe you're right. But let's get back to your problem. Why would these casino executives jeopardize good, secure, high paying jobs by engaging in some high-risk marker rip off?"

"There's a possibility of the owner selling the operation in order to get his estate together. Sam Logan has spies all over the place. Not much escapes his attention. Even if Logan could talk Mr. Davenport out of selling, he couldn't talk him out of dying. Aaron Davenport is at least twenty years older than Sam Logan. Someday he will lose out to new blood. He can see the future. Call this his retirement planning. If the markers are never paid, which I believe they won't be, then I'd be forced to take Logan's word for it that it's just the luck of the draw, and write them off our books as a bad debt expense. He pockets the money and calls his travel agent for a lifetime vacation after Aaron sells or dies. Now I have a question for you. *If* the casino is issuing bogus markers and bogus players are walking out of the place with several million dollars of our money, how are you going to prove it?"

"I'll start with that Helen Enges that Steve told me about. If she can spot that player again, then I can attempt to ID him. If he's not the player the casino tells you he is, then we can go from there."

"Let's assume he's not a player. Let's assume he's not from Hong Kong. Logan could just say he was duped. That he was a victim as well. That's why I can't go to Aaron with just my suspicions now. I need solid evidence."

"Don't worry about it, or concern yourself about how I perform my job. We can look at the different possibilities when I know more. Then I will tell you about your options."

"Okay. One last point. Go through Steve Berkich on anything you may find. If I need you, I'll contact you. Also indicate on your billings that they're for employee background checks. I'll make sure they get paid."

*

Hamilton was barely out of Mannerheim's office when the phone rang. Within less than a minute Betty was announcing over the intercom, "Mr. Yarbrough on line one."

"Thanks Betty."

"Randy, still can't find a better use for your money than giving it to Ma Bell?"

"Paul, I'm the best thing that could happen to that place. Remember my promise, I'd make sure you're provided for. My word is my bond."

"*My word is my bond!*" Mannerheim knew a con man when he heard one. It was true, Mannerheim could probably work his own deal and add a couple bucks to his pocket if he provided his influence with Aaron, but he also knew this guy's interest was not along the lines of "buy and develop." Yarbrough was a "buy and sell for a fast profit" type of guy. Mannerheim remembered his lunch with Susie. At this point, his faith was in Susie and Elliott, if a buyout occurred at all.

It did seem odd to Mannerheim that everyone wanted to buy something that was not even for sale, until the obvious was examined. Half the reason, Mannerheim figured out long ago, was the *status* of owning a casino. Sort of like becoming Rick in your own movie version of Casablanca. Mannerheim thought it must be similar to the apparent common desire of owning restaurants, which must also appeal to one's ego, judging by the number of people who started them despite their high rates of failure. The other reason was the main difference between casinos and restaurants... most casinos actually made money.

"Consider it Paul. You'd be a large part of my management team. I'd keep an arms-length approach as far as the day-to-day operations are concerned. I have no desire to move out of New Orleans. Together we can make some needed changes. A fresh breath of air will do the place some good. You know the lack of efficiency there. Think of it like a needed business cycle, waste is examined and eliminated, productivity and profits go up."

"I know you see a fast buck in a larger bottom line, but being I'm just a mere employee, I'm comfortable with the current status quo."

"You could substantially increase your comfort level. I can afford to be very generous. I could even be talked into a five-year contract, at say... double your current salary."

"You're getting ahead of yourself, Randall. To the best of my knowledge, Aaron doesn't have any interest in selling. If and when he does, I must admit your offer of employment does sound interesting. Maybe one day things may change. If they do, I'll consider it."

"You do that. Also, trust me when I tell you, Aaron *will* sell. In the meantime, I've altered my latest proposal for Aaron's consideration. My secretary is faxing the update to you as we speak. I hope you will pass it on to him, with a kind word. I'll get back to you in three or four weeks when

Aaron returns."

"Okay. Talk to you then."

Suddenly it flashed.

"Wait a minute! How did he know Aaron would be back in three or four weeks? Who else has he been talking to?"

CHAPTER 9

Wednesday, October 19
6:45 p.m.

Scott was at a crossroads. His current path of hustling the rich might continue for a few more years, but he realized it did not lead to a secure retirement. Stories of his party maneuvers were far too commonplace.

Last year he perfected the technique of throwing an old skeleton key in a keyhole from a distance of four feet. He located an old door and had it custom installed in a friend's house just prior to a celebrity tennis party. That earned him a cool fifty thousand dollars, less the cost of the door.

Since passing fifty, Scott worried that one day his body might fail him. One slip and all he had worked to accumulate would tumble down. He felt defeat nipping at his heels. Sometimes the mark of brilliance is knowing when to quit before that day arrives. As much as that worried him, the thought of the cost of living, and future rates of inflation, worried him more. The trap was his own creation. No longer the hunter, he was, like his prey, living an overly affluent lifestyle. As a result Scott had developed, like them, and unlike his father, a lifestyle that yielded nothing of any importance. Glancing down at the ice in the bottom of his glass he realized, like the glass, empty.

Scott turned and looked out the window of his hotel suite. Across the street stood the massive fourteen story structure belonging to Aaron Davenport. It reminded him of a long-standing invitation, which now appeared to be coupled with good timing. Any problem is best discussed with a friend. *"Maybe I should call my old football buddy for lunch, and talk to Vic. One old athlete to another."*

*

Vic quickly returned Scott's call and accepted his invitation for lunch at noon the next day. Though it was Scott's invitation both knew Aaron was going to end up with the tab for the meal. As Casino Host, Vic Welles' comp, or *comp*limentary privileges were the most liberal in the place, just short of Aaron's and Sam Logan's. But neither Aaron nor Sam Logan came close to Vic when the monthly totals were accumulated.

*

Thursday, October 20
12:00 p.m.

Vic met Scott at the Garden Restaurant. Scott came from the pool at the Golden Palace. Vic came from bed. This was still early for him. Scott arrived on time. Vic managed to arrive twelve minutes late, which for Vic was about as close to being on time as possible.

"Vic, glad to see some hostile husband hasn't shot you yet, on the grounds of justifiable homicide."

"Well it's fortunate we live in a nation of poor shots."

They were friends for many reasons, aside from being former athletes. Both were Southerners living among Yankees, both were raised dirt poor, and both were now accustomed to the finer things in life. They first met at a Vegas party six years ago while enjoying those finer things.

After about twenty minutes of small talk Vic decided to find out why Scott ventured out so early in the day, aside from snappy conversation and a free meal.

"So what brings you to my part of the woods. Something I can do for you?"

"Oh, I've been considering a career change, but I've got a small problem. As Shakespeare said, '*My large style agrees not with the leanness of my purse.*' So far, I've managed to do all right for myself, but it's getting more difficult with each passing year. I'm getting the feeling it's time for a career change. I was wondering if you could provide some suggestions."

"Wow! I'm impressed. I didn't know you could even read, let alone read Shakespeare. I tried to read him once, but the racing form made more sense. You know something, you're a lot smarter than you look, but I suppose you'd have to be. But speaking about your career change, I happen to be working on a little scam that has room enough for both of us. In fact, I've been looking for someone I can trust. That, and your unique ability to judge human nature, make you the perfect choice. If things work out like I think they will, you're looking at the next Casino Manager around here. That would provide a vacancy for my job. It pays beyond belief, with enough perks to make that White House job look pale by comparison. Don't suppose you know anyone who would want to be the new Casino Host?"

"I assume you're talking about me. But I don't know anything about that."

"Now I've got a quote for you. Sam Goldwin once said, '*The most important thing in acting is honesty. And once you learn to fake that, you're in.*' It's the same with casinos, only more so. Based upon your past experience you're already there. Give me a couple days to help you scope out the territory, get to know the cast of characters, learn a couple buzz words, and you'd fit into this like you were born to it. It's not like you need to learn something that is really difficult... like football."

"I'm getting tried of associating with people that confuse having money with having brains."

"Just think of it as our duty to separate one from the other, and help them straighten out that illusion."

"That doesn't sound much different from my current line of work. Okay, I'm interested, but why do I get the feeling the current Casino Manager doesn't know that he's vacating his job?"

"Oh, he's just a little slow finding out about these things."

"So what's the scam?"

"Let me tell you about it..."

CHAPTER 10

Friday, October 21
6:00 p.m.

Poker night. The third Friday of every month, with one exception - the holidays. They were the busiest times of the year. December was definitely out and sometimes November, depending on what day Thanksgiving fell on. Otherwise a small group met every month for a game of poker. They were composed of Sam Logan; Casino Manager, Vic Welles; Casino Host, Carl Desmond; company President, James McPherson; Hotel Manager, Lenny Goodrich; Food & Beverage Director and Paul Mannerheim; Controller.

Aaron held a standing invitation to the game, but never was in attendance. Someone told Mannerheim that Aaron did show up once, about fifteen years ago, but he was too much of an intimidating presence. The then-Hotel Manager got so nervous he kept spilling his drinks and most everyone dropped out every time Aaron raised the pot. After that night, Aaron never returned.

No one remembered the game's origins. Its beginnings were lost to the past. Somebody thought it began in the late '50s. The original members were distant shadows. But, their legacy now was a time-honored tradition. The game was always played in one of the two bedroom suites in the hotel. The bedrooms were unnecessary, but the two bathrooms and a well stocked bar came in handy. A cocktail waitress popped in twice a night to bring fresh ice and check the liquor inventory. In order to keep Carl happy, Lenny always made sure she was a "Looker". Meeting at the hotel provided the convenience of "room service" in case anyone became hungry, which all did at one time or another. Any food orders were filled by one of the gourmet restaurants, and their chefs, bypassing the normal room service kitchen. Those advantages, plus the fact that no wife wanted to host the event, made the hotel a logical choice.

At first Mannerheim wondered why Logan bothered attending this monthly event. Later he remembered that anyone with a gaming license, such as a Casino Manager, is prohibited from gambling in his place of employment. It was also considered bad form for someone like Logan to be seen gambling in another casino. It showed poor character. This way Logan was able to enjoy himself without public comments. Usually none of Logan's Shift Managers ever attended the game. Mannerheim assumed it was because Logan did not want any of them to beat him at his own game. They also probably felt it was safer not to embarrass their boss. On rare occasions, when the number of players fell below five, Logan drafted one of them into the game in order to have a minimum number of players. When those times occurred, they were transformed into very cautious players. Mannerheim once briefly thought of suggesting Susie as a replacement player, but quickly came to his senses.

Money affects emotions. The game was not intended to bring out anger, greed or hard feelings, therefore, the table stakes were kept small. It was a rare day anyone lost or won over fifty dollars. Vic did not like playing with nickels and dimes, so he found some chips from an old casino in Jackpot, Nevada that was going out of business. After their doors closed he managed to obtain all their then-worthless chips for the game. By necessity their values changed. The red five-dollar chips were now equal to five cents. The green twenty-five dollars chips were equal to twenty-five cents, and the black one hundred-dollars chips were equal to one dollar. It did not change the stakes any, but everyone seemed to enjoy tossing a hundred-dollar black chip into the pot. In order to assure no one became overwhelmed in the spirit of the moment, a one o'clock a.m. quitting time was strictly observed.

Mannerheim felt he was included because they needed an accountant to act as Treasurer of the chips. Whenever Mannerheim was unable to attend, and cash-out time arrived for the players at the end of the night, the bank was always off. Not because of dishonesty, but because of clerical ineptness. Besides, in keeping with tradition, Mannerheim's predecessor was a regular, so it seemed only natural for Mannerheim to assume his spot. Mannerheim was not all that fond of poker, but he knew the advantage of meeting his fellow workers in a far more casual setting. It created a rapport that carried over into the workplace. That rapport varied from friendly to tolerable, depending on the individuals involved.

As usual, the game started at six o'clock. It was straight poker. No wild cards. Draw, stud and a few low-ball hands were the norm. McPherson was going to be late, due to a meeting that was going over schedule.

Vic started the game off as the first dealer.

"Hello pigeons. Stud is the game. The color of the ante is green."

Everyone tossed in a green twenty-five dollar chip representing twenty-five cents as Vic dealt one card, face down, then a face-up card to each player.

Logan was seated as the first player to Vic's left, then Mannerheim, an open seat waiting for McPherson, Lenny Goodrich, then around to Carl Desmond, who was seated to the right of Vic.

Logan drew a king, which was high-card.

"King is worth a red one."

As he tossed in one, with everyone in turn, responding in kind.

Without even looking at Mannerheim, Logan asked,

"Your auditors happy?"

Knowing he was talking about the marker inquiry Mannerheim responded,

"Happy? Who can tell? At least they've moved on to a new subject."

Wanting to take the issue off the front page for now.

Vic dealt out the third card. The bet fell to Lenny who drew a pair of fours. In his enthusiasm he quickly threw in a green chip. Desmond, then Mannerheim dropped out as the betting went around the table.

Logan threw in more than his chip.

"Thanks again for keeping those children happy and out of my office. I'm getting too old to entertain their whims and stupid questions. They think nothing can succeed without their portable computers, cellular phones, faxes and college degrees."

"It's the way of the future, Sam. Can't stop progress."

"Your future, not mine. Nevada is losing its character as more casinos hand their operations over to a bunch of soulless corporate animals and number crunchers, instead of old pros who know people and made the casino business great in the first place. The men that had the guts to take the risks are gone. Some of the old-timers would go over to their competition and shoot craps in order to cover payroll back at their own club. They lived with disaster on a daily basis just to get this industry off the ground. Now it's just a business, and nothing more."

"I agree, it seems the bottom line is all that counts."

Mannerheim worked for several other companies where management's idea of managing was just to cut expenses, so the bottom line theoretically goes up to a desired number. This was done without regard for quality, or even trying to come up with ways of increasing revenue. What normally resulted was a loss of customer satisfaction, and resulting customer revenue, which caused an additional round of cost cutting. Too often they acted more like accountants than he did. It was also one of the main reasons Mannerheim wanted to work in a profitable operation, even if Aaron went too far in the other direction. So in large part, Mannerheim agreed with Logan.

With genuine amazement, Logan responded, "Being you're an accountant, I'm surprised to hear you say that."

"Without profit, none of us would be here, but those 'experts' seem to forget what generates that bottom-line profit. They develop tunnel vision. Nowadays each and every department has to show at profit, even food & beverage. They don't understand they were intended as loss leaders to draw people into the casino. All they seem to understand are line items and cash flow, and not what makes people act and react."

Feeling a little relaxed, Logan's thoughts drifted again to different times.

"In the early days, our cash flow was so tight we had to hold checks already made out to local merchants. If we had a good night in the pit, we would send some out a check. One angry merchant called us up and told us... *'If we didn't pay me, I'm going to tell everyone in town that we did pay me'*. We were so concerned everyone else would think we had some money, we paid the guy."

Logan smiled to himself. Then, as if talking to himself, his thoughts moved to the present as he said in a slightly lower voice...

"When Aaron goes, this place will probably become like all the other casinos in the state."

Logan won the hand with pair of kings and pulled in the pot, along with the deal. The game switched to draw. As Logan was about to deal, McPherson arrived from his meeting. Before he closed the door, an extremely good-looking cocktail waitress followed him in, to check on the ice and see if anyone wanted anything to drink that was not in stock. As she walked in, everyone cast an eye over in her direction. Poor McPherson did not even rate a hello.

Desmond leaned over to Goodrich and asked, "Is she new?"

"Hired last month... and not married." Anticipating his next question.

After checking the ice and the liquor stock she headed back to the Lakeview Room. The bet was to Vic. But his mind left the game, and his head was still looking in the direction of the door as the pretty cocktail waitress disappeared from sight.

Goodrich kept looking at Vic, expecting him to make a bet, and finally said, "Earth to Vic. It's your bet."

"Sorry boys, changed drugs this week... bet a green one."

Everyone stayed in.

Logan first looked at Mannerheim to see how many cards he needed.

"These are... *adequate*."

McPherson drew three cards, as did Goodrich. Desmond dropped out again. Vic and Logan also drew three. The first bettor checked to Mannerheim's pat hand. He tossed out a green chip. Everyone but Vic folded. As they showed their hands Vic pulled in the pot with a pair of kings, as Mannerheim revealed a pair of fours. Mannerheim knew Vic. He never folded and Mannerheim wanted to encourage this tendency with a small pot so he could count on it later in the evening.

Knowing Logan's negative view of accountants and auditors, Mannerheim wanted to distance himself from that image and establish some common ground, other than more talk about numbers and audit inquires. After all, he was there to build a working rapport with his fellow workers. It was corporate survival rule # 12. Their common military backgrounds seemed like a good topic.

"Sam, understand you served in Korea," as he dealt the next hand of draw.

"Sure did. Marines, Alpha Company, 43rd Battalion. But we didn't do much better than you did in Vietnam. Didn't you fly when you were over there?"

"What bar does she work out of?" Vic asked.

"This week she works the Lakeview Room," responded Goodrich.

"Yeah, flew in a low-flying, night-flying, twin-engine observation plane called a Mohawk. Flew right-seat, and operated navigation and infrared equipment. Found targets that generated heat, like campfires and generators, then adjusted artillery on them. They may have won the war, but at least they were cold and wet while they were doing it. How about you, Sam?"

"Infantry all the way. Bet a red." Everyone followed suit.

"Paul, what did you get out of the experience?"

"Other than fear?"

"Did you find it interesting?"

"Yeah. To be honest, I found it the most exciting year of my life. If I could have gotten a guarantee from God that I wouldn't have gotten killed I would have stayed another year. I found the whole experience fascinating. What was your experience?"

"Fascinating!... Yes, that and more. I found war a true preparation for life. Each generation in this century has been strengthened by hardship. World War I, the Depression, World War II, molded our fathers and grandfathers. Korea and Vietnam molded us. This current generation has had nothing demanded of them. They only take, and still demand. It's made them soft and spoiled. They lack discipline."

"Sam, there's a small flaw with your theory, this preparation for life of yours. It's that it has the minor inconvenience of sometimes getting oneself killed."

"The price of strength, commitment and discipline."

"Makes you want to hate peace and prosperity," inserted Vic.

"Think of it Paul. Recall your history. The Roman Empire was not destroyed by her enemies. She fell due to her internal weaknesses. Look around. Take New York City for an example. Their population has *not* increased over the last fifty years, yet illegitimacy is up fifteen times, welfare cases are up sixteen times, and murders are up thirty-four times during that period. Crime is at an all-time high all over the country. There's no regard for order. Just a bunch of social programs for the weak and lazy."

Mannerheim considered bringing to Logan's attention the fact that they were not exactly constructing kidney machines on the casino floor. It would make for a more lively discussion if he turned the conversation in the direction of how their industry affected society, but thought better of the impulse. It would defeat his purpose of attending the game in the first place. Instead, he offered the comment, "What about concern for the weak?"

"Lenny, do you think she was a natural blond?"

Desmond voiced his concern. A shrug of the shoulders was his reply.

"As it was with you in Vietnam, and me in Korea, there comes a point where the perimeter is broken, the battle is lost, and you can't change the situation. One should only concern himself with whatever it takes to survive."

"Are you referring to war, New York or the casino industry?"

"Your bet, Paul."

A little over six hours later the game ended as usual, except Vic had a run of luck and broke even. Mannerheim made about five dollars. McPherson lost thirty-three, and Goodrich about forty. The difference going to Logan.

CHAPTER 11

Saturday, October 22
7:34 p.m.

Mannerheim usually skipped dinner, but planned an evening out with a pretty escrow officer he recently met. Mannerheim gave up dating cocktail waitresses on general principal. His date came down with the flu at the last minute, but his stomach was still expecting to be fed.

Two nights earlier, Mannerheim took a party of six up to the gourmet restaurant on the top floor. That night he used his "comp" benefits and signed for the five hundred dollar meal. He indulged his stomach with too much rich food and spent most of the last two days watching his weight. He wanted to be ready for the anticipated Saturday night's meal. Mannerheim enjoyed the perks attached to his job as Controller. On a monthly basis he enjoyed almost two thousand dollars in non-salary benefits. In addition to almost unlimited food and beverage privileges, he also enjoyed free auto maintenance, laundry and dry cleaning.

Tonight Mannerheim decided to try the Mexican restaurant, instead of one of the two gourmet restaurants. Knowing Berkich worked the swing shift on Saturday nights, he invited Steve to join him. When it came to Mexican food Berkich could not tell one meal from another, so he placed his standard order from any Mexican restaurant menus, combination #4. He would eat whatever arrived.

"Paul, did you hear what happened at the Golden Palace last night?"

"Spent the day stacking a cord of fire wood before we're hip deep in snow. Haven't heard a thing all day. What went on?"

"Seems a team of players took them for over one hundred thousand dollars."

"How? Craps?"

"Roulette!"

"Steven my boy, somebody must be pulling your leg. Nobody but little old ladies play roulette. Never have I heard of any real gamblers playing that game."

"True, until now. The Palace figures they must have rotated in and out, over the last few months, and observed every turn on that particular roulette wheel. Recorded every winning number. They must have fed them into a computer until they found out what section, or quadrant yielded the highest percentage of winners. Remember, a roulette wheel is just a mechanical device, and with any

67

mechanical device, it can never be in *perfect* balance. They found out what effect this *microscopic* tilt had on the outcome of winning numbers. They came in and loaded their bets in that quadrant. After six hours of play they were up a cool one hundred thousand."

"Why didn't the casino pull the wheel before six hours went by?"

"They walked in on the graveyard shift. The poor pit supervisor didn't realize what was going on. About six in the morning their Casino Manager walked in, took one look and immediately replaced the wheel. As soon as that happened, this team of four players got up with their winnings and left."

"Not bad, and perfectly legal. I'll have to check into our system narratives and make sure the casino rotates our roulette wheels on a monthly basis. Thanks Steve, I always appreciate your little war stories. I use them to help keep our procedures as tight as possible."

"Always happy to contribute to your continuing education."

One of Mannerheim's main responsibilities was internal control. In order to write those procedures he must anticipate the ways someone could rip off his employer. Very seldom were casinos robbed by someone on the outside. Ninety percent of the time it was by an employee. A good Controller shares many similar traits to that of a good cop. You must think like your opponent, and anticipate the unusual, then write control procedures to keep someone from doing it. In that regard, Mannerheim always enjoys listening to Berkich's rip-off stories.

"Amazing, it's always a constant battle to keep some devious mind from enacting some similar scheme on us."

"Speaking of devious minds, that brings us back to Logan. What did you think of Matt Hamilton?"

"I guess he'll do."

"His attitude a little abrasive?"

"How'd you guess? The guy must have enough work to support that attitude."

"Don't take it personally. It's a hangover from his standard approach as a cop. Diplomacy was just a token job requirement. Why do you think I never hire ex-cops as security guards? But don't worry. He'll do a good job for you, and he should even warm up a little after he works with you a while."

"I'll look forward to the thaw. Meanwhile, I'll give him a try and see what he comes up with. Want to hide my tracks if I'm wrong about this, so I asked him to go though you instead of me, if that's all right?"

"No problem with me."

Berkich was enjoying the possibility of the hunt, especially if it involved the pit. Security was getting far too routine.

"What's on your schedule for the weekend? They're sponsoring some boxing matches at the Golden Palace. I intend to pick up some easy money betting with the tourists... Cortez is fighting."

Billy Cortez was a rotten boxer. His only saving grace was that he was a local and accustomed to the six thousand plus feet of elevation. Some first-class opponent from Los Angeles, or Chicago would murder him during the first three rounds. Then the altitude kicked in and from then on, Cortez controlled the fight. Eventually his winded opponent finally went down, gasping for oxygen. During the third round, locals would find tourists who anticipated the outcome based on the amount of Cortez's blood laying on the mat up to that point. It just convinced Mannerheim never to accept an obvious bet based upon somebody else's suggestion.

"No thanks. Looking forward to watching some football games this Sunday. My team is playing the Saints. How about taking the Saints if I give you six points?"

If you live in Nevada you found a severe shortage of home teams to cheer for. The closest professional team was San Francisco Forty-Niners, which was the team Mannerheim was referring to.

"Not me. Even if Montana isn't playing anymore. They should still win by at least a touchdown. But I'll tell you who would take that bet. Try Vic. He'll take the Saints at the drop of a hat. That's the team he used to play for when he was young and dumb."

"I didn't know that. I knew he played pro football, but I never knew the team. So he played for the New Orleans Saints!"

"Four seasons."

"Interesting."

*

9:18 p.m.

Later that night Mannerheim made a swing though the casino. He went through the casino floor, the health club, three bars and two restaurants until he discovered his goal. There sat Vic Welles talking to a good looking waitress.

All executives in the place had access to meals that were the envy of French kings. However, Vic indulged more than the rest of them. His years as a football player developed a frame that was more the shape of solid barrel, which required constant feeding and exercise. Within a few more years his body's metabolism would change and show the effects of the same amount of feeding, with less amount of exercise. Even now, his body was catching up to his eating habits. Last month Vic complained about a loss of energy. According to his doctor, based upon a blood sample, Vic was accumulating high levels of uric acid and was close to developing the gout. Mannerheim also remembered Vic complaining about the strict diet his doctor put him on. As Mannerheim approached his table, he saw Vic bite into a big juicy steak, stuffed with oysters and mushrooms.

"Vic, I thought your doctor restricted your diet?"

"Paul my man, please don't mention that sadist while I'm eating. If he had his way, all I'd be able to eat is celery, cardboard and Alpo. Let's talk about anything else. Pull up a chair, pour some wine and make yourself comfortable. Say, what are you doing here, didn't know you moonlighted, or did your payroll girl tell you about my last advance?"

"Another advance! You've got to get a bookie who accepts American Express."

Vic reminded Mannerheim of a tax client he once had. The man had a unique philosophy. He did not want to own a million dollars, he wanted to owe a million dollars. He figured he would have the same lifestyle either way. But if he owed a million, when he died, he would be better remembered.

"No, I'm not here to hassle you about your payroll problems. I had to check something in the cage."

"Good. Say, I sure enjoyed our little poker game last night. Entertaining for a country boy like myself to listen to all the different ways of looking at things that come around the table."

"Yeah, Logan was more talkative than normal?"

"Oh, I've figured out Logan. Reminds me of old Robert E. Lee."

You lost me on that comparison. I'm a student of history, but I fail to see any similarity between the two."

"Oh, I didn't mean the man. I was thinkin' of my granddad's old plow horse. We named him Robert E. Lee."

"Okay, I'll bite. Lay another one of your southern home-spun stories on me."

"Well, my granddad bought this beautiful new plow horse, during the early thirties. He would harness that horse up to the plow, and every time he tapped that animal on the rump, that horse would leap six feet into the air, taking my grandfather and the plow with him. When my granddad would finally finish the row, he would look back and see barren ground between deep ruts."

"Okay, okay, you've got me hooked. Where you taking this?"

"My granddad finally figured out he bought himself a stump horse."

"Stump horse?"

"Didn't they teach you city boys anything? A stump horse is a horse used to pull tree stumps out of the ground. They were trained to give it everything they have for a couple of seconds, then wait for the next time. From what the family tells me, they never could reeducate that animal to pull a plow. My granddad finally gave up. After that, all that horse was good for was carrying the children around the farm."

"And you've got some comparison between this stump horse and Logan?"

"Sure. Logan can't learn other ways of doing things either. Everything is changing around him. Some for the better, some for the worse. No matter how much things change, Logan is too set in his ways to feel comfortable with what's going on around him."

"Now you showed me a different way of looking at things. You've convinced me. I'm going out and buy a book about the wit and wisdom of Will Rogers."

"My pleasure. Say, if you're available, I'm throwing a party for some players in a hospitality suite on the eighth floor. You're welcome if you don't mind associating with nobody sober."

The party probably consisted of a bunch of Vic's worthless friends, and a lot of pretty female employees. Mannerheim was not going to take inventory of the guest list, but thought he should at least play the part of Controller.

"You entertaining a junket? I thought it was your off-season?"

"Really it is. But today I found out alcoholism is a disease and not my fault. And all this time I thought it was a result of my poor character. That's got to be something to celebrate."

"I'm sure all that's on your diet. Sounds entertaining, but I've got to pass, got an early morning. Got to review the cash requirements in connection with our commercial paper procedures, being I have to roll it over the first thing Monday."

"What's commercial paper?"

"Nothing you'd be interested in. Just boring financial stuff."

"No, I'm trying to expand my knowledge. Somebody told me there's more to life than wild women, fast horses and old whiskey."

So summed up Vic's philosophy of life, which Mannerheim admired for nothing less than its simplicity.

"I don't believe them, but I could always be wrong."

"Oh, its just how we invest our surplus money. Our major money requirements fall on the weekend when there are more players. That's when we need our largest amount of cash. On the weekdays our cash requirements are at their lowest, but most companies have just the reverse cash needs. They need it on the weekdays and not the weekend, so I invest our surplus weekday cash with our broker, Piper-Wilson. They buy short-term, four-day commercial paper of major companies. We convert it back to cash in time for the week-end activity. That way we pick up another hundred thousand dollars in interest income each year that we otherwise would lose if we left it just sitting in our vaults, or checking, or with the bank's low interest savings accounts."

"I was right! There is no more to life than women, horses and whisky."

"But I applaud your attempt."

With the bait planted, Mannerheim headed off to the cage, which occupied a large built-in area along the west wall of the casino floor. The cage provided a hub of activity, it served as the in-house bank for the entire operation. If chips were added to, or taken from any gaming table, they went through the cage. The cage also cashed chips, checks and made change for customers. In addition, it also served as custodian for the change banks of food and bar registers, and housed all unpaid casino markers. Every day the revenue from all operations of the hotel/casino ran though the cage, which prepared the daily deposit to one of several possible banks. The early cages, like early banks, had bars separating the cashiers from the customers, hence the term "cage."

Being that was where the money was stored, occasionally some desperate idiot would try to rob a casino's cage. It was like robbing a bank located in the middle of Grand Central Station, covered by fifteen overhead surveillance cameras and surrounded by a dozen private security guards. For that reason, Mannerheim had never heard of anyone trying to get to the vault, but several had attempted to rob cashiers. It was not a common crime. In fact, it had only happened once during Mannerheim's tenure, and the individual was quickly apprehended.

Mannerheim approached the cage through the side alley. He walked past a security guard who had just received a fill and was heading back toward a crap table. By routine, Mannerheim turned his head back and looked at the security guard. Due to the historic low pay given to security, and resulting high turnover, it was difficult remembering their faces. This almost subconscious procedure by Mannerheim was due to a story Berkich once told him.

It happened to a new casino in Vegas. Seems an individual walked past the front cashiers and down the side alley of the cage. This area was not meant for the public, but for the use of security and pit personnel. Whenever a table needed chips (called a "fill"), it was not practical to wait in customer lines, so this side alley provided quick access. Security or a pit supervisor then told the cage cashier the table number, the amount and denomination of the fill. This guy obviously had the jargon down. He boldly walked up to the side cashier and announced, "Ten thousand, black, BJ-12." (Meaning, I need ten thousand dollars worth of one-hundred dollar black chips for blackjack table #12.) The busy cashier hurriedly prepared the fill and pushed the rack of chips toward the man, dressed in a nice three-piece suit, for his receipt and signature. The man scribbled an unreadable signature on the required fill slip, turned and headed off toward the pit with the rack of chips in hand. The money never arrived on blackjack table 12. As he was never found, nobody ever found out if he was an employee, or not. They did know they were missing ten thousand dollars in negotiable chips. New casino or not, management quickly made sure the cage cashiers knew the faces of all security officers and pit supervisors.

A cage cashier saw Mannerheim at the entrance and hit the button that released the door lock. She flashed a formal smile to her boss's boss, which Mannerheim returned. Mannerheim knew the names of a couple old-timers, but cashiers also turned over with consistent regularity. With the sound of the buzz, Mannerheim went through the door. He immediately saw his Cage Manager, Robin Hale, reconciling some paperwork at her desk.

Robin heard the buzz and looked up to see Mannerheim, "Evening, Paul. What brings you out on a Saturday night?"

Robin was an excellent Cage Manager. Some twenty-eight years ago she started out as a bank teller, and quickly rose to become their Branch Manager. Mannerheim first worked with her as a customer, when he needed a loan to buy his condo, and appreciated her competency and friendliness. When he had a vacancy in his cage, he hired her as his Cage Manager. It did not take much to talk her into making the move. She was already vested in the bank's pathetic retirement plan, and at fifty-four she was ready for a change, but not ready to knit afghans. It helped that Mannerheim beat what her prior employer was paying her. In order to get the salary package approved, he did have to pull some strings with Susie.

David Hannuksela

All the casinos in the area paid "competitive wages." That meant that they all paid more-or-less the *same* for each position. Unfortunately for the employees, they all paid low. It resulted in a high turnover for everyone except executives and those employees who received "tokes" from the customers. Low pay, coupled with the high cost of living in a resort area, resulted in an *average* turnover of three hundred percent among the total employee population. Some departments were less, some more, depending on the department.

Robin approached the cage like it was her bank, and did not take any lip from the pit. At least once a month Logan complained about her aggressive style. Mannerheim always managed to focus the complaint to some Gaming Control Board requirement, or some internal control procedure, and away from her style. Not that Mannerheim thought the world evolved around rules and regulations, but wanted a Cage Manager to have enough of a backbone to keep the cage from becoming a wimpy yes-*man* to the dictates of the pit. Besides that, it amused Mannerheim that Logan was forced to deal with a woman. Probably the only woman in Logan's life who he did not intimidate. At her stage in life, Robin was even more independent than Mannerheim. He still had need of continued employment and, as a result, still needed to play the political game.

"Here due to a combination of my stomach and my curiosity."

"Being I never claimed to cook, you must need my help with your curiosity?"

That remark only reflected the truth. Once Mannerheim attended a dinner at the home of Robin and her husband, Bud. Robin cooked and it took three days for the heartburn to die. Mannerheim figured she must own stock in Rolaids. Robin's comp privileges were on a par with those of Berkich's, but hers always amounted to twice his average monthly totals. However, Mannerheim *never* suggested she reduce her use of their restaurants. He figured it was not just a privilege for her, but a life preserver for Bud.

"You're right. Fortunately, I just fed my stomach at the Mexican restaurant. I'm here because I need you to keep an eye out for any *large* markers being issued to any unfamiliar players."

"Like the kind of unfamiliar players Fitz was asking about last week?"

"Just that kind."

"As I was pulling their credit applications, and comparing them to their current marker balances, I could see why you were interested. Talked to Fitz yesterday, he told me you talked with Logan on Tuesday concerning the lack of documentation. He tell you anything that would shed some light on those players?"

"Please, don't ask me about Logan so soon after eating. But to answer your question... not much. I'm trying an alternative approach. I'll let you know when I get something solid."

"In the meantime, you want me to run up a flare when I see any more similar markers?"

"Yeah, let me know as soon as you can. If I'm not in my office, call my condo. And I'm not curious enough that you need alert anybody else in the cage. Keep this between you and me."

Normally Mannerheim would never suggest that Robin do anything else but keep it confidential. The fact that he mentioned it at all conveyed to Robin how sensitive the matter was becoming.

"You got it, boss. By the way, I see your old friend is playing the tables again."

"Being I only have a handful of friends, you're assuming I can figure that out, but you're going to have to give me more of a clue than that."

"Sarge. He's been on table 32 for the last two days."

"Two days! How's he doing?"

"Same as always, he's losing. It's just taking him longer to do it."

With that Mannerheim left the cage and headed to table 32. Sarge was easy to spot. He had been there so long he was falling asleep. The impatient dealer had to touch his hand in order to wake him up long enough for him to determine if he wanted another card.

"Sarge."

"Hey, kid... how's it going?"

"Better than it seems to be going for you. How about calling it a night? Let me arrange for a hotel room for you. I don't want you falling asleep behind your wheel on the way home."

"Thanks, but I'm doing fine... don't worry about me."

"Sarge, you've lost just about everything. You're now playing minimum bets. The little you have in front of you won't get you even. Call it a night."

"Paul... you don't understand... getting even has nothing to do with it... all that counts is staying in the action."

Mannerheim paused for a second. He then remembered his experience in Vietnam. To the surprise of his relatives, Mannerheim wanted to stay for another tour of duty. He really did enjoy the *action*. Like an adrenaline junkie, the action also hooked him. Luckily he was never shot down, so the grim reality of the situation never touched him. Wars eventually end, unlike the availability of gambling.

"Okay, Sarge. We'll do it your way."

Mannerheim then went over to the security booth occupied by one of Berkich's officers. Berkich was also there, standing next to the booth.

"Steve, do my a favor. Keep an eye on Sarge. I'm going to arrange a comp room for him. Could you make sure he gets there?"

"Paul, I don't see why you care, but I'll make sure it gets done. Looks like it won't be long before he's totally broke or totally asleep."

"Thanks Steve."

With that accomplished, Mannerheim picked up the security phone hanging on the wall next to the booth, and dialed the number to the hotel's front desk.

*

About noon on Monday Mannerheim got the call he was expecting.

"Mr. Mannerheim, this is Ron Irving with Piper-Wilson. I understand you requested we notify you if anyone inquired as to the purchase amount of your commercial paper transactions. We did get a new inquiry concerning a purchase at 4 1/2%. I would suggest..."

"Excuse me Ron, but I've got one quick question. From what location did the inquiry came from?"

"New Orleans, sir."

"Thank you. That's all I wanted to know. Complete the best available transactions at your own discretion."

Now the source was known. Vic was feeding inside information to Yarbrough. Mannerheim rolled it over in his mind. *They must have met when he was playing for the New Orleans Saints. Probably envisions himself to be the next Casino Manager. This could be useful. No need to disclose this to anybody for now.*

CHAPTER 12

Saturday, October 22
10:24 p.m.

If a person wanted to blend into the scenery, the perfect place to do it was in a casino. Tourists, players, locals, dealers, waitresses, the hopeful and the hopeless just occupied their space and time waiting for the gods to smile down on them. All had mentally spent their future fortune they expected to come with the next card, or roll of the dice.

A little knowledge is not a cure, but a hook. Dealers see the lost bets, but still assume they are privy to some magic secret. Many casinos feed on their own. They pay their employees with cash instead of by check. They figured their employees returned 40% of their salary back to the casino in additional food, liquor and gambling revenue before they ever get out the door on payday. Mannerheim never liked the practice but was unable to override the casino's appetite for revenue, no matter the source.

Matt Hamilton was about the only person on the floor with different agenda. He sat in the bar's darkest corner for his third night of surveillance. He hated the long hours of stakeouts, and was starting to hate Diet Pepsi. But as stakeouts go, this was fairly easy, as it was out of the snow or rain. Even the chair was almost as comfortable as his car seat. So he sat in the bar waiting for a signal from one little old lady about thirty-five feet in front of him. Helen was the one doing all the work.

Helen found it difficult to concentrate. She was expected to keep track of the cards being dealt, as well as look for a face she saw briefly only three times before, most recently a good month ago. It was fortunate Berkich guaranteed Helen her standard one hundred dollar profit if this hurt her game performance. The first night she had to take him up on it after a frustrating experience where she was lucky to break even. The second night she achieved her hundred dollar goal. Normally she would not even be working three nights in a row, but Berkich stressed the importance of finding that player. She was beginning to regret she ever mentioned him to Berkich in the first place. If she had not, she would be watching Jeopardy! right now.

"There! The man two tables over... Talking to the Shift Manager. Talking to... McWhat, McDuff, Mc... McDonald, that was it, McDonald. He is talking to McDonald. Now what? Oh yes, take off my coat."

Within one minute after Helen slipped off her coat, Matt Hamilton made his way through the crowds and was in the seat next to her, with a two dollar bet on the table. By the time Helen could roll her eyes in the right direction, the player was signing a marker slip.

The casino employee was dressed in a dark, well-tailored suit. He looked to be in his mid-forties, stood a couple inches under six foot and weighed about two hundred and twenty pounds. He was joined in the pit by another well-dressed individual in his mid to late fifties. The older man also signed the form, and tore the yellow middle copy out and slid it down the chute on the table's drop box. He handed the white bottom copy to the waiting player. The two pit employees then turned and went to the small cabinet in the center of the pit, where they slipped the top copy of the form in a drawer. Hamilton noted all that from the corner of his eye, for his main focus was on watching the player.

The player received a large pile of black chips, which Helen had informed him each represented one hundred dollars. By Hamilton's rough estimate, there was at least thirty thousand dollars in front of him. He then started playing a single chip at a time. Hamilton went over each and every notable feature of the man. One thing was sure, the man was not an Oriental. Not that everyone with money, and came from Hong Kong, had to be Oriental. He did not fit the physical profile of Hamilton's version of a "high-roller". No close shave, perfect haircut, or fine tailored suit. Maybe the player was on vacation, and not at work. Hamilton decided to cut him some slack over his shoddy appearance.

Ten minutes after receiving the first marker, the player received a second marker and was standing up, preparing to leave. Hamilton was right behind him. Two minutes behind him was Helen, who was out the casino doors in hopes of catching the final question on Jeopardy!, and glad to be through with this game of hide-and-seek.

*

Sunday, October 23

The sound of the phone awoke Mannerheim at 4:16 a.m. It was almost expected. Some four hours earlier, two large unpaid markers were issued to another "unfamiliar" player. When they were transferred from the pit to the cage at the end of swing shift, Robin called him from the cage to report the news. There was no need to alert Hamilton, as Mannerheim knew he was already on the job. Besides, the markers were a couple hours old by then. This time the call was from Steve Berkich, who got right to the point.

"Paul, I just got a call from Matt. Our player showed up last night. He signed a couple markers, placed a couple small bets, then took off with the money. Matt managed to maintain contact with him as he made his way through the crowds down to the Starlight."

The Starlight was a small operation three blocks away. If it ever went out of business, Mannerheim was sure the state of Nevada would block any future owner from establishing a similar operation. It did not conform to the current psychology of "style and class" established with the large casinos. The Starlight was one of a half dozen small "mom and pop" operations that were under a grandfather provision, made under more liberal rulings thirty years ago.

"He saw the player wait at their bar for fifteen minutes. The man was met by someone who Helen previously identified as Todd McDonald, the Shift Manager who approved the guy's markers just an hour before. They talked for less than a minute. Matt saw the player pass a large, thick envelope to McDonald. Then they both left."

"That's it, then. We've got him! But you're the ex-cop. You tell me, do we have them?"

"Depends on who you want. Todd McDonald may be Logan's Shift Manager, but he's not an independent thinker. Being he won't blow his nose without Logan's approval, we both know he would never attempt something like this without the full knowledge and support of Sam Logan, but try to prove that to a jury. And what we do have probably won't even hang McDonald. He'll just say he met a good player by accident and said hello to him. As far as the envelope goes, it could have been recipes their wives were trading. You'll have a rough time convincing a jury that it was our chips in that envelope."

"Great! What about the player? Did Hamilton manage to follow him after he left the Starlight?"

"Yes. He kept with the player and followed him over to the Golden Palace where he checked into one of their hotel rooms. He paid for it with cash and disappeared into the elevator. Even though he was the only one in the elevator, it stopped at six floors as it went up from the lobby to the eleventh floor. I checked with my counterpart at the Palace and had him confirm the name and room number. It was registered to a Wayne C. Smith. My friend even had a maid pretend to bring new towels to the room. She found it totally undisturbed and empty."

"Smith! The pit never was creative. Does Hamilton think he went through that because he saw him and tried to cover his trail?"

"Not a chance. If Hamilton was following me I won't even know it. No, he thinks that was just part of their pre-established plan. It shows they thought this out and were as careful as possible."

"So we have nothing!"

"Not exactly. We have a picture of the player Hamilton took at the Starlight. He will give us each a copy in the hopes we may know the guy. I ran up the employee data files on my terminal and showed Hamilton the computerized image scan of McDonald. He confirmed Helen's initial identification. More important, we have Hamilton's total enthusiasm that there's a real case here. He wants to bring in an additional employee just to handle future night photography and help him with surveillance. He also wants to run his own check of all those bogus players on your most recent marker listing."

"There's only so much I can bury under the topic of 'employee background checks', but give him the green light. Just have him keep each individual billing under my $1,000 authorization limit so I don't need a second signature on the checks. By the time the auditors question them we will probably be heroes, or out the door anyway. We both know how vindictive the pit can be if we attack them and can't prove it."

"In that same vein, Hamilton is providing both of us with gadgets to put on our phones to detect bugs. He also wanted to know if you own a handgun."

"Don't you think that's a bit extreme? I know it's a job perquisite to be a little cold-blooded in order to be hired for the pit in the first place, but I've never pictured Logan reacting with violence."

"Paul, we're talking about millions of dollars, and you just said how vindictive the pit can be if we're wrong. Think about their attitude if we're right, where they could be facing long jail terms for the rest of their lives. Logan will react anyway he has to if he feels threatened."

"Yeah, you're probably right. Tell him I'll get one tomorrow. I had a Colt .45 in the army. I think I can still remember how to shoot the thing."

*

Monday, October 24
7:26 a.m.

Mannerheim was just coming out the casino bar with his morning cup of coffee in hand. Within ten feet he noticed Max Gray coming across the casino floor from the opposite direction.

"Good morning Max."

"Good morning Paul."

Mannerheim was never known as a decent singer, but he made an attempt.

"Off we go, into the wild blue yonder, flying high into the sun..."

Max just looked back and smiled.

*

8:45 a.m.

First thing Mannerheim did when he arrived at his office was pull up the swing shift activity on the computer. Two large markers were issued. In total they amounted to fifty thousand dollars, and were issued to a player with three hundred thousand dollars of markers already on the books.

Fitz walked in and handed Mannerheim his review of all players with marker balances above one hundred thousand. Mannerheim put the paperwork into a large manila envelope for Hamilton, via Steve Berkich.

*

Hamilton received the manila envelope from Berkich late that afternoon, and immediately started to work on it. He went to his computer, activated his modem program, and started to access the Super Bureau database, a side road on the information super highway unknown to the general public.

When he was a police detective he had access to government databases, but after he retired he learned to navigate the available public databases. To his delight, almost all the information he once obtained through the police department was still available through public access. He did miss access to the FBI's computer database, referred to as NCIC (National Crime Information Center). But those computer databases available to Hamilton provided him with criminal records, driving records, marriages and divorces, real estate holdings, civil lawsuits, bankruptcies, business applications and history, and the color of the subject's underwear. In several cases Hamilton worked on investigations involving governmental agencies, and found out how handy the Freedom of Information Act can be. About the only information not available to him were copies of tax returns. The IRS does not share with anyone, at least not yet.

Included on each player's application was their social security number, a useful piece of data to aid in research. Since most of the suspect players were identified as Hong Kong citizens, there were no social security numbers. At least that was the explanation indicated on the credit application. Even with the few that had a number, no great benefit was achieved. With each number Hamilton typed in he noticed the name belonging to the social security number did not correspond with the name of the player. From there it just got worse. Nothing tied to anything. Even if they were all foreigners, they were required to have some papertrail. Casinos were required to withhold a percentage of their documented winnings, usually from a big slot machine payoff, and send it to the IRS to await a non-resident tax return for any income earned in this country. That's how the system should work. But not in this case.

Even with numerous databases at his disposal, Hamilton had the same lack of success as Fitz.

CHAPTER 13

Tuesday, November 8
3:12 p.m.

Berkich's small office was not on the second floor with the "executives." It was tucked away in the most obscure corner of the casino floor. Over half of the people who attended the Thursday management luncheon did not even know where the office was located. All this was fine with Steve Berkich. Being out of the limelight, and out of the line-of-fire, provided additional job security. Job security that he was about to put in jeopardy.

The overhead cameras were the responsibility of the Surveillance Department, but "courtesy" cameras were installed in the security office. Since it was not his department's responsibility, Berkich did not assign a security officer to monitor the cameras. But Berkich did encourage his people to study them whenever they were in the office. He felt it trained them to always be on alert.

Today Berkich was on the phone with one of his security officers. The youngster was giving one excuse after another as to why he was unable to show up for his evening shift. Due to the low pay earned by security officers, and the high cost of living in a resort area, Berkich was used to dealing with less than professional employees. As his employee was developing his third lame excuse, Berkich's mind was on auto-pilot, and his eyes were searching the office for something more entertaining than the conversation. Suddenly, his eyes focused on one of the six surveillance cameras. Currently the camera was directed on pit three, crap table two. Without saying good-bye he dropped the phone and headed toward the pit.

Marcus Adams worked for the casino for six years. For two of those years, he had been a "Stickman." In that position he was responsible for the speed of the crap game, calling the numbers thrown, and determining who had control of the dice from moment to moment. Prior to that, he dealt blackjack for three years. He was about the age of Logan's first son from his second marriage. Logan was at the point that he just numbered his marriages, similar to how historians number our world wars. The only difference was Logan had twice as many marriages as the world had world wars. Besides age, Adams also shared enough similar features with his son that Logan took it upon himself to take Marcus under his wing. In return, Adams followed any and all orders given by Sam Logan. He knew the basic glue that kept the casino together, and it was *not* loyalty to Aaron Davenport. Few of the casino personnel had seen Aaron, and even fewer talked to him. No, the glue that held everybody in the pit in place was their loyalty to Sam Logan. And Marcus Adams maintained blind loyalty to Sam Logan. For that reason, as opposed to any natural talent, Adams quickly rose through the ranks until last year, when he was promoted from Stickman to Boxman, the name for the supervisory position on the crap table.

Casinos provided their managers and supervisors with salaries that almost guaranteed their employees a very comfortable standard of living. That practice was based on the assumption that if they were not in desperate need, they would not be tempted to dip their hand into the till. In keeping with that theory, Marcus Adams was already in an upper income bracket. Unfortunately, he maintained a taste for drugs that exceeded the financial benefit offered by his employment, and far exceeded almost anyone's cost of living. Marcus' loyalty to Logan did not preclude him from stealing Aaron Davenport's money. After all, it was not as though he was putting his hand in Logan's pocket and taking his money.

Marcus sensed several people approach the crap table on his left side. Expecting anxious players with their blank looks and sweaty hands, he was surprised to see Steve Berkich and two of his security officers. Knowing that Logan would be called, Berkich decided not to wait for that "no-win" confrontation in the middle of the pit. Any delay would work against him so Berkich had his security officers literally lift Marcus and carried him off. Since both security officers were taller than Marcus he found himself moving his feet, but neither managed to find the floor. As they made their way back to the security office, Berkich looked over to a bewildered Ethan Scott, the Casino Shift Manager on duty, and asked him to follow them. Better to invite him along, as opposed to leaving him there to alert Logan.

Marcus was at first stunned. That feeling quickly turned to anger. Once all were in the office Berkich shut the door and took charge of the conversation.

"Take off your jacket. Now!"

Marcus just sat there and looked at the Shift Manager for help. By nature, Casino Shift Managers were not a timid group, but Ethan Scott was out of his comfort area, and the situation was beyond his immediate understanding. In lieu of instructions from Logan, who was not available, Scott was no more than a curious spectator. Berkich waited only a few seconds before he nodded to his officers and the coat came off. With it three one-hundred-dollar bills fell to the floor.

As Berkich had watched on the camera, whenever Adams received a hundred dollar bill from a player, he then placed the bill over the slot above the drop box. He then placed the paddle, with his right hand, on top of the bill and appeared to push it down into the waiting drop box attached to the underside of the table. However, a trained eye would observe that as the bill was disappearing under the front of the paddle, it was being pulled up the other side, by the left hand of Marcus Adams. If performed properly, an individual just a few feet away could not see Adams palm the bill. Unfortunately for Marcus Adams, Steve Berkich had a trained eye.

Berkich's long-held suspicion was correct, Marcus was a thief.

*

That evening Mannerheim and Berkich met at the Lakeview Room. Marcus Adams no longer worked for Aaron Davenport, but neither was he in jail. Hotel/ Casino operations are reluctant to publicly prosecute most of their dishonest employees, especially those who were there to insure the game's honesty. The line workers, such as the dealer who palmed the ace, would be sacrificed to set an example to the rest of the staff, but seldom a pit boss. It would embarrass a casino to admit that they had hired employees with such poor character and placed them in such key positions. It made the image of dishonesty in the industry a reality. And in the casino industry, *image is everything*. Generally, the employee just walked away, forever blackballed by the industry, while the Nevada Gaming Control Board quietly revoked their gaming license.

Mannerheim was quick with the opening greeting, "Hello, hero."

"No hero here. I can't even say I was just doing my job. You know Paul... If it had happened just a couple weeks ago, I can't say with any honesty that I would have taken the same course of action."

Mannerheim chose not to argue the point. Berkich did not share as secure a position as many who had a direct rapport with Aaron. Taking down one of Logan's lieutenants was risky. If he was wrong, Logan would attack him with all his power and influence. In order to keep peace in the family, Aaron would most certainly terminate Berkich. If he was right, he would forever be on Sam Logan's hit list. At some later date Logan would extract his revenge. Even after Marcus Adams was caught and terminated, Logan angrily tried to defend and reinstate him, but it was too widely known by then. Even if Carl Desmond wanted to save Adams, it was beyond his control. The Gaming Control Board, specifically Jeff Meyers, was made aware of the situation. On paper, they were in the immediate area performing a standard audit review, and just happened to document the arrest. In actuality, Mannerheim phoned Jeff as soon as he heard of the confrontation.

"Quite a chance you took."

"Between us, the *only* reason I took the risk was because of the marker investigation. After Hamilton's surveillance I feel we're committed. If we are going out on the limb, another few inches won't make that much difference. In the end it will be him or us anyway. Besides, I enjoyed it. It reminded me of the days when I took a course of action because it was right, not because it was politically correct. That, and my frustration with the dealer case, prompted me to do something."

"Yeah, how's that case coming along? As I remember, you needed to find the dealer's missing partner in order to save the case. Any luck?"

"No, not yet. Couple days ago the District Attorney called me and suggested we drop the charges for now. He said we could always recharge the dealer when we find his partner. Then we could play one against the other, and get the conviction down the road. I'm afraid I had to agree. I've been looking for the guy, but no luck so far. Seems that we can't ever get anybody in jail. Everything has just been so frustrating lately."

"I know what you mean, but don't overreact. I suggest you start watching your back. At least for the next few weeks, you better not get any further out on that limb. I'd hate to see Logan saw it off."

"I know ... I know."

"Just be glad you didn't see Logan's reaction up in Desmond's office. The fact that Adams ripped us off was of absolutely no concern to him. All Logan cared about was defending someone loyal to him. In any other industry the whole conversation wouldn't have taken place. Even in the military, loyalty to a general, admiral, or even the President, doesn't exceed that due the Constitution or the code of military conduct."

"What was Desmond's reaction?"

"Luckily, it was out of his hands after the Gaming Control Board got involved. All he could give Logan was some sympathy. If it had to come down to Desmond, I would have hated to depend on him to do what was right."

"We, and Hamilton, better come up with something we can use against Logan before he starts to plot against us."

"Right you are."

*

Tuesday, November 15
3:26 p.m.

Mannerheim was on his way to the computer room when Fitz approached him. Mannerheim sensed Fitz was amused about something by the angle of his mustache.

"Okay, what's up?"

"Did you heard what Max Gray did in the slot department?"

"He took the airplane out!"

"Nope, but he did take out those twelve three-reel slot machines and replaced them with twelve four-reel machines."

An additional reel will multiply the odds by another 76, which in effect took the odds from 440,000 to one, up to 33 million to one.

"Paul, you're into astronomy. How often does Halley's comet come by?"

"Once every seventy-something years as I remember."

"Well, the next time he has to worry about giving away another plane is sometime after Halley's next two visits. Max claims he can now sleep at night."

Mannerheim also started to smile as he headed off to the computer room.

"Can't say as I blame him."

By necessity, Mannerheim was responsible for the computer department. He was the logical person to manage it, but found the department his most difficult area to manage. Computer programmers were in a group by themselves. They almost make accountants look normal. They seemed to hate working with people. They just wanted to retreat to their computer room and play with their bits and bytes. Every few months they would pop out and announce they just completed some grand program that was designed to help the front desk, or the pit, or some other department. What irritated Mannerheim, was their habit of never asking the departments for their input regarding problems or solutions. As a result the end-user department always hated the program. It did not fit their needs, it was difficult to use, and therefore they did not want to use it. Changes were an insult to their creation. Even when Mannerheim suggested moving a comma, it was always met with the same response. *"It would take two programmers a full month to make the change."* From start to finish, Mannerheim's roughest problem was to get the programmers to sit down with the end-user, and work as a team.

As Mannerheim entered the computer room he stepped up on the raised flooring that supported the large mainframe computer placed in the center of the room. Underneath the flooring were air conditioning ducks that served to cool the computer and keep the monster from overheating. Mannerheim had toyed with the possibility of establishing a similar network using small PCs for each department's needs, but decided to wait until he could get another year's worth out of the current system, mainly to justify the massive cost already invested in the mainframe. When the time arrived, he anticipated a major battle with Dale Hawkins, the head of his Data Processing Department. Dale would surely guard his pride and joy for all his worth.

Adjacent to the computer room were several working offices for the programmers. The walls separating these offices from the computer room were constructed with solid wood panels on the bottom and glass panels up to the ceiling. That way the programmers could always see and bond with their mainframe. In one office Mannerheim noticed Adam, Aaron's grandson, busily hitting keys as he glared into the computer monitor at the workstation.

Adam was a common sight in the computer room. He was never with friends his own age, and never seemed to go out of his way to communicate with others. Over the last couple years, as Adam roamed around the computer area, Mannerheim tried several times to strike up some conversation but could not seem to find any common ground for a discussion. Mannerheim attributed the problem to the fact that Adam bore the handicap of being a product of the public school system.

One of the major drawbacks of working in an organization that had a single owner was the risk of working for, or with, that individual's relatives. Since Aaron's wife, daughter and older sister had already died off, most of the remaining relatives, other than Desmond and Adam, were cousins, nieces and nephews. There was always the possibility that a conflict with any one of them would force Aaron into a position of choosing between Mannerheim and one of his own relatives. Fortunately for Mannerheim, most of Aaron's relatives did not want to work in the accounting department, or anything connected with too much work or too many numbers. The other departments associated with Mannerheim also required a certain degree of competency. The pit excitement was better suited to their collective abilities and temperament. Logan learned to sacrifice minor employees in order to be on the good side of the relations he was saddled with. The relatives, in turn, learned not to attack Logan or his inner circle. But Adam was not a relative Mannerheim could totally ignore. Paul knew Adam could easily be *his* employer in another few years, Mannerheim thought it was in his best interests to make one more attempt to be on the kid's good side.

"Afternoon Adam, how goes the battle?"

"Fine."

Another snappy response. With this kid's personality Mannerheim thought he was destined to develop into the perfect computer programmer.

"What are you working on?"

"I'm trying to debug this program that determines the amount of laser blasts the Enterprise can sustain without damage to its shields. It's one of the elements of a game I'm working on with Dale."

Mannerheim quickly thought, *"If the kid likes Star Trek, he can't be all bad."*

Dale Hawkins contributed the vast majority of Adam's knowledge about computers and programming. They were sort of "kindred spirits." Which generated major doubts with Mannerheim concerning the kid's future ability to relate to the rest of the world.

"Your dad tells me you may be interested in working in the pit when you turn twenty-one."

A comment that was more of a hope than a statement of fact.

"That was his idea, not mine. Thinks I should learn the business. I've told him it's not a business I care about. Just an excuse to rob and steal. I intend to do more useful things with my life."

"Well don't worry. Your generation will have its turn to screw things up."

"Well I won't! And I won't have this rotten business to worry about."

"How do you figure?"

"Dad says grandfather will be leaving soon and we'll have more money than we need. To do anything we want."

"Did your dad say the reason your grandfather will be leaving?"

"Not really. Something he's working on with that lawyer... Elliott."

"Now Elliott is working with Carl Desmond! Taking advantage of all the love in that family. Interesting!"

CHAPTER 14

Monday, November 14
5:00 p.m.

As happens during mid-November, the weather could not seem to decide whether it was time for winter, or still wanted to cling to fall. Mostly it rained, mixed with days of light snow. This day it was snowing just enough to make driving miserable. As the sun set, and the temperature dropped three degrees below freezing, the thin wet slush on the roads turned to "black ice". The road may look bare, but this thin layer of ice caused cars to totally lose control. Even four-wheel drive vehicles had no assurance of a safe trip home. In fact, the mast majority of accidents involved four-wheel drive vehicles. Their drivers paid the price for being over-confident and pushing their mechanical advantage beyond the margins of safety.

Don Soreng had just gone off duty as the Day Shift Security Supervisor. For the last four hours he had monitored the local radio station that gave special emphasis to weather reports, road conditions and traffic accidents. After going into gruesome detail concerning the injuries incurred in the fifth accident report, the disc jockey finally reported the Nevada Highway Patrol had issued a traffic advisory. Unless urgently required, they suggested it was best to stay off the highways. Soreng decided to phone his wife in Carson City. She answered on the first ring.

"Hi honey. Have you been listening to the weather reports?"

"Yes. You going to stay over?"

"Yeah, I think it would be best. I don't want to take a chance on going over that pass. I should have gotten new tires on the Ford. In fact, I should have done it months ago. Promise, I'll do it Saturday."

"Okay, but please do me another favor. Stay away from the tables."

"I will... I will. See you tomorrow, honey."

With that promise in mind, Soreng headed for the hotel front desk to take advantage of the fifty percent employee discount available during marginal weather. Even with the discount, Soreng made sure he got a standard rooms, nothing fancy. He could get by without an extra telephone next to the toilet, a basket of fruit, or a mirror on the ceiling over the bed. All he needed was a comfortable bed, and not a wild time in the fantasy land of casinos. The discount served the advantage of both the hotel and the employee. As long as there was space available, the hotel made additional revenue, and the employee saved a dangerous trip home. As with most employees, Soreng carried a small bag in his car trunk. It provided him with extra clothes and the needed essentials necessary for the stay.

After Soreng checked in, and deposited his bag in the room, he turned on the television. Ten minutes of watching traffic accidents did not excite him, and decided to go for a walk before dinner in the employees' cafeteria. His boss, Steve Berkich, had some 'comp' privileges, but it stopped at his level. Even though Soreng carried the title of Shift Supervisor, he lacked restaurant privileges. The job barely provided enough income to meet the needs of his second wife and newborn baby girl. Most security officers were single, as few could support anyone else on their salary. Aside from the executives on the second floor, all decent salaries were confined to casino supervisors.

Five years earlier, his first marriage ended as a result of his gambling habit. Since then he faithfully attended his Gamblers Anonymous meetings. He toyed with the idea of leaving Nevada, but his family and boyhood roots were there. During this low period of his life, Soreng met Sandy, who would become his second wife. Shortly after they married, they decided to buy a small home in Carson City. For them, Tahoe was far too expensive. For the first time in his twenty-eight years and after finally paying off his debts from the past, Soreng was now free to enjoy life.

Soreng's walk ended in the lounge, where he ordered a beer. The beer and the Keno runner arrived at precisely the same time.

"Care to fill out a ticket?"

Keno is a lottery type game where the player selects a set amount of numbers out of the possible eighty numbers available. A bingo type cage is turned, and twenty numbered balls fall out. If a certain number of your choices are selected, you win. The odds against winning big are equivalent to those of a state lottery. The hook lies in the fact the bet could be as low as a dollar.

"Sure, for a dollar I'll try it."

It would provide him with something to watch while he finished his beer prior to heading down to the employees' cafeteria for dinner. Ten minutes later the numbers on the large Keno board in the lounge began to appear. By the time Soreng first took notice, four of his seven numbers were lighted up on the Keno display. He was already a winner. Then a fifth lit up. A minute later the sixth blinked on. Finally, the last of the twenty numbers flashed on the screen, and filled out Soreng's set of numbers. He just won twelve thousand dollars.

Within five minutes after he collected his winnings and filled out the required forms, Soreng was back on the phone to his wife.

"Honey, guess what? I was having a beer and played a dollar on a Keno game, and we won twelve thousand dollars."

Technically Keno was not a table game, but it was still gambling. Just ask *Gamblers Anonymous* as they add more chapters in states were lotto/lottery games have been established. In one form or another, the only states that do not permit gambling are Utah and Hawaii. Even if state governments did not use gambling to raise revenue, then every Indian tribe with more than three members were busy building casinos on tribal property. There were almost one hundred Indian casinos operating across the land, with more opening their doors with each passing month. The Blackfoot were now dealing blackjack to their white neighbors. It was their way of taking back the West from the evil white man.

Notwithstanding his promise to her, this was not the time for Mrs. Soreng to lecture her husband regarding his fall from grace.

"Oh honey that's great! At last we can finally afford to put up some decent drapes in the living room, and maybe... visit my folks in Houston?"

"Sure, whatever you want. We can finally afford to take some of my accrued vacation time, and actually go someplace. I'll just pull enough out to have a good meal in the restaurant, instead of the slop they serve in the employees' cafeteria. Saturday we will celebrate together with a great meal in Carson City, right after we buy new tires, and pick up those airline tickets to Texas."

"Okay, but I worry about you carrying all that money around with you. Can't you put it on deposit with the cage until you're ready to come home?"

"Just what I was planning to do with it."

"This is just wonderful. I'll turn you loose so you can get something to eat, while I phone my mom with the news. Try to get to bed early, and I'll see you tomorrow evening. Lov' you dear."

"Love you too."

Soreng went to the cage and deposited everything but one hundred dollars. Then he headed for the Lakeview restaurant, where a waiter, who was much better dressed than Soreng, served him a juicy steak and an Australian lobster tail. In the spirit of celebration, he also ordered a small bottle of red wine. Craving replaced celebration, as the wine was followed by several shots of scotch and water. By seven o'clock he was feeling no pain, and kept remembering the great return he generated from his minimal amount of effort. He still had thirty dollars of his hundred left. At that moment, he decided to try and duplicate his success. If he won, so much the better. If he lost anything, it was just the last of his fun money. The promise to his wife was forgotten somewhere between his second and third scotch.

It took just four minutes, after Soreng arrived at Blackjack table #28, to lose his remaining thirty dollars. The speed of the loss amazed Soreng, and just instilled within him the desire to remedy this minor injustice. He headed for the cage.

Three hours later Sam Logan was making his rounds as he swung through the pit. He located Todd McDonald.

"Evening Todd, so what's happening?"

"It's turning into a good evening, boss. Babcock is back, over at craps three. He's sure not hurting us. As usual, his luck is rotten. Of course, a little more skill at the game could drag the final outcome out a little longer. As it is, we can plan on another twenty grand in drop before he's out of here."

He then double checked his memo pad that recorded the shift's win/lose trend.

"How do think an accountant, who works for an insurance company, can afford to lose that kind of money?"

Logan managed one of his rare smiles.

"He can't. Keep an eye on him. Sometime soon, you'll see a couple of guys from some law enforcement agency show up, slap some handcuffs on him as they take him away."

Last year a player arrived with fifty thousand in cash. Instead of holding that large amount of chips in front of him, he placed the money on deposit with the cage and played against it. The Cage Manager, Robin Hale, became curious about the player and ran the information from his driver's license through Central Credit. It turned out the guy was wanted on a felony warrant from Minnesota relating to embezzlement charges. Before she reached for the phone to call the Sheriff's department, she notified Logan of the situation and her intentions. Logan stopped her until the player finished losing the last of "his" deposit on the tables. A blind eye was maintained until the transfer of funds was achieved. Money being king, it ruled over lesser values.

"Anything else?"

"Yeah, see the guy on 28. If he looks familiar, it's because he's a shift supervisor with security. Name's Don Soreng. Got lucky at keno, but managed to lose all twelve thousand over the last three hours. He now wants a marker for a thousand. You know what security gets paid. He's not qualified, and more than half drunk. Initially I turned him down, but thought you might be interested."

"Security! Yes, I'll be glad to talk to him."

Logan walked over to Soreng's blackjack table as he was busy receiving another free drink from a cocktail waitress. Knowing introductions were not required, Logan started the conversation.

"I hear you need some credit. I've always felt we should provide our fellow employees the same benefits we provide our regular customers. I understand you'd like a thousand dollar marker."

Even in his foggy state, Soreng recognized Logan and immediately felt uncomfortable in his presence. It was the equivalent of one end of the food chain coming face-to-face with the other. Soreng only nodded.

"Then it will be my pleasure. Good luck, and enjoy yourself."

With that Logan turned back to McDonald, approved the issuance of the marker with his signature and, in a low voice, gave his instructions,

"Bury him."

In another two hours Soreng was in debt to the amount of five thousand dollars. All the while, inhaling more drinks than he could remember. He would have continued to stay at the tables, signing his name to more pieces of paper, if it were not for Steve Berkich. Steve got word of the situation from a sympathetic dealer, and arrived to pull his supervisor off the tables.

*

Tuesday, November 15
12:40 p.m.

Mannerheim and Berkich were having lunch. The quality of the meal was lost on Berkich, who was having trouble digesting much of anything.

"I can't believe Logan. He deliberately took his revenge over the Marcus Adams incident and set out to ruin one of my supervisors."

"Steve, what did you expect? We knew Logan would find a way to extract his revenge."

"But against me! Soreng was an innocent bystander. Logan set out to ruin a man just because of who he worked for. Soreng phoned his wife about the keno win. Instead of a twelve thousand gain, they are now looking at a five thousand dollar debt. Besides losing the money, he probably lost the trust of his wife. This could ruin his marriage. And speaking from experience, I know what that

95

can do to somebody's life."

"Unfortunately, Soreng was just a target of opportunity. Knowing Logan, it was just his style. He knows you could recover from an attack better than Soreng. He wanted to give you something that would haunt you. By the way, better clue Soreng into our tax reporting requirements."

"What do you mean?"

"The keno department is required to take down the name, address and social security number of all big keno winners. We send that information to the IRS, and Soreng gets a 1099-form at year-end, indicating that keno win as taxable income."

"But he lost it!"

"Which is why he better go hunt up Todd McDonald and get him to sign a statement, as a representative of the casino, verifying he witnessed Soreng lose those winnings. Soreng can then safely deduct his losses, equal to his winnings, and avoid a tax bill. But he better document it, because we don't send notices of table losses to the IRS to offset that keno notification."

With barely a thanks for the tax advice, and leaving what was left of his lunch, Berkich was gone and in search of Soreng. Berkich's sympathy increased for Soreng, knowing his underling had to again face his embarrassment.

Mannerheim took a few extra minutes to finish his lunch before he headed back to his office. Just prior to reaching the stairs Mannerheim saw Logan walking from the cage on his way to the pit. Mannerheim stopped and waited for Logan to reach him.

"Just found out about Soreng. Really Sam, that was a cheap shot for you."

Why Paul! I'm surprised. Based upon my knowledge at the time, I was led to believe he's free and over twenty-one."

"Granted, he's responsible for his own actions. But correct me if I'm wrong, shouldn't we selectively provide opportunities to our customers based upon their ability to handle them? The guy was too drunk to know what he was doing."

"Paul! We're an equal opportunity vice. A dollar bill looks as big as a bedspread to me, no matter who's holding it. No matter if drunk, sober, tall, short, lame, crippled or crazy. Subject only to our state's law on minimum age requirement relating to gambling, of course. As for being drunk, why do you think we feed our customers free drinks while they're playing anyway?"

Logan's background supported his position. He entered the casino industry in the mid fifties as a young blackjack dealer. It was a period in Nevada's history most state politicians would just as soon forget. The depression and the world war of the previous decades were behind the nation. The only thing that was exploding now were the economy and the income it generated. The nation wanted to celebrate and Nevada offered them the opportunity. It was wild, and open to almost anyone. "Anyone" included individuals from little Italian "families" who lived back East. Logan was never part of their inner circle, just a spectator in the gallery. As he rose through the casino ranks in Las Vegas, these "pioneers" were being phased out of the industry by the state, or aggressive competition. Still, their approach and philosophy left an impression on Logan. It served as his basic training all the way up to his post-graduation work. Human weaknesses were something to be exploited and not corrected. Money, and getting it, were the only factors that defined success. He also learned any challenge to his position was only encouraged if it was not answered with a swift and sure response.

Mannerheim knew debating ethics or morals with Logan was a losing endeavor. Besides, for this time, this place, logic seemed to side with Logan's argument. He also felt he was not a fit subject himself to champion Soreng's cause. Mannerheim just nodded and resumed his walk back to his "glass" office.

*

Five hours later Soreng, in anticipation of a future tax audit, was standing by the front door, waiting for McDonald to arrive for work and sign a statement witnessing his losses. Even his still massive headache could not distract him from the horrible thought of facing his wife the next day. Unknown to him, Sandy was spending the afternoon consulting a divorce attorney.

CHAPTER 15

Wednesday, November 16
11:12 a.m.

Carl Desmond's secretary showed Scott Sherman into her boss' spacious office. Desmond was quick to greet his visitor with a wide smile and a warm handshake.

"This is a great honor, Mr. Sherman. Being a weekend tennis player myself I'm glad to have this opportunity to meet a master. Would you care for some coffee, or maybe some tea?"

"Tea would be appreciated, Earl Grey if it's available."

Desmond nodded to his secretary as she closed the door.

"I assume you're looking for a sponsor for a celebrity tennis tournament, or maybe an introduction to some of our local charity programs."

"Thanks, but I'm here in another capacity. I'm the new spokesman for the Nevada Silver Shaft Mining Corporation."

"Oh, I think you've made a mistake. We would only sponsor organizations that contribute to the tourist industry. Mining is a little out of our area of interest."

"No, I think the mistake is on your part. We are not looking for a sponsor, or your endorsement. I'm just here to notify you that we intend to start operations in the area. Sort of a welcome wagon visit in reverse."

"Oh, I wasn't aware of any mining operations in the Tahoe area. You sure the Virginia City area isn't more in tune with mining? We are more of a tourist area. Exactly where were you planning to start your mining operations?"

Scott walked over to the Desmond's window, with Desmond in tow. He pointed to an area of grass between two paved parking sections.

"We thought we would start there."

"I'm sorry, but you're pointing to the middle of our parking lot."

"Exactly."

"But we own that property!"

"That's only partially true, you may own what you can see, but the Nevada Silver Shaft Mining Corporation owns the mineral rights under your property, and we hereby give notice we are going to exercise those rights."

*

Mannerheim was in the middle of a procedural discussion with Jeff Meyers when the phone rang. It was Carl Desmond's secretary. Her customarily squeaky voice was even higher than usual. Mannerheim's presence was required immediately in Desmond's office. That caught Mannerheim's attention. Never had Carl Desmond ever worked on anything that required anyone's immediate attention. Sheer curiosity drove Mannerheim down to Desmond's office.

As Mannerheim walked in he could see Carl Desmond, Thomas Elliott, and an unknown man sitting in a chair drinking a cup of tea. Mannerheim guessed his age as late forties, or early fifties. He immediately wished he was as thin and trim when he reached that age in another few years, or even now for that matter. Desmond was sitting down, looking a little confused.

Elliott was visibly agitated, and was the first to speak.

"It seems we may have a little problem, Paul. Mr. Scott Sherman here says he represents a company which claims to have the mining rights on our property."

"Claim is not a totally accurate description. We do own these rights, as documented by the copies of Mr. Drew Williams' will, the deed of sale of this property to one Aaron Davenport, and a copy of the sale of the mineral rights, as recorded in the Douglas County Assessor's Office."

Feeling the need to say something, Mannerheim asked, "Who is Drew Williams?"

"Drew Williams was the rancher who sold Aaron Davenport this property some forty-one years ago, this coming December," responded Scott.

"However, Mr. Williams did not sell the mineral rights that went along with the property. Those he retained, up to the time his heirs sold them to the company I represent. I would guess your owner, Mr. Aaron Davenport, didn't consider them of any value to justify an increase in his initial purchase price for the property."

In an effort to come on like a lawyer, Elliott announced,

"You may or may not have rights to mine-scrap metal on the moon, but I will tie you up in litigation for so long your children will be complaining about their social security benefits before you ever dig a shovel full of dirt on this property."

"I gather you are not an attorney who specializes in mineral rights."

"I normally specialize in labor negotiations, but I'll be glad to make an exception in your case."

"And am I correct in assuming you didn't obtain your law degree in the state of Nevada?"

"The law works the same in all fifty states. File a lawsuit, delay, judgment, appeal, delay, judgment, appeal. I don't know the financial depth of your company, but trust me when I tell you we can outspend and outlast you."

"Oh, I doubt that, but to help set the tone, let me inform you about some unique characteristics concerning Nevada history and its related law. Nevada became a state on October 31st, 1864. That was during the Civil War. Their claim to fame was the vast amount of gold and silver they produced. Later, I believe, President Grant personally came to Virginia City to thank the miners for providing the silver which helped finance the Union's war efforts. Nevada is still responsible for 32% of all the silver production in the United States. Which is why the state's nickname is the 'Silver State'. Am I boring you?"

"Aside from a history lesson, what's your point?"

"You see, in Nevada, mineral rights have priority over all other property rights. Those old miners made sure of that. Nevada only got around to creating legalized gambling in 1931, and they gave very little thought to removing those old mining laws from the books. You know the priority you lawyers give to adding, as compared with removing laws. You sue us, knowing the full weight of Nevada law is on our side, and we will claim it as a frivolous lawsuit and countersue you for an amount equal to the value of this hotel/casino. And we will win! Even if it takes years in the court system."

"Would you excuse us for a minute while I confer with my clients?"

Win or lose, Elliott realized more than anyone in the room, that this could drag his own plans into a bottomless black hole, consuming massive amounts of time and money.

"Take all the time you wish. We won't be starting our rotary drills for at least a week."

This time Desmond felt the need to say something. "Did you say drills?"

"Yes, it's for the core samples, but it shouldn't be too noisy. But when we start sinking our tunnels, we will have to do some blasting."

"Blasting?"

"Yes. I would suggest you notify your guests. We don't want anyone phoning 911 and declaring an earthquake alert. You might consider giving them a little notice at the point of checkin."

Because Elliott wasn't saying much anymore, Desmond thought he could cut to the heart of the solution.

"If all you say is true, would your company consider selling your mineral rights for a sizable profit?"

"Not really. And I wish you all a good afternoon, and thank you for the tea."

With that Scott turned, opened the door, and headed down the hall toward the elevator.

Over the next few minutes the three of them just stared at each other. Finally Desmond spoke.

"You two are supposed to be the college kids. Got any ideas?"

Elliott took those minutes to run the problem over in his mind.

"Okay, the way I see it, we have four alternatives. First, despite his threat, we could still file an injunction in local court. We have at least five judges who owe favors to Aaron, not to mention a few hundred thousand in reelection campaign funds this place has given them over the years. That's not even taking into account the judges I know personally. I've never heard of this outfit. Even if they have money, they couldn't have the political clout we have."

Mannerheim thought it interesting that Elliott knew so much about Aaron's political contributions. But now was not the time to ask Elliott about the reasons he acquired that information.

"And choice two?"

"If what he said was true, we could have some of our legislative friends pass a new law to reverse, or repeal any provision of the law that would permit them to engage in mineral exploration in the Tahoe basin."

That was the good news, soon to be offset with the bad.

"There's only one problem with that solution."

It did not even have to be said. Both Desmond and Mannerheim knew the problem. Unlike California, where their legislators meet in almost constant session and as a direct result have produced the thickest constitution in the history of the known world, the state of Nevada permits their lawmakers to meet only three months once every two years. Most of the time they ran over the three months, but then taxpayers stopped paying them for their overtime. It's Nevada's way of limiting useless laws. The last session adjourned about three months ago. The next legislative session would not meet for almost a year and a half. To get the Governor to call a special session solely for the business interest of one casino was a possibility, but they could get better odds on the roulette wheel.

"What's the third choice?"

"We could get the environmentalists and the press to mount a campaign to shut them down. Recently environmentalists kept an old couple from building their retirement home on their own property, just because it's within the Tahoe basin. They should jump at a chance to close down mining operations."

Mannerheim liked that option.

"That sounds like a good idea. We spent almost a million fighting the

102

environmentalists so we could build our new parking structure. It's about time they do us some good. Any downside with that?"

"This company could just deny they are even engaged in actual mining. They are just sinking a few exploratory core samples every week, for the next few years, in order to determine if there's anything to argue over. They could say they are within their legal rights, but would be flexible to the environmental concerns if they ever decided to sink an actual shaft. Remember, this is Nevada, not California. The environmental movement carries less weight over here. They could mount a case of a basic state industry in battle with some Greenpeace extremists, all in the name of state's rights. It will play well with the locals who are tired of these tree-huggers anyway."

"What's left?"

"We just buy them out. This whole thing smells like a blackmail scheme anyway, and it would sure be faster. But we need to know who we're facing. Paul, let's research these guys. Let's turn their story inside out. Got any bright ideas?"

"As a matter of fact, I have been working with a highly competent investigator who's been doing some minor employee background checks. I could have him investigate this company and trace their money all the way back to the mint."

"Sounds fine. You research their financing, and I'll research our legal and political options."

Desmond made a valid point when he asked,

"Don't you think we better notify Aaron?"

"Certainly, and as legal counsel I would suggest I should be the one to brief him on this legal situation. However, let's better evaluate our options prior to alarming him of something that may prove superficial. Agreed?"

"Agreed." The last thing Desmond wanted to do was bring bad news to Aaron.

*

As soon as he returned to his office, Mannerheim paged Matt Hamilton.

"Better start hiring some extra help. We just expanded our need for your services."

It took Mannerheim only a few minutes to give Hamilton the little he knew about Scott Sherman, the mineral rights claim and the Nevada Silver Shaft Mining Corporation.

Thanks to a contact at the Public Records office in Carson City, it took Hamilton less than an hour to call back with some initial information.

"The Nevada Silver Shaft Mining Corporation only came into existence last week. So they have no business history at all. Looks like it's not much more than a shell of another company. All their stock is owned by an offshore corporation called the Caribbean Mining & Exploration Corporation. Their business application, on file with the Secretary of States' office, indicates they have three officers. One you already met, Scott Sherman. He is listed as the Vice President of Public Relations. Another is Rob Mayo, a local Reno business attorney. His office is also listed as their official business address. The last is one Edward Kendall. Looks like a non-resident alien. His address is also the official business address of the holding company, a PO box in Georgetown, Grand Cayman Island. Wherever that is."

"It's the largest of three islands under British dependency. Collectively they are known as the Cayman Islands, located just south of Cuba."

"Geography one of your interests?"

"It is when it's a tax-free refuge for foreign funds and has numerous branches of most major European and American banks. My bet is Mr. Kendall is a banker at one of their more silent banks, or maybe another attorney. This figures. They set it up like I would have. With as few tracks as possible for us to follow. Anything else?"

"Yes, one other item. Their application lists no liabilities and only one asset, and that's a checking account located with the Tahoe Bank and Trust."

"Did they indicate the dollar amount of that account?"

"Yes, at the time of the business application, they indicated an account balance of five million dollars."

"Five million! They want us to know they have deep pockets. They put that much in a checking account! They don't even care about making any interest on it. Money to burn, money needed to engage in a legal fight. Interesting."

"Better start checking into those three officers and that holding corporation. We might consider the need for you making a trip down to the Cayman Islands and see how cooperative the local natives may be with any available business records."

"If the British set the place up, they must have a public records office."

"Don't dust off your passport just yet. Find out anything and everything you can at this end first, and keep in touch."

Mannerheim put down the phone and realized they may never be able to determine the source of those five million dollars and the identity of the real individual behind this scheme, but his gut feelings tilted toward New Orleans, and Randy Yarbrough.

*

Mannerheim walked into the Tahoe Bank and Trust within twenty minutes after it opened. Before he was able to reach the manager's desk, the manager had spotted him and was already closing the distance between them with his hand extended. Every bank manager within the Tahoe Basin knew Paul Mannerheim. Aaron and Desmond developed a policy of spreading goodwill in the community. When that philosophy came to banking it meant spreading their banking needs among all the banks in Tahoe, and even some of the larger ones in Reno. Mannerheim always thought it was a major nuisance to establish eight different checking, and twelve savings accounts among so many different banks, but it was Aaron's decision to keep all the locals happy.

"Mr. Mannerheim, how may we be of help to you today."

Paul always felt like a celebrity whenever he walked in any of the local banks. His mother never gave him so much attention. Anyone on the signature card of the bank's largest account will always be appreciated by the local banker.

"Good morning, Richard. How's business?"

"Very good, thank you, but we always have room for some more of your surplus funds."

Bankers are never shy when they have the need of your money, as opposed to their outlook during the times you may have the need of some of their money.

"Everything been satisfactory with our service?"

"I'll know in a minute. I need to see a signature card for one of your checking accounts."

"Mr. Mannerheim, as valued a customer as you are, you must know that's very confidential. I can't just show you something that would violate the privileged information of another customer, not to mention various banking regulations."

"This is of major importance to us. Of course, I could have Aaron call and discuss our needs with you, especially concerning who's on the checking account belonging to the Nevada Silver Shaft Mining Corporation."

"Do you also need their current balance?"

Within ten minutes Mannerheim knew everything the banker knew. Most confirmed what Hamilton had already discovered. The account consisted of five million dollars, less a twenty thousand disbursement recently made payable to Scott Sherman, which was the only disbursement made from the account since it was opened. Three individuals were listed on the signature cards. Two were already known; Rob Mayo, the Reno business attorney, and Edward Kendall, the Cayman Islands representative. The new name was that of a Mr. John Stremel. Scott Sherman was not on the signature card, even though he was the one who opened the account and provided the bank with the completed signature card. The account required two signatures for any disbursement. The business tax identification number probably belonged to the holding company, but Mannerheim would pass it on to Hamilton for confirmation.

CHAPTER 16

Thursday, November 17
12:45 p.m.

Sam Logan mentioned his pending vacation as a minor comment during the normal Thursday afternoon luncheon meeting. Made by anyone else it would normally have been received as just that, a minor comment. But coming from Sam Logan, Mannerheim considered it a major announcement, especially when Logan was asked by the Hotel Manager, James McPherson, where he planned to go. The answer... the Bahamas.

Mannerheim wasted no time walking over to the Golden Palace, picking up a public telephone, and paging Matt Hamilton. Thanks to a cellular phone, the page was returned in less than a minute.

"What's up?"

"Better dust off that passport. Sam Logan is leaving on a sudden vacation, as of tomorrow."

"Is that unusual?"

"The last time Sam Logan left on a vacation Ronald Reagan was still in office, and that was because his eighty-something-year-old mother was dying. But what really got my attention was where he plans to go... the Bahamas."

"Let me guess. Besides being a tourist spot, it's also another one of those quiet little islands that serves the needs of those with money to hide."

"Exactly. Not the one I would have chosen, but adequate for his needs. It's another little country where the British encouraged international banking and use of sun tan lotion."

"I suggest I have him followed from the time he walks out of his office till he returns with his tan. But I'm going to need some help to maintain twenty-four hour coverage."

"Do whatever you have to do. I can now bury the cost in the Cayman Island investigation. Just find out what he's up to, and I'll bet he's not going down there for a tan."

"Remember, I'm no betting man, but even my father wouldn't touch that one."

*

Friday, November 18

Sam Logan was on vacation. Carl Desmond took his son, Adam, to Disneyland for a long weekend, and Lenny Goodrich had relatives in town. The monthly poker game for November was therefore canceled.

*

Friday, November 18
8:12 a.m.

Sam Logan boarded Western Flight 223 for Miami. He sat in first class, while Hamilton went tourist and as far back in the plane as possible. After a two hour stopover, they both took another flight which went directly to Nassau.

Since his departure from Reno airport Hamilton had been in climate controlled, or air conditioned environments. As he disembarked from the plane, he walked into the clear, but sweltering air of the Bahamas. He felt like he walked into a sauna. In the span of just the last few hours, the temperature increased by more than fifty degrees. Hamilton quickly reached for the sunglasses he purchased at a gift store he visited in the Miami airport. Even from the view obtainable from the top of the passenger ramp, he was surprised any scenery could produce so many different shades of green.

The Spaniards first discovered the Bahamas via Columbus, but it was the British who colonized the islands in the seventeenth century. Fortunately for both Logan and Hamilton, this resulted in English, instead of Spanish, being the national language. Over two hundred and fifty years later it was converted from a British crown colony to an independent nation. Independent on paper from England, but not in truth from the United States. Each year, each resident mingles with ten tourists. Prior to this stable support by American tourists, the economy was temporary sustained by American rum-runners during Prohibition, who were preceded by Confederate blockade-runners during the American Civil War. Their economy, otherwise, was dismal. Even with tourism and a thriving international banking center, the nation still suffered a high rate of unemployment. A condition Hamilton was about to take a *small* step to cure.

Because he was going to work in a foreign country, Hamilton knew he would be uncomfortable with the local environment and customs, so he wired ahead and hired a local private investigator to provide backup. They met at the airport. The local was a young investigator named Tommy Freeman. His only "professional" claim to fame was looking in open windows with a camera, usually after midnight. Half the time he was employed by the future ex-spouse of one of the parties at the other end of the lens. The other half served to replace the need for cable television. When he was not working as an "investigator" Tommy was a deck hand on a sports fishing boat, or a part-time tour guide for one of the large passenger cruise boats when they arrived in port. Not the professional Hamilton was looking for, but it was a matter of any port in a storm.

Based upon pre-arranged instructions, and an advance of expense money, Freeman arrived at the airport with two cellular telephones and a pager. He handed Hamilton one of the phones and a piece of paper indicating the numbers of the pager and phone that Freeman retained. Hamilton pointed to Logan as he was standing in line awaiting customs inspection. With that Freeman was off and running. Matt Hamilton would normally attach himself like a second skin to his subject, but this time he let Tommy, and a cabbie he claimed to be some relation, do most of the shadow work. They could blend into the scenery much better than he could. Hamilton did not want to be noticed by over exposure.

Logan went directly from the airport and immediately checked into the Grand Banks Hotel. Within forty-five minutes he left the hotel, and flagged down a cab. Surprisingly, Logan dress was casual. Usually he wore a three piece suit, but today he just had on a two piece suit. In keeping with his normal habits, Logan also wore black cowboy boots. In fact, almost all the executives at Aaron's, including Mannerheim, wore cowboy boots with their suits. They were more comfortable and far warmer, especially in the winter. Logan's dark, wool suit was made for the temperatures of Tahoe, and not the Bahamas. Instead of serving the effect of blending into the masses, Logan's conservative attire only made him stand out in the otherwise colorful crowds. While the suit made Logan feel presentable, it made Tommy feel amused.

Initially, Hamilton held some doubts about Tommy, but as it turned out, his money well spent. He knew everybody. He knew the cabbies, hotel workers, old people and young kids. One of Tommy's contacts was an underpaid hotel clerk who informed him Logan checked into room 402. Another was a maid who let Hamilton into the room while Logan was out. If Logan headed back to his room, Freeman was instructed to call Hamilton immediately, so he could vacate the room. The call was not needed. It all resulted in a wasted effort on Hamilton's part. It was a scavenger hunt that yielded nothing of interest.

After the search Hamilton found himself with some free time. Even if Logan was turning this into a business trip, there was no reason for both of them to be monks. In a few weeks Hamilton would be looking at ten feet of Tahoe snow. Might as well take back some pleasant memories. Time for some of the world's best diving.

Hamilton learned to scuba dive on a vacation to San Diego. He tried it once in Lake Tahoe. After that attempt, it took three days for the blue color to disappear from his lips. It was like swimming in the Arctic, with about the same view. The bottom of Lake Tahoe consisted of nothing more interesting than an empty beer bottle embedded in the empty white sand. He soon found a dive shop, and headed for the coral reefs of the island. As he submerged himself in the crystal clear water, Hamilton contemplated whether to discount his hourly billing rate to Mannerheim for the time involved.

Later that evening Tommy found Hamilton at the bar he suggested at the airport that morning. Hamilton indicated he wanted a location that was not usually visited by tourists, so they could be assured Logan would not walk in on them. He was not fully prepared for Tommy's suggestion. It appeared to be home for every two-legged, and four-footed dock rat on the island. The place looked like the maid quit years ago. Hamilton ordered a beer, and fully intended not to use the glass that accompanied it. Hamilton, always confident he could take care of himself, still welcomed a friendly face.

"Evening, Tommy. Our subject nice and bedded down?"

"With a guardian angel looking through the peep hole in the opposite room. Just to make sure he does not sleep walk."

Hamilton was glad the local labor rates were reasonable.

"So, where did our subject go, and who did he talk to?"

"The cabbie took him to our local branch of the Singapore National Bank. He stayed not even an hour before returning to the hotel for late lunch. He then used telephone in the lobby and made several overseas calls using credit card. I must tell you this man is exceedingly boring. He can not be a dealer of drugs. They at least know how to party."

"You make a valid assumption."

When your whole life rests with your power and your position, you do not know what to do with yourself when you are out of your element.

"Can you find out what he did at the bank?"

"That I already know. He opened savings account. Deposited five thousand United States dollars."

"I assume your friend is the Bank Manager, and he told you this."

"Oh no! My friend is computer clerk who recorded the new account info.

Bankers have no known friends. Bank Manager is modest, quiet little man. He about as boring as your Mr. Hopkins."

"Wait a minute! Did you say Hopkins?"

"Yes. Mr. Henry Hopkins. The man at airport this morning. The boring man we follow all day. The man you keep calling the Subject."

Hamilton then pulled out a picture provided by Mannerheim, from the employee database files, and showed Tommy the computerized image scan of Logan. "Are we talking about this man?"

"Yes! Mr. Hopkins."

"Tommy, I'm impressed. You just justified this whole trip."

Hamilton took a moment to wash his smile down with a slug of his beer before his train of thought changed direction.

"I also have a little problem down in the Cayman Islands. Don't suppose you know anyone there?"

Feeling better about Tommy, Hamilton decided to hop an island flight to the Cayman Islands to see what he could find out about the Caribbean Mining & Exploration Corporation and their subsidiary, the Nevada Silver Shaft Mining Corporation. Operating in his own environment, Tommy could follow Logan around town better than he could anyway.

CHAPTER 17

Wednesday, November 23
11:15 a.m.

Due to a previously scheduled meeting with bankers and investors, Elliott delayed his trip to Alaska to brief Aaron by one week. He would have preferred to have made the trip sooner. It took him countless hours to persuade Aaron to sell out in order to better settle his estate. Now this mineral rights problem put a dark cloud over any pending sale. He did not want that hard-won conclusion to be reversed on this technicality. Elliott was not a sentimental person, and was not overly concerned about missing Thanksgiving with his family the next day. After all, it was a matter of priorities.

Elliott had lined up four money brokers in Reno and two in Vegas to put together a financial package to arrange the buyout. They represented a faceless consortium. After the dust settled, the face of Thomas Elliott would emerge, and step into the position of power that belonged to him alone. Elliott had figured out how to bring in his own appraisers and lowball any possible selling price. As Elliott waited for his flight, the wheels inside his head were turning. *"Maybe this mess could be a blessing in disguise. This could drive the price even lower. Just have to keep a tight leash on my loose cannon. Just can't let the old goat decide to dig in, or back out, and screw up my whole plan"*.

Elliott hopped an Alaska Airlines flight out of Reno, with a brief stopover in Seattle, then on to Anchorage. At the Anchorage airport he changed to Bush Express Air Service where he was scheduled to fly a twin-engine prop craft that would take him the final leg into Kodiak. As he left the terminal and started his walk to the loading area, he was greeted by a plane that looked like a reject from some ancient war. Elliott had his secretary request first class. Now he understood there were only "seated" class throughout the narrow airplane. He sat next to some overweight salmon fisherman from San Diego. Looking around he discovered everyone looked like fishermen, mixed in with a dozen or so women and children. He was the only one wearing a tie. He hoped this airline at least served drinks or this was going to be a long flight into Kodiak.

An hour later Elliott looked out his window as the plane was lining up for its final approach into Kodiak. Besides the harbor, he could see little that held his interest. A mile or so on one side of the airport was a military base. Unknown to Elliott, it was the largest Coast Guard base in the United States and one of the busiest. Many a fisherman, alive today, owed a debt to the efforts of the U.S.C.G. in the Gulf of Alaska. The base also serves as the community's largest single employer. On the other side of the airfield lay Kodiak's harbor, filled with a several hundred fishing boats. Several large canneries awaited the harvest of not only salmon, but halibut, herring, and cod. The small commercial and residential areas were nestled along the adjacent slopes. Within these boundaries Kodiak housed less than seven thousand people, smaller than several communities around Lake Tahoe, but large for an Alaskan town. The main intersection consisted of four streets converging in the middle of town. To the locals, if more than two cars arrived at the stop signs within the same few seconds, it became the accepted definition of "gridlock" to the locals. Also scattered around the island were various little native villages that increased the total population to sixteen thousand. If the population were equally spread over the entire island, it would result in a little less than four people for every square mile.

What immediately struck Elliott was his own hand, hitting his neck, as he attempted kill a mosquito that was in the process of extracting a quart of blood. The mosquito is jokingly considered Alaska's state bird. The town had a small, but challenging nine-hole golf course. It was short on caddies and finely groomed fairways, but long on rough and mosquitoes, who were almost big enough to carry their own clubs. Even the hardy Alaskans sought relief. They imported a colony of bats to a cave located next to the course, in the hope the bats would dine on the mosquitoes. In the end, the mosquitoes won out. It was the opinion of the locals that the mosquitoes looked at the bats as a source of nutrition instead of the reverse.

Soon after his landing, Elliott was approached by Stan Austerman. Aaron had sent Stan to retrieve Elliott. Elliott wondered how he knew who he was without asking him his name. Stan was a little over fifty and was considered one of the best salmon fisherman on the island. He alternated between being a surveyor and a hunting & fishing guide, depending on the season. Over time he tried his hand at being a bartender, working on halibut boats or in canneries, among other occupations of convenience. He had lived on Kodiak his entire life and was not impressed with lawyers, expensive suits or famous people. What impressed him was a thirty pound King salmon on the end of a twelve pound test line as he stood on the bank of a clean, fast moving stream. Aaron also impressed him. He liked the old boy. He found Aaron honest and unpretentious. For someone from the lower forty-eight, he was not in a big hurry to get down the road. He would spend some time talking with the guy on the other side of the counter as he ate his hamburger. They also liked the same brand of beer. Stan could see this lawyer was not cut out of the same cloth as Aaron. He could leave as soon as he wanted and Stan would not be any the sadder.

They used a battered four-wheel-drive Jeep to make the ten minute trip to a seaplane airport. That is assuming you can call a small lake, and eight seaplanes floating along a small dock, an airport. Only about ten percent of Kodiak Island was available by roads. Almost none were paved and all were as rough as cobs. Each spring, graders ran up and down the roads with fresh gravel in order to level out the potholes. If you wanted to reach the rest of the island, seaplane or boat were the only options available. Elliott glanced at the Jeep and again was not impressed. When Alaskans visit the lower forty-eight, they even assume the cars are newer than theirs. Its not that Alaskans have older cars, its just that people in the rest of the country wash their cars occasionally.

The seaplane they crawled into was a de Havilland Beaver, and looked like it was lucky to lift even its own weight, let alone its passengers. It's single engine was attached to an inflated whale of a fuselage. That twin-engine antique that Elliott just left was looking better and better. Looking out the window he could not believe the mountain of gear and groceries Stan and the pilot were loading in the side of the aircraft. He immediately looked for the end of the lake and tried to judge the distance required for getting the thing airborne. Just when he was about to say something, Stan and the pilot were in, and the door slammed shut. With the shortest preflight check Elliott had ever witnessed the engine was generating an ear shattering amount of noise as it moved toward the northern end of the lake. Like it or not, he was stuck.

The plane lifted off half way across the length of the lake. At a couple hundred feet of altitude, the pilot made a sharp bank to the right and headed south. As the plane continued to climb, it quickly passed over the outskirts of Kodiak. While continuing to bank, Stan pointed out antique gun bunkers constructed over a half of century ago to defend against the Japanese during World War II. The Japanese did invade part of Alaska's Aleutian Island chain, and if they had succeeded in working their way further up the chain, they could have occupied Kodiak. The gun emplacements were a haunting memory to the "Forgotten War". Elliott looked down on these silent defenders of another era, and wondered if the military compared the value of what they were defending to the cost of the bunkers' construction. In a rare moment of diplomacy, he remained quiet about his thoughts concerning this economic equation.

Dotted with bays and inlets, Kodiak claims the longest coastline and is the second largest of any island in the United States. It is a place filled with rugged beauty. Sparsely covered with trees, the terrain is thick with underbrush providing ample cover for its world renowned brown bears, and other wildlife. The hills and jagged peaks would make someone from the highlands of Scotland feel right at home. But all Elliott wanted was down. The trip was planned to last a little over forty minutes, but ended up closer to an hour because Stan asked the pilot to make a couple turns over the bay and a mountain ravine. Stan's intent was partly due to the fact that he liked to fly, and partly due to figuring out that Elliott did not.

Much to Elliott's relief, the plane finally landed at one of the more remote inlets on Kodiak Island. It was a hundred miles southwest of town. The camp was located on some high ground between a small lake and the ocean. The plane landed on the lake, floated over to the shore and beached itself on the bank. Normally the plane was tied up next to a small dock, but a storm the week before had caused it to break in two, and repairs were still in the works. Elliott was the first out. He looked around and saw five old shacks, ranging from medium to small, all painted red. He was hoping this was some kind of storage area and they would be moving to the main lodge shortly. His hope vanished when Stan announced, "Welcome to the Allan's Bear Camp."

It was November, late in the season for the camp. Soon it would close for winter. Kodiak benefits from the Japanese current and the island's weather is moderate by Alaskan standards. Most of the inhabitants of Kodiak had never seen an Eskimo. When enough workable snow was available the locals would construct a few igloos for the benefit of the children and a few tourists, but not for necessity of shelter. This area of Alaska was not covered with the layers of snow that the people from the "lower forty-eight" imagined. However the island received *an abundance* of rain, about seventy inches annually. Today was typical. There was a dampness hanging in the air, helped along by a light mist and lingering fog. The high temperature reached only into the mid-thirties, although it seemed colder due to the constant blowing wind. The overcast was dark and gray. A depressing condition for Elliott that the "natives" seemed not to notice. As Elliott looked around, even by Tahoe standards, the last description he would apply to the weather was "moderate."

For a moment Elliott wondered why a man who owned a five star hotel considered coming to this God-forsaken place. It just confirmed his suspicion that Aaron Davenport's bypass surgery last year was messed up, and his heart was not pumping the required amount of blood to his brain.

As they were walking up to the main cabin, Stan pointed out the smoke house where they smoked the salmon, the boat house, the bunk houses, and the shed where they salted the bear hides before they shipped them to various taxidermists in the lower forty-eight. Stan told Elliott about the immense size of the Kodiak bear. It represented the largest of all bears. Many weighed over 1,500 pounds and stood ten feet high. The people assigned to such things estimate there was about one bear for every square mile of Kodiak Island, which makes for a lot of bears. Looking at it another way, it worked out to about four humans for every bear. A few years back an unwitting National Geographic photographer made the mistake of walking between a mother bear and her cubs. The end result was one less photographer for National Geographic. Stan felt obligated to inform the tourist of the cost of carelessness. He also held the common belief that lawyers give bears indigestion. All this was lost on Elliott.

As Elliott entered the main house he expected to see Aaron. Instead a perky gal in her mid-thirties approached him.

"Hi, my name is Jill. My brother owns this camp, but being he spends all his time in the bush, I'm the one to see if you need anything during your stay with us."

"The only thing I need is Aaron Davenport. You got one handy?"

"Not for the next couple hours. He's out on the boat right now. How about if I show you where you're going to bunk tonight."

For the first time it dawned on him that he had to stay over. Elliott was beginning to feel ill.

About three o'clock the four hunters and two guides returned to camp. They had spent the last three days at the *outcamp* located in the high country. Elliott found it hard to believe that anything could be more primitive than his current predicament. They came in with two bear skins and a massive hunger for some of Jill's cooking. Dr. Bradley Remington, a plastic surgeon from Kirkland, Washington, came through the door and headed immediately toward the small kitchen. The last time he ate was six hours ago, and it was a sandwich of peanut butter between two pancakes. His immediate concern was the nature of this evening's bill-of-fare.

Half an hour later Aaron's boat arrived and beached itself in the rocky shore. In keeping with the family tone of the operation, the boat was piloted by Jill's twin sister, Joan. Jill had informed Elliott that Aaron shot his bear last week, but wanted to stay on to do some fishing. Aaron was the last of three passengers off the boat. His rumpled white hair looked as if it had not been near a comb or a barber since his arrival in Alaska. He also looked very tired but, despite Joan's offer of assistance, he insisted on lifting his thirty-six pound salmon out of the boat and up to the lodge.

Aaron looked up and saw Elliott approach.

"Hi Tom, I see you made it in without hurting your legal briefs. How do you like this catch? Nice, isn't it?"

Elliott would have been more impressed if it were covered with butter and served by someone with a French accent.

"Looks beautiful. Got some time to talk?"

"Later, after dinner. I'm just one of eight guests here, and dinner doesn't rotate around when I'm available to eat."

Dinner was on the table by six o'clock, and even Elliott had to admit that it was excellent. The main course was smoked salmon, mashed potatoes, biscuits, and some kind of mystery meat which everyone, except Elliott, knew was moose. All that was followed by the local variety of blackberry cobbler. The meal was washed down with a choice of beer, wine or milk. All selected beer, except Aaron, who went for milk, and Elliott, who tried the wine.

Aaron and Elliott went off to one of the bunk houses while the rest of the party swapped hunting tales and another beer. In typical lawyer style it took about forty minutes for Elliott to lay out the circumstances of the mineral rights claim. He related to Aaron how the claim threatened to throw a monkey-wrench into any possible sale of the property, and their legal options. He finished with an eloquent summary opinion that would have inspired the defenders of the Alamo about the righteousness of their cause, and the need to fight on.

Aaron was not as educated, or as polished, or as sophisticated as Elliott, but he knew horsepucky when he stepped in it. Aaron discovered long ago that people who are more polished become that way in order to project an image they feel suits the audience they happen to be facing at the moment. Usually that develops into conversations that are less sincere, and less honest. For that reason Aaron never really trusted the honesty of "polished" people. Aaron knew Elliott would never consider the difference between book knowledge and common sense. Elliott would never understand that if someone did not have one it did not mean he lacked the other, or visa versa. Aaron had met his share of educated idiots, and he resented the fact that Elliott always talked down to him because he lacked a college degree, and the fact he was well over seventy years old.

"I hear what you're saying and I don't care. And I can hear you fine."

It annoyed Aaron that Elliott still spoke to him two levels above normal conversation. Just because he was old, Elliott assumed Aaron was also hard of hearing. Each time they talked Aaron had to tell him to quit shouting at him. Years ago Aaron fired and hired lawyers with the change of the seasons. Finally he decided they were all alike, so he better stick with one in order to minimize his learning curve in dealing with the necessary evil.

"You said Mannerheim thinks that New Orleans clown, Yarbrough, may be behind this con job. That's fine with me. It means that he's real eager to get his hands on my property. If he developed this little smoke screen he won't worry about it and drop his price, because he knows that if he haggles over the price it would give us time to foil his little plan and find other buyers. Looks like he developed this so he's the only possible buyer. I figure he must want it too much to quibble over a few million. So as far as I'm concerned, he can have the place."

Elliott almost went into shock.

"Are you just content to let him blackmail you, and get away with it?"

"For one hundred million dollars, I'll try to bear up under my grief."

"But other parties have expressed interest in any possible sale. You've got to keep all your options open."

Elliott could not believe either his poor luck or his poor timing. It took him months to convince Aaron that it was in his best interests to sell out and get his financial house in order. The heart surgery last year, combined with his lack of true concern for the daily details of the property, had suitably cultivated the groundwork for Aaron's decision. Now it looked like some unknown third-party would come in and reap the harvest cultivated by all Elliott's hard work.

"I know what the market will bring. Yarbrough kicked up the price enough on his last bid to be in the area I was looking for. Any other bidder won't go much above him to warrant wasting my time. I can only spend it so fast now. Besides, he's one man, one voice. As you keep reminding me, I haven't got too many years left. I don't want to share what time I've got left with a bunch of buyers, and their blood-sucking lawyers, none of which can make up their little minds, or can't agree on a course of action, without a hundred meetings. I like the idea of looking in the eyes of one man."

"You just want to give up the fight? What about your old friends? With Yarbrough in charge, all your friends, who have been with you all these years, will be at his mercy."

"As for my friends and employees, Mannerheim is also right when it comes to them. They have been working at half speed for me for years. I can't protect them from life forever. They've had a good run with me. It's time they take their chances and face the prospect of working for a living. The change may even do them some good."

"So what's your bottom line?"

A masterpiece of poor timing, especially for an attorney, and Elliott knew it as soon as the words left his mouth.

"You and Mannerheim are to start negotiations with Yarbrough as soon as possible. Provide full disclosure of our financial position, and all potential legal matters, including this mineral rights issue. But hold firm on the price. I anticipate one hundred million out of this deal, after taxes. It seems like such a nice round number. So get our number crunchers, and his number crunchers, working on ways to minimize my tax liability."

As Aaron finished stating his position, the lights went out. It was 8:30 and the generator was turned off throughout the camp in order to conserve fuel. The morning would start again at 4:30 a.m. Everyone but Elliott was asleep by 8:45.

CHAPTER 18

Thursday, November 24
Thanksgiving
8:45 p.m.

Mannerheim uncorked a nice bottle of red wine and poured himself a glass. Then he slid open the sliding glass window of his condo. He moved his telescope from the corner of the living room, and carefully placed it on the outside deck. He then went back and retrieved his glass of wine, and picked up a reference book on astronomy.

One of the side benefits of working in Tahoe was the absence of city lights. The air was cold, but the sky was usually clear and beautiful. The job of Controller also had the benefit of being basically a day job. Mannerheim never could get used to working nights, and on a night like this he was glad he was not working for the casino, and stuck in the pit looking at six 21 tables. The stars were calling him tonight.

Even with the best telescopes available to him, Mannerheim could only find a pinpoint of light and just imagine what it truly must look like. Recently images from the orbiting Hubble space telescope, as well as other satellites, were copied on CD ROMs for computers. These CDs look just like the music CDs, but these had text, sound and photos that Mannerheim could access from his personal computer. Aside from being able to call up beautiful images of planets, comets, nebulae and several thousand galaxies, they provided much clearer and better images than anything generated by a small amateur telescope, but Mannerheim still liked the idea of seeing the stars with his own eye.

Usually Mannerheim would limit his wine to two glasses. Any more than that and he had trouble sleeping, but tonight was different. He knew he would not sleep much anyway tonight, so he prepared a third glass of wine. His mind kept reviewing the marker investigation. Besides the investigation, that could be his undoing, he was bothered by something he normally overlooked.

He was walking from the parking lot that morning and noticed a small child outside the doors of the casino. Children are not allowed in a casino. At noon, he and Susie went to eat at an nearby restaurant. The same child was there as they were coming and going. That night, as he left the casino, the child was still there. For an instant, their eyes found each other as he headed for his car. Mannerheim figured her age somewhere around six or seven. He knew the

121

child was waiting for one, or both, of her parents to come back from gambling so they could go home. He also knew the parent would be broke. Somebody may get lucky on the short-term and win, but nobody wins on the long-term. And if the parent spent that much time in there, they were trying to recoup their loses. That child was one of the losers, and she did not even get to make a bet. He thought how a child that age always thinks her parents can do no wrong, and as an adult, will look back on an old parent and think of how he or she did nothing right.

Still thinking of the child's face, Mannerheim's mind drifted back twenty-five years to his service in Vietnam, and a public dump outside a coastal town of Vung Tau. As with most third world dumps, it housed more than the castoff possessions of society. It also housed society's human castoffs. There were hundreds of children living in a mountain of garbage. Each sifting through the new garbage of the day in hopes of finding something they could use to add one more day to their hopeless lives. While Mannerheim and a sergeant friend, who had to dump something, were checking out the local sites and found the site. Mannerheim got more local color than he intended. He remembered turning and almost falling over a child who was standing behind him. He looked into the eyes of that filthy child, and did not know what to say. It was just as well they did not speak the same language. A candy bar was his only solution. Later, Mannerheim toured the local area again, but made it a point never to go back to the dump.

He saw the same look in the eyes of the child today. In many ways he wondered which child was better off. The child outside waiting for a parent who had more interest in a crap table, or the child in Vietnam who was thrown away by his parents because they were out of options, or probably dead. That Vietnamese child would at least be able to understand and possibly forgive his parents. One child was a casualty of an endless war and a backward economic system. The other child was a casualty of nothing more than greed and a weak character. Whatever the reasons, the end result was two shattered childhoods.

Every now and then Mannerheim drifted into periods of melancholy. It was not so much a result of his tour of duty in Vietnam, as his understanding of human nature. Part of it was also due to the fact that it was Thanksgiving and he could not make it out of town to spend the holiday with his brother's family in Phoenix. *Enough of this.* A candy bar was not the solution to the world's problems back then, tonight, or any other night. It would have provided as little relief today as it did twenty-five years ago. Sadly, he could not change governments, economic systems, or qualify the world's population as parents. As an alternative to his limitations he swung his Celestron telescope toward the stars. He turned his thoughts to things that were clean and bright and distant.

*

Friday, November 25
11:00 a.m.

Lt. Robert Danbury arrived at the garage of the Reno Police Department and immediately noticed Captain Pete Jansen and two lab technicians. They were standing next to Willie Grant's 1983 Olds Delta 88. One of the technicians was Rick Larsen and the other he did not know. He was glad to see Rick. They worked together on another case about three years ago and Danbury trusted his skills.

"Pete, Rick, glad to see you two. I appreciate your help with this case. Especially the day after Thanksgiving."

"Robert, it's good to see you back in the big city."

A remark that would have sounded ridiculous to anyone living in Los Angeles or New York, but compared to South Lake Tahoe, Reno was a massive town.

"I'd like to introduce you to David Rainwater, who's working with Rick."

As Danbury shook his hand he wondered how a black man ended up with a name like Rainwater, but decided to postpone any inquiry.

"Rick, have you had enough time to come up with anything useful?"

"Only that the guy who owned this must have been born and raised in this piece of junk. This guy was a real slob. Aren't neat people ever killed?"

"Seldom it seems."

Rainwater added his revulsion for the car by adding,

"I'm amazed it even managed to make it down the hill. I could get rich putting this thing back in working order."

"At least it's in better shape than its owner."

"Speaking of the owner. Willie wasn't the one who drove the car down here and left it at the airport. According to the preliminary report you faxed us, your murder victim was only five foot, seven inches. Judging by the position of the driver's seat when he left it, the last driver must have been at least six foot. In addition to that, we found the radio was fixed to a different station other than one of the five preset stations... make that three, two didn't work."

"Anything else, Rick? How about prints?"

123

"Tons, except on the steering wheel. Due to the shape and texture of most steering wheels, it's difficult enough to pull anything more than a partial print, but the driver took the time to wipe it clean. As for the others, it will take us some time to separate the various prints and determine who's who. The ashtray is full, with a mix of a half-dozen different brands of cigarettes and cigars, along with the residue of some marijuana joints. We'll sort them out and see if there's anything that stands out. However, based on the steering wheel, I doubt if our murderer was stupid enough to leave behind a cigarette with his DNA on it."

"You never know. Haven't seen too many mental giants murder anyone."

"Could be he was at least smart enough to watch enough television and know enough not to leave fingerprints. Ever think we're only smart enough to catch the dumb ones?"

Said more in jest, than fact, by Larsen. Of all crimes, murder had the highest success rates for conviction. All present held the belief that the court system should view the final sentencing with the same concern that they viewed the arrest, but that was another issue.

"Speak for yourself. What else did you find?"

"We also found a varied collection of trash, ranging from matchbooks to unwashed laundry. But we'll make out a listing and turn it over to the lab for examination. After they're through with the rubbish I'll make sure they bag it up for you. You can eventually bury it as easy as we can. That's about all for now. Give us another day or so, and we'll see what else we can find."

"Sounds good, and gives me some time to check out how the autopsy on good old Willie is coming along."

*

Sunday, November 27
4:13 a.m.

Elliott arrived back at the Reno airport early Sunday morning, after leaving on the late flight out of Anchorage. He spent an extra two days trying to talk Aaron out of selling to Yarbrough, but to no avail. Additional dialogue just seemed to cement Aaron's decision. The delay had not been totally by his own choice. He had to wait until the seaplane made its next scheduled trip back to the camp. He felt like he was just released from prison.

Again the wheels were turning. Like a salesman, a rejection could only be answered by another, larger assault to overcome his empty-headed subject. He had a golden opportunity to gain control of one of the more profitable, and best located casino in Nevada. Instead, his new fortune and future were about to be pulled out from under him, by an old man who was not his equal. Elliott would not let it go without a fight. *If Aaron did not want to deal with a bunch of attorneys and judges, then that was exactly the area to hurt him.* Plan "B" was about to go into action.

*

Monday, November 28
11:50 a.m.

Not a patient person to begin with, Mannerheim was eager to see Hamilton upon his return. As usual they arranged to meet offsite from the casino, and away from curious eyes and ears. In the age of high-tech, no room was really secure. The site location was Mannerheim's selection. By design, he worked Thanksgiving Day. He wanted to go skiing but did not want to fight the throngs of tourists in the lift lines. Therefore he postponed his holiday until after the weekend. There are literally a couple dozen quality ski resorts around the Tahoe Basin, including Heavenly Valley, Kirkwood, Alpine Meadows, Sugarbowl, Northstar and Incline. But Mannerheim's favorite was Squaw Valley on the California side, site of the 1960 Winter Olympics and still the official U.S. Olympic training center.

They agreed to meet at the Squaw Valley ski lodge at noon. Mannerheim arrived several hours earlier and hit the slopes. Like most locals, Mannerheim skied frequently soon after he moved to Tahoe. Then, being a local, he evolved into a pattern where he did not ski during bad weather, poor or icy snow, weekends or holidays. Soon he found he did not ski much at all. Mannerheim's first run down the slopes was not a thing of beauty. Ugly was a more accurate description. What especially disturbed Mannerheim was the sight of a dozen children, all under the age of ten, zipping past him, as represented by various blurs of color. After a few shaky runs down the hill, Mannerheim felt more comfortable as his form and speed improved, and he was starting to have some fun.

The area formed part of the Sierra Nevada mountains. Some hundred and fifty years ago, and less than ten miles to the west, a wagon train became stranded in the mountains during one of worst winters on record. The surviving members of the Donner party managed to come through the experience by renewing the practice of cannibalism. Mannerheim was informed they, and their descendants, later moved back to Nevada, opened a casino, and continued the practice of feeding on their fellow citizens. Until recently, Mannerheim took little note of the story.

Shortly before noon he skied over to the lodge, took off his skis, buried them in a snow bank near the steps, then made his way over to the bar and ordered a warm ham sandwich and a cold beer. He found an empty bench on the deck and looked up at the slopes. For a few minutes Mannerheim sat back and enjoyed the blue sky, and the clean, white, snow-capped mountains. For amusement, he watched beginners and flatlanders crash into each other. He was sure his form and style looked only slightly better, but it helped him to visualize he could be worse. He then heard a familiar voice behind him.

"Great to be back in God's country."

Mannerheim turned around to see Hamilton. He was also in a ski outfit, holding his skis and sporting a nice deep tan. In fact he had a much better tan than Logan, who he saw last Friday, fresh from his vacation.

"Oh, I think God may have had a hand in the making the Bahamas. Have a good time?"

"Better than some of the holes where I've followed people around." Trying not to crack a grin.

"I hope you made it back in time to spend Thanksgiving with your family?"

"Arrived back late Wednesday night, just in time to keep my wife from killing me."

Berkich was right. Hamilton was becoming more casual with exposure.

"Glad it worked out. So what have you got for me?"

"Hopefully, enough to justify the trip. First, Logan has developed a new identity. He's using the name of Henry Hopkins. He opened a bank account with that name. Probably has a passport with that name on it."

"Well how did he manage that?"

"It's fairly easy. There're several ways to develop the needed paperwork identification in order to get a passport. Usually people research death certificates of children who died shortly after the time they were born. Most counties don't cross-reference birth certificates with death certificates. Besides, most people move around so much, few people die in the same state or county where they were born. So you just request a copy of 'your' birth certificate and use it to apply for a new drivers license. Probably claimed he just moved to the state and lost his old one. Then he could have ordered some magazine subscriptions, which would have gotten him on a ton of mailing lists. Within short order he has a post office box jammed with credit card applications. Starting a bank account wouldn't be any problem in this country, let alone in the Caymans. Then walking down and getting a passport wouldn't be too difficult. Within a short time Mr. Henry Hopkins has all the paper identification you or I have."

"It can't be that easy. What about a social security number?"

"If you do your research you could find someone who died back then who was old enough to have been issued a Social Security number. Just pick it up and start using it. The original Henry Hopkins won't be complaining. Or he could have just made up a number. By the time some big government computer generates an inquiry, Logan will be out of the country and past the point of caring. It will have served his purpose by then."

"So what you're saying is that Logan could have created a phony paper person with genuine identity. Or maybe even several different identities. If he takes off he could be lost forever. He could just leave the United States and never return."

"Or he may even come back to the states and assume that identity. A lot of people are doing that with the blessing of the government. Ever hear of the Witness Protection Program? The only difference is the Feds generated the identification there. Here Logan did the grunt work."

"Great! Did you find out how much he deposited?"

"Yes. Surprisingly it was only about five thousand."

"No, that was no big surprise. I've got the answer to that. It's another example of government watching our every move. Claiming to be going after counterfeiting and money-laundering, the Bureau of Engraving and Printing, out of their new Ft. Worth plant, have started to alter all new hundreds, fifties, twenties and recently, ten-dollar bills. They have embedded these bills with a green polyester thread, along the left side. They are sandwiched inside the bill, but they can be seen if you know where to look. If you hold them up to the light, they're more obvious. Haven't you noticed them?"

"Hundreds, fifties and twenties don't linger long in my wallet before my wife finds some useful purpose for them."

"Well, these 'security' threads are traceable by electronic scanning devices. Some say this new currency even contains a hidden bar code across the bottom of the bill. Any information can be encoded on that bar code. The Feds are a little closed mouth about this, but I've heard rumors that each bill's serial number is encoded in the thread. Also, if enough of these new bills went through an airport metal detector, it would set it off. Or so I hear. Which is one reason

Logan may not have taken much money with him to the Bahamas."

"How did you learn about this?"

"Recently a Treasury agent gave all the casinos a seminar on counterfeiting. At that time the thread was just out, and he enjoyed talking about their new traceable money. He also discussed the ink they use in the printing process. It seems each bill also contains a certain amount of 'magnetic ink' on the face side, but doesn't have any on the back side. Some currency counters can detect any variation in the amounts of magnetic ink on a bill. So when a counterfeit bill goes through one of these counters it causes it to stop the counter, and the bill is detected."

"So has all that managed to slow up counterfeiting?"

"Counterfeiting was only a minor concern. Its real purpose was to create a cashless society, uproot the underground economy and keep tabs on all cash in the economy. Having everyone pay their taxes was their primary concern, not counterfeiting. Big brother is working toward that goal."

"You don't sound happy about all this."

"It's not that. I'm not hiding anything for them to find. All my income is subject to its fair share of taxes. What bothers me is that our currency, and its effect on the economy, is only backed by the full faith and integrity of the U.S. Government, the biggest debtor on the face of the earth. It's what backs our currency, not how it looks, that concerns me. Since 1971, when Nixon cut the final tie to gold, we have ushered in twenty years of higher inflation, falling living standards, huge Federal deficits, and bigger government. I'm not for going back to the gold standard, but I am for balanced budgets, or our economy is headed for disaster. But that's enough of my soap box."

"I guess I should have taken that economics class in high school."

"Anyway, that's the long answer to why Logan took so little money with him."

"So it seems Logan can't just pack a suitcase with currency and grab a flight to his Bahamas bank. Correct?"

"Right. He's going to have to convert it to other assets, or arrange for a money mule to take it out of the country for him. Knowing Logan, he's *not* a trusting person. I can't picture him ever trusting a mule. He won't want to bring anyone else in and enlarge the circle of people involved. His loyalty only extends to his followers in the pit. My guess is that he may take it out of Nevada on a domestic flight to another city within the country, but not on an international flight that would be subject to customs. He will probably convert it some other common convertible asset, like diamonds, and move them out of the country himself, or through McDonald. Speaking of Todd McDonald, Logan's Shift Manager, he also must need new paperwork if he intends to leave with Logan. You might try to learn what name he's using."

"McDonald may not be ready to move yet. Based upon what you've told me, Logan always has to be the one in control. I bet Logan was the first one to complete the needed paperwork, so he could make that initial trip to the Bahamas. He wouldn't trust anyone else to make the arrangements. So there's a good chance McDonald isn't ready yet."

"All we can do is keep an eye on McDonald and wait for him to make a move."

"Consider it done."

"What about our other little problem? During your side trip to the Cayman Islands, what did you find out about the Caribbean Mining & Exploration Corporation and their subsidiary, the Nevada Silver Shaft Mining Company?"

"Not much. The business address in Georgetown turned out to be the law offices of Edward Kendall, the guy listed as an officer of the Caribbean Mining & Exploration Corporation. I couldn't get past his secretary to even talk to him. Seems he isn't taking any new clients at this time. Lives in a villa, with high walls and ample security around it. Public records in the Cayman Islands are not nearly as public as they are here in the states, but from the little that was available, they show the same information we already knew from our public records office in Carson City. It does appear our Mr. Kendall is a very high-priced corporate attorney. All in all, that side trip added up to a waste of time."

"Well, looks like you got off to an adequate start, but we better keep digging."

Digging would wait for the next day. Both Mannerheim and Hamilton headed back to the slopes after their conversation ended.

CHAPTER 19

Reno, Nevada
Monday, November 28
2:00 p.m.

Lt. Danbury arrived at the Washoe County Coroner's office to meet with Dr. Kim Bailey, to discuss the results of her autopsy on Willie Grant.

Over the weekend Danbury reviewed and cross-referenced numerous arrest reports in the computer systems of both Washoe and Douglas Counties. He looked for any associate, relation, accomplice or enemy of Willie Grant. Based upon eight arrest reports, Danbury identified nine people who knew, or were friends of some degree or another, of the victim. All had to be checked out. This morning Danbury drafted two of his better deputies into service in tracking down and interviewing those named so far. By the end of the week they reported back that almost all loaned Willie small amounts of money over time, but most had recently been paid back. All were in agreement that Willie had recently come into some money, as evidenced by their mutual surprise that they were ever reimbursed. Aside from some general boasting Willie made about some new and unnamed partners, none could, or would, provide any specific details as to how Willie came into procession of this new-found wealth. All volunteered a name of someone who had argued with, or been on the short end of some deal with Willie in the past, but none had been current enough, or emotional enough, to warrant his death. Experience had taught Danbury that in Willie's world, even an apparent minor reason could result in death. The next step was to be locate and interview those new names.

This was Danbury's first time to work with Dr. Bailey, who recently replaced the retiring Doc Bjork. Danbury only met Doc Bjork a couple of times due to their difference in county jurisdictions. In keeping with those boundaries, Lt. Danbury normally used the Douglas County coroner, but for this case, he wanted the better lab in Washoe County. Besides, due to the fact Douglas County's need for a coroner was so infrequent, their coroner function was performed on a part-time basis by their local country doctors. And Lt. Danbury had very little trust in him even when he, or his own family, needed medical services. Danbury often wondered if the old boy moved to a rural environment just because of the lack of competition. It once occurred to Danbury that he became coroner in order to bury his own mistakes. Compared with the known option, he quickly chose the unknown commodity of Dr. Bailey.

The coroner's offices occupied space in a basement belonging to one of Reno's three hospitals. As Danbury entered the lab, he was taken back by the various peculiar odors that seemed to be ingrained in the walls and furniture. He had visited this and similar coroner offices before and always wondered how anyone could get used to the smells, or the nature of the work. Looking around the lab he noticed two men pulling a pale rigid body out of a stainless steel opening built into the side of the one of the walls. Present also was a young woman sitting at an old wooden desk in the corner of the room. On top of the limited amount of desk space sat a computer, to which she was giving her full attention. Figuring it was safe bet none of the men was named Kim, Danbury approached the woman.

She wore her hair in the younger "light-socket" style that looked like she just had gotten out of bed. He was glad his wife was raised in a previous generation, and silently made a note to himself: From now on, he would stop complaining to his wife about the time it took her to get ready to go anywhere. A smoldering cigarette was dangling from the woman's mouth. Every minute or so, some ash would drop off the end of her cigarette and land on the keyboard. Not too disturbed by this combination of gravity and a politically incorrect habit, she would blow it off as the need required. She was dressed in a white smock, still covered with a plastic liner. Since the arrival of AIDS, even the dead can attack the living. Anyone who examines corpuses must take extra care to avoid contact with blood. This caution did not extend to a hastily eaten meatball sandwich that left several ketchup deposits on the plastic liner. The desk looked like the end result of a bomb squad exercise. He hoped she was more competent than she was neat.

"Good afternoon doctor. I'm Lt. Danbury with the Douglas County Sheriff's Department... here about your examination of Willie Grant."

"Sure, have a seat. As you can see, I'm still working on my report but I can fill you in on some of the high points."

"Great, and welcome to Nevada. I understand you recently moved here to take the position of Coroner."

"Technically I'm a Medical Examiner; thus, I was appointed and not elected. And yes, I just relocated from San Diego. Unfortunately, my move caused me to be out of the office and unavailable last Friday. I was busy talking to Bekins movers when I should have been talking to you at the crime scene. This morning, I made it crystal clear to my staff the importance of tracking me down for all future murder investigations."

"Sorry, it never occurred to me either. In Douglas County, our coroner never wanted to face the elements in order to merely view a body. Figured he could take its temperature in the comfort of his office. But, it would be my pleasure to wait for your arrival in the future."

Lt. Danbury was also making some mental notes about the future. As with this case, he planned to jump the jurisdictional fences so he could use this willing professional on future murder investigations. He was already feeling very comfortable about his decision to try this unknown doctor, messy as she was, compared to his choice back home in Douglas County.

"Good. A body can tell you volumes, if you know what to ask. Measuring only its temperature will result in seeing a very small piece of the total picture. For example, based upon how the blood settled in the body, I believe the victim was not moved around too much and was probably buried soon after he died. So, he was killed at or near the site where you found him, as opposed to being killed somewhere else and just being dumped there. I would be more confident telling you that if I examined the body at the scene, before you moved it."

"Point made, doctor. If your staff doesn't find you, I'll make sure I track you down myself from now on."

Danbury was beginning to sense that Kim wanted to show off. Considering that she probably wanted to make a strong first impression, it was understandable. Because it was taking the form of a lecture, he thought it was time to move on to another subject, and still keep it upbeat.

"I understand you worked part of Saturday to finish your examination on the murder victim."

"I was able to work on him Friday afternoon. Came back early Saturday to continue some lab work and get started on the paperwork."

"I really appreciate the urgency with which you approached this case."

Which was spoken with true sincerity.

"Well, this case was far from routine. I understand most of the cases through here need an autopsy as just a required formality. The facts are usually well known by the time my office enters the picture. It's either an accident or the suspect is already behind bars."

"If you think that's true here, you should see the lack of mystery cases back at Tahoe. When people lose their fortunes on the gambling tables, they usually just shoot themselves instead of someone else."

"I'm not sure I can provide much crucial detail for you. Our Mr. Grant was shot once, by what appears to be a 9mm bullet. It penetrated back to front, on a downward plane, lodging in the lung, just to the right of the heart. Death would have occurred within seconds."

A 9mm. That was disappointing to the lieutenant. It was a caliber that was as common as mud. In Nevada, mud might even come in second. To see a 9mm pistol, all Lt. Danbury needed to do was look down at his own holster. It was so common because the majority of state and federal law enforcement agencies, as well as half the street gangs in the country, converted to 9mm semi-automatic weapons.

"When do you think Willie assumed room temperature?"

"I can only give you a real spongy estimate of the time of death. Based upon the temperature of the body on Friday, the recorded overnight air temperature in the immediate area where the body was recovered, the amount of clothes he was wearing, as well as the estimated soil temperature, I would estimate the time of death between 3:00 p.m. and 9:00 p.m. Thursday."

"Can't you get it any closer?"

"With all those variables, you're lucky I can narrow it down to Thursday. If your officer had taken some pictures of the burial site, before the earth was totally removed, I would have a better idea of the conditions around the body. I hate going into court and tell the opposing counsel about my 'best guess' methods. Even under the best of conditions, when the time of death exceeds twelve hours, things tend to cloud up my crystal ball."

"Okay." Danbury would have to live with it. "Anything else?"

"Police files indicated the victim was thirty-two years old, but based upon my autopsy I would have estimated his age to be at least forty. He had high levels of fat in his liver, probably from a history of excessive alcohol consumption. His lungs looked like they belonged to a coal miner." She looked at the cigarette still burning in her fingers. "Which reminds me of the promise I made to myself, at the time, to give up the habit myself."

Danbury, a non-smoker himself, quickly responded, "Good idea."

Turnabout was fair play. Since Bailey decided not to open the conversation up to any more sermon-like comments, she was now the one who moved on.

"The toxicologist was in this morning. He took the usual fluid samples... blood and urine, as well as hair samples. From what I saw, this body was a case study in poor nutrition and the effects of substance abuse. I wouldn't be surprised if the toxicologist confirms drug usage, but you'll have to wait a few days to confirm that theory. The bottom line, in a few seconds that 9mm bullet accelerated a process that would have dragged out his death another ten or fifteen years at most."

"If you're finished with the slug, I'll take it with me. Maybe I can talk the ballistics department into matching it with any other slugs they may have in their open files? Maybe this isn't the shooter's first time."

"Based upon their workload and the size of their open files, you better be a real good talker. That could take a couple man-hundred hours. While you're at it, you can sign for his clothes and personal effects. They're already bagged and ready to go."

"Okay. Is that it?"

"Just some minor details. Mr. Grant has more-than-average his share of scares and tattoos. Pictures will be included in my report. If you're curious about his eating habits, I'd say he consumed some meat, maybe a hamburger, no more than two hours before his death. Even when dead, his stomach acid was converting anything else he may have eaten into history. Other than that, there's nothing else I can tell for now."

Danbury figured that last bit of information could not have been discovered without the need of a nose pin. Considering the obvious lack of windows, he hoped they had at least purchased a heavy-duty ventilation system.

"Thanks Doc, and would you please forward the pictures and a copy of your autopsy to my attention, care of the Douglas County Sheriff's office, Stateline substation?"

"Sure can. My report will be finished as soon as I get the results of the lab work. Figure a couple more days. Give me a call if you have any questions."

CHAPTER 20

Tuesday, November 29
9:13 a.m.

Toward the end of the previous week, Elliott assigned his secretary the chore of setting up a Monday meeting with Mannerheim. She managed to contact Betty before she left for her Thanksgiving holiday, and was informed Mannerheim was taking Monday off. Elliott took the opportunity to catch up on his sleep and formulate his game plan.

Elliott arrived back at the hotel early Tuesday morning, and proceeded straight to Mannerheim's office. He was obligated to inform Mannerheim of his meeting with Aaron, and Aaron's decision to sell out to Randall Yarbrough. Elliott just wanted to fulfill the requirement.

It was a brief meeting. The bombshell to sell the whole operation, and the basic mechanics involved in achieving the task, lasted just twenty-two minutes. Per Aaron's instructions, Mannerheim was to make contact with Yarbrough and arrange the time and place for the negotiations. Elliott did almost all the talking. As with most attorneys, it was more monologue and than dialogue. The facts were supplemented with Elliott's disapproval of the decision, and his instructions they should take their time in order to make sure the sale was done properly. Without taking time for questions, Elliott got up and left at 9:35.

*

At noon Elliott met Carl Desmond and Susie Parsons for lunch, off premises. That meeting lasted three hours and ten minutes.

*

Mannerheim thought over Aaron's decision. From Aaron's point of view, Mannerheim concluded it was a sound decision. A quick sale at a good price, continued enjoyment of his retirement, and an easy estate settlement for his heirs when the time comes. From Mannerheim's viewpoint he could not see how he could be hurt either. Yarbrough had mentioned several times his desire to retain Mannerheim. In fact, he as much as stated his willingness to sign Mannerheim to a five year contract at double his current salary. Of course if they did it prior to the sale, and it was discovered at a later date, then Mannerheim would be opening himself up to a lawsuit for a conflict of interest. Elliott could make the case that Mannerheim was really working in the interests of Yarbrough and not Aaron. It would be an easy case for conspiracy. He briefly wondered what the jail term would be for that. No, he would have to *trust* Yarbrough to keep his word after the sale. *Trust!*, not a long suit among employers and employees in the casino industry. Always a percentage player, Mannerheim realized he would need to keep his alternative options open.

After a few minutes of thought Mannerheim picked up his phone. He decided to call the three New Orleans numbers until he tracked down Yarbrough himself. He trusted his secretary, Betty, but something like this required as few to be involved as possible.

He first reached Yarbrough's office. They were expecting him to return from lunch shortly. Mannerheim forgot about the time difference. He then tried his car phone. Yarbrough answered on the first ring.

"Randy, Paul Mannerheim. Thought I'd check. If you're still interested in buying, we *may* be interested in selling."

"Music to my ears. Interested enough for me to make a trip to Tahoe?"

"Yes."

"Great! Give me a few days to confer with my team and check my financing arrangements. We'll fly up and be there by next Tuesday."

"Let me know what airline you're coming in on, and I'll have transportation arranged for you in Reno."

"No airline, I've got my own plane. We'll fly into that small Tahoe airport instead of Reno. I would appreciate transportation from there to the hotel."

"How many in your party?"

"Eight, including me."

"Fine, I'll have two limos and a van waiting for you when you get here. Let me know when your pilot figures his estimated arrival time. I'll also make reservations for you across the street at the Golden Palace. If you stay here it will probably be discovered and feed the rumor mill. And I don't think it's advisable to have eight dark suits marching into the lobby with briefcases and computers in hand. Dress casual."

Only with casinos would the sight of people carrying briefcases and computers be conspicuous, while two limousines would be standard and routine.

"I will be the soul of discretion. Looking forward to next Tuesday."

Even after the conversation ended, Mannerheim was still thinking about

Yarbrough, the arrangements he had to make, his own options, and the pending negotiations. The phone was still resting on his shoulder. As he realized he better put the receiver down he heard a faint click in his ear. In an instant he realized he had not yet installed the bug detector Hamilton had given him for his phone.

*

That night Mannerheim quickly arranged for a meeting with Steve Berkich and Matt Hamilton to discuss damage control. This time he called them from a pay phone, located a block from the casino property. He had to inform them both that a pending sale of the property was in the works. Both had jobs where confidentiality was a part of their job descriptions. Besides, Hamilton would not even be affected by a change of ownership, and Berkich had a job that should not be in the line of fire if the new owner started to let heads roll.

On paper, the Surveillance Department reported to the president of the company, Carl Desmond. The truth of the matter was that it reported indirectly to Sam Logan. Wally Lowe, the head of that department, was an old friend of Logan, and obtained his job though Logan's efforts. If Mannerheim's phone was tapped, which Hamilton confirmed, it was probably by somebody loyal to Logan. They had to assume the pending sale of the hotel/casino was now known to Sam Logan.

Mannerheim was embarrassed that it was his mistake that caused this meeting. To make sure that there was not a possibility of any additional leaks, they decided to meet in a hotel room located on the north shore of Lake Tahoe, at the Hyatt. First Mannerheim gave a summary of his meeting with Elliott, and the phone call with Randall Yarbrough. He then opened it up for discussion.

Hamilton was the first to speak.

"Do you think Logan will use his influence with Mr. Davenport to try and stop the sale, or maybe get rid of you?"

"Doubt it. Based upon the brief discussion I had with Elliott this morning, if he couldn't talk Aaron out of it then I'd say he has his mind made up. One thing about Aaron, dynamite won't move him once that happens. Right or wrong, once he's committed, he can make Stonewall Jackson look indecisive. In fact, this sale will be safer for me. Without a sale, and in the event of open warfare between Logan and me, it will boil down to Aaron choosing between Logan and me. When Aaron looks at that political battle, he will find it easier to replace his accountant instead of his Casino Manager. But with a sale, Aaron will really need me, and my knowledge of the numbers, more than he needs his Casino Manager. During any negotiations Logan won't be of much value. And after the sale, Aaron will end up with a lot of money, and no employees anyway. So the pressure from Logan won't have any effect for now. But, if that sale doesn't go through, I'm history."

Besides being a friend, Berkich also knew Mannerheim protected him on several occasions. With the absence of Mannerheim, Berkich would be facing Logan alone. "If the sale doesn't go through, we're both probably history."

"Knowing Logan, you can count on that. Remember, it doesn't matter if you're flying first class or tourist if the plane goes down."

With that said, Hamilton made a mental note to send his billings on a more frequent basis. If Mannerheim lost out, he did not want to be holding any uncollectable receivables himself.

Berkich then said what they were all thinking.

"So there's only one thing left that makes any sense. Any change of ownership will necessitate a complete review of the books, including the status of all outstanding, unpaid marker balances. Logan's position and explanations won't justify those accounts to a new owner. We've got to figure that will force Logan and McDonald to move up the timetable and turn rabbit on us, taking their millions with them to their new bank account in the Bahamas."

Hamilton was in quick agreement, as was Mannerheim.

Mannerheim then addressed the next topic when he asked, "Both of you were once police detectives, you tell me, do you think we have enough to take to the sheriff's department?"

Aside from the glitter and glamour of the casinos, South Lake Tahoe was a rural environment with most of its population located on the California side. The Douglas County Sheriff department was the primary law enforcement agency for the Nevada side, as opposed to a local city police department.

Berkich first expressed his opinion.

"Not yet. Logan could just say he was doing his job and issuing markers to some foreign players. He will claim they are still good receivables and will be eventually repaid. It could be months, or even years before he would finally acknowledge them as uncollectable. Then he could just say he made an error in judgment, but by that time he and McDonald would be long gone anyway."

Hamilton echoed the sentiment.

"There's no law against taking a vacation to the Bahamas, or even opening a bank account in a foreign country."

Mannerheim was getting frustrated.

"Well what do we need to do in order to get him? I've got over twenty thousand dollars of Aaron's money invested in investigative fees trying to prove his Casino Manager is ripping him off, and I still can't bring him proof that I'm right. And what's worse is the fact he's probably about ready to leave the country."

"Paul, the best evidence will be Logan holding the money in his hot little hands. Money that doesn't belong to him, and money he can't explain. That's how the Feds got Al Capone. They couldn't prove Capone made his money from bootlegging, but just that he couldn't *explain* how he got all his money. So they finally got him for tax evasion. The possession of those millions will provide what's needed to hold Logan. Combine that with a documented, long-term examination of the bogus players and we could get a conviction. That would be a combination that Logan would have major problems explaining away."

"*Could* is not a word that provides me with all that much comfort."

"The truth is we may have to settle for something short of that, or risk losing out entirely. Tell you what. Even though we may not have enough for a grand jury, I could take what we have and bounce it off somebody I know in the sheriff's department."

"Okay Matt. I'm willing to try anything. I checked our insurance policy. Specifically the clause relating to employee theft. We need either a conviction, or solid evidence of an actual thief. Poor management decisions won't cut it. Right now the insurance companies can just say that Logan made an error in judgment in granting those markers. Aaron is out three million instead of the insurance companies. Even if we can't get all the money back we need to document that the theft occurred for those picky little insurance auditors. Right now I'll settle for that. We need a smoking gun. My fear is that we're running out of time." Mannerheim paused a few seconds, then finally said, "All right, who do you know in the sheriff's department?"

"A good guy named Robert Danbury. He's a lieutenant. I worked with him several times when Washoe and Douglas Counties had some mutual cases."

"Well, go ahead and bring him up to speed on what we have so far, but swear him to secrecy. If this investigation becomes known, and can't be proved, then I might as well start looking for my next job now. Logan will accuse me of misusing company funds for this investigation. Unless I can prove it legally, I can't take it to Aaron and count on him choosing my view of this mess as opposed to Logan's explanation. Logan will claim it was based on a personal witch-hunt against him and not valid, supportable business reasons. I'll be lucky to get a job as the Controller of the local Taco Bell."

CHAPTER 21

Wednesday, November 30
10:23 a.m.

Lt. Danbury was reviewing the ballistics report on the slug which killed Willie. Based upon its final appearance, the experts determined the slug was a hollow point, 124 grain, hydra-shok 9mm. The bullet was designed to mushroom out, which caused protruding barbs to rip and tear vital organs as it journeyed through the body, generating maximum destruction. It was one of the more lethal bullets available for that caliber, but Danbury just needed to read the autopsy report to make that determination. Even with the desired mushroom effect, the side of the slug still provided ballistics experts with enough markings to match it with the rifling pattern caused by the murder weapon, assuming it was ever located.

Danbury also received the report on Willie's car from Larsen and Rainwater. They found seven different fingerprints, not counting Willie's. Three belonged to ladies who had an evening occupation, and total lack of exposure to the sun practically assured them they were not at risk of skin cancer. The remaining four belonged to some of Willie's friends. All shared backgrounds and character flaws similar to the deceased, but all had reasonable alibis for the afternoon and evening in question.

One of Danbury's deputies located a young Burger King cashier who remembered serving Willie a hamburger the day of his death. The day was fixed in her memory because she was upset she had to work on Thanksgiving. She immediately recognized his picture. She still recalled the overpowering smell of beer that he exhaled when he burped in her direction.

In addition to the other items, Washoe County sent over a billing which requested reimbursement, in the amount of three hundred and forty dollars, for the pending cremation of Willie's last remains. There would be no funeral because nobody stepped forward to request one, or wanted to pay for one, which was the only news item that Danbury was interested in knowing. Despite the billing, there were no current plans for a cremation. Dr. Bailey put a hold on it until after the investigation's conclusion, or another six months, whichever came first. Danbury knew full well that his own coroner would have made Willie into toast as soon as possible, just to keep the place tidy and his desk clear of the paperwork. As Danbury was wondering if Washoe County would bill him for cold storage, the phone rang.

"Lt. Danbury, its been about four years since we worked together, but this is Matt Hamilton calling."

"Matt. Of course. I heard you retired a couple years ago."

"Almost three. I became a private investigator."

"I heard that too. Is that why you're calling?"

"Sure is. I've got a case that's developing on your turf. I'd appreciate a brief meeting to show you what we've got so far. I think you'll find it interesting. We would also like to keep you advised of our progress."

"We?"

"Me and my clients. I can go into that when we meet."

"Well, I'm in the middle of a heavy case right now, but I can spare some time for an old friend. How about coming down to my office this afternoon, say three o'clock."

*

Hamilton reached Danbury's office at the appointed time. It was just off Highway 50, about five miles north of the casinos clustered along "Stateline." There were a couple four-wheel drive Sheriff's vehicles parked along the side of the building. Due to the high maintenance cost associated with four-wheel drive vehicles, the Sheriff's department only used them when weather or road conditions demanded. The building contained a couple of small offices, some lockers for the deputies and a temporary holding tank for prisoners. The main jail for Douglas County was down in the valley, in a town called Minden, at the eastern foot of the Sierra Nevada Mountains. Several small farm towns and ranches were nestled in the strip of land along the base of these majestic peaks. If you ventured too much further to the east, the landscape quickly changed to the wide open spaces of the Nevada desert. From there you could drive and not see much of anything until you reached Salt Lake City. If you missed that, it would be a long, empty drive until Denver. The road going southeast toward Las Vegas, Highway 95, goes through terrain so desolate a traveler would think they were on the surface of the moon. Being it does not amount to much that would interest anyone was the main reason the Federal Government still owned over 86% of Nevada.

Hamilton arrival needed no announcing by Desk Sergeant Patrick Miller. Lt. Danbury heard the door open, recognized Matt's voice from his office, and turned the corner to greet him.

"Matt, glad to see you. Step back into my office. Care for coffee?"

Hamilton declined the coffee and stepped into an office about a third the size of Mannerheim's. Due to the mutual trust Danbury had with his desk sergeant, he almost always kept his door open. Hamilton made a point to close it.

Hamilton went over the case. He had Mannerheim prepare a written analysis of the marker receivable figures because he wanted an accountant's explanation of the problem and not his layman's interpretation. Hamilton told him about his surveillance of the bogus player, the passing of the envelope between him and McDonald at the Starlight, the player's disappearance after checking into the Golden Palace, Logan's Bahamas vacation to establish a bank account under a false name.

Looking at an accountant's spreadsheet was not the best way to attract the initial attention of Danbury. Nevertheless, he sat patiently and listened to Hamilton describe each phase of the investigation. At last Hamilton laid down the surveillance photos he took of Logan, McDonald and the bogus player. When the photo of the player landed on Lt. Danbury's desk he came to full attention. It was a picture of Willie Grant.

*

Mannerheim was entering the office of the Food and Beverage Director, Len Goodrich, for a scheduled meeting to discuss showroom procedures. Just as Mannerheim was a foot within the door of Lenny's office his secretary buzzed in. Lenny had to take an "emergency" call from some temperamental chef, so Mannerheim found himself waiting next to the desk of Lenny's secretary, with Lenny looking at him through his office doorway as he held up two fingers.

The showrooms provide a lot of glamour for the casinos' image, but Mannerheim tried to keep as far away from it, and the "entertainers", as possible. He was part of an industry that did not lack for egos, but performers elevated theirs to new heights. They acted like gods and expected to be treated accordingly. Mannerheim would speculate that if they did not live in this century then they would probably have been failures in any previous period. Entertainers just kept dreaming up things for their "wish list" and never dropped anything from their old list. One "big name" demanded two full floors of the hotel for himself and his freeloaders. In addition, he demanded silk sheets on his bed, an on-call limo driver and a French chief. All this resulted in his, and most other entertainers' contracts, for a weeks' engagement, being several inches thick. Subsequent contracts were as thick as the constitutions of most countries. They also held the assumption that all the hotel facilities were there for their personal use. In the end, it was the massive amounts they demanded for their services that had caused most casino operations to either drop their showrooms, or go to more controllable in-house variety shows. Country and western entertainers were usually more down-to-earth and much better to deal with, which was probably the reason Mannerheim developed an appreciation for their music. Mannerheim was hoping Aaron would see the light and just convert the showroom into more convention space. Soon a new owner could examine that option.

Lenny was still on the phone when Mannerheim's pager went off. He decided to pop into a nearby empty office and return the call. Paul usually did not carry his company pager because he considered it a leash anyone could jerk to demand his attention. But this was a different pager, not his company one. The number was known only to himself, Matt Hamilton and Steve Berkich. This call was from Hamilton. Due to the fact Mannerheim first responded with the caution that he was using a company phone, Hamilton just identified himself by his first name, followed by a phone number. As soon as he hung up, Mannerheim advised Lenny's secretary that he had to take care of one of his own little emergencies and would reschedule their meeting. As previously arranged, Mannerheim went off to locate a public phone and called Hamilton back.

It took Mannerheim just a few minutes to reach a bank of public pay phones located a block from the hotel.

"Mannerheim here."

"Ready for a news flash? Remember that bogus player I followed to the Starlight, who met with McDonald? He's dead, murdered last week."

"Murdered!"

Mannerheim was surprised. After a tour in Vietnam, and seven years of working in the casino industry, Mannerheim thought he understood human nature. He certainly accepted the concept that Logan was capable of murder, but until now he just thought greed, theft and his job security were the only aspects involved.

"You sure it was murder?"

"Unless he managed to shoot himself in the back with a 9mm, and bury his own body, I'd definitely rule out suicide. By the way, his name was William Grant, commonly referred to by his few friends and numerous enemies, as Willie. He was a low-life with a long, but undistinguished, criminal record."

"Other than the fact this Willie character received a marker from Logan, does Lt. Danbury have anything that would tie him to Logan?"

"Not yet. Willie committed most of his criminal activities while in Reno. Even though Willie had no arrest record for anything in Douglas County, Danbury's sergeant remembers his picture, but can't recall where or when he crossed paths with him."

Hamilton then provided Mannerheim with a recap of the investigation Danbury was conducting into Willie's murder.

"I assume you think Logan murdered him?"

"Who else? Either him or Todd McDonald."

"But why would Logan have one of his own killed?"

"Grant was just a bit player. Logan needed a strange face on the other side of the table to sign for the money. A faceless non-entity, that was Willie. He fit the bill perfectly. Shortly after you questioned him about the validity of the marker activity he decided to start to clean up his loose ends. Willie Grant was a loose end that needed to be taken care of. He was the most expendable, and not part of the inner circle. It also confirms that Logan is getting ready to leave. Especially if he now knows the place will be sold, and his forced retirement will be forthcoming under a new owner."

"Sounds reasonable. What have you told Danbury?"

Not that there was anything that Mannerheim wanted to hold back, but he felt a little uncomfortable totally putting his future in the hands of a government employee.

"Everything. I laid out our cards before he could show me his."

Said with a light-hearted tone that disturbed Mannerheim. He was getting the feeling Hamilton was enjoying this mess. No doubt a memorable case for him to tell his grandchildren when he was old and gray. Mannerheim was sure he would take the situation more seriously if it was his future on the line.

"What does he want to do now? And don't tell me he wants to discuss everything over with Logan."

"Matter of fact, that's exactly what he wants to do. But relax, I know him. Give him some credit. Danbury is not your normal hick cop from the back waters of Mayberry. He has had some experience with Logan himself. And after what I've told him about Logan, he knows he could just disappear if he feels too threatened."

"Yeah, and Logan is not your normal street punk. He has made a long living sizing up people. The casino is littered with the broken careers of people who made the mistake of underestimating the old boy. There are also a massive number of poorer players who thought they could pull something over on him. He plays the fool for nobody."

"Danbury assured me he will approach him as a possible witness, and not as a possible suspect. Seems the victim was a known small-time gambler. It's only logical that Danbury would ask around the local casinos for information."

"You're not a big comfort to me, but I guess this whole mess is rushing out of our control anyway. Just try to keep your Lt. Danbury as low-key as possible."

"He will be the soul of discretion."

That made Mannerheim feel worse. That made two people in as many days that expressed to him their discretion. Mannerheim was a methodical person. He was also somewhat of a cynic, and it served him well in life. The last person Mannerheim truly trusted was the doctor who delivered him. From there it had been downhill in the trust department. Now he was forced into a position of trusting two men... one he barely knew, and another he did not know at all.

*

South Lake Tahoe
Thursday, December 1
3:00 p.m.

In the scope of the big picture Hamilton was more concerned with the activities of Sam Logan than his minor accomplice, Todd McDonald. But Hamilton told Mannerheim he would keep an eye on him, so he drafted another private investigator, Ben Weaver, to follow McDonald around. He decided to use Ben instead of a team of two or three in an effort to keep the budget within reason. At seventy dollars per hour, the costs were mounting up for Mannerheim. Ben was a casual acquaintance, but not really a friend or even an investigator Hamilton held in high esteem. He had no police experience, and worked on cases Hamilton would normally turn down.

Ben was working the case because he had no other cases pending. His hourly billing rate was lower than Hamilton's, but subcontracting under Hamilton made it even lower. He knew Hamilton was probably charging his client his normal fee structure for the work *he* was doing. He calculated Hamilton was passing on less than half that amount to him. Hamilton probably rationalized he deserved it for *supervising* Weaver.

With that in mind, Weaver decided he would adjust his hours accordingly. It was determined his subject did not require round-the-clock coverage, and he was working alone. Weaver decided he could always find McDonald in the casino pit eight hours of every working day. He would inflate the time report to reflect at least four of those hours, and another four of McDonald's off time. In actuality Weaver planned on putting in less than five hours of labor. That way he could "adjust" his effort to correspond to a "proper" hourly rate.

Weaver started his third day of surveillance by stationing himself outside McDonald's house and waiting for him to head to work in a couple of hours.

*

Carson City, Nevada
4:40 p.m.

A nervous man was waiting in line at the Carson City office of the Nevada Department of Motor Vehicles. At last he was at the head of the line.

"Excuse me miss, but I'm afraid I've got a little problem. I just moved here from Florida and was robbed my first night here. They took my wallet, which included my old Florida driver's license. I managed to get a job at the Nugget as a waiter, but it's hard to even cash my payroll check without a driver's license. Could you *please* help me apply for a Nevada driver's license?"

Robbing tourists was not all that uncommon, and unlike murders, the police had a poor case-by-case rate of arrests. It was twenty minutes till closing time and home. The last thing the clerk wanted was a problem. She still had four impatient people behind this person, and they fully expected their problems to be solved before she closed up.

"Do you have *any* identification?"

"Yes, I anticipated you would need something, so while I phoned back to Florida for some money, I also had them fax me a copy of my birth certificate. It's right here."

The clerk examined it. Even though it as only a photostat, she was impressed by the signatures along the bottom, the image of a ribbon and seal along the right side, and the footprint of a newborn baby along the left side. Proof of identification was not anything that the state of Nevada required she examine with any great detail. The only requirement was that a person present *some* proof of identification. After a long day this will do as well as anything.

"So what's your current address, Mr. Finn?"

David Hannuksela

*

South Lake Tahoe
5:10 p.m.

After two hours and ten minutes Ben Weaver decided he better get a closer look. He got out of his car and started to walk along the street. As he came to McDonald's home he paused and peeked through the window of the garage door. Nothing but an oily garage floor. *The clown must be running errands*. He decided to head to the casino and pick him up there. It was nothing that needed to be included in his report.

CHAPTER 22

Monday, December 5
4:48 p.m.

Lt. Danbury made a point to inquire at every casino at Stateline before he called Sam Logan. Unlike Reno or Vegas, where you have many large hotel/casino operations scattered over a large area, Tahoe has just a handful clustered along the Nevada side of the one main highway passing through the Nevada/California border, and all within two blocks of the state line. As with any business, the people in the casino business got into a daily pattern that becomes routine and boring. Lt. Danbury knew that news of his murder investigation would travel ahead of him from one casino to another. By the time he approached Sam Logan he should feel comfortable that it was not directed at him personally.

The pipeline among the casinos was equal to that of any political environment. It half amused Danbury when immigration agents showed up. The housekeeping departments of all the hotels paid so poorly that the bulk of their staff was composed of illegal aliens. Within ten minutes after immigration agents went in the front door of the first hotel, hundreds of illegal aliens were going out the back door of all the hotels. Anyone standing there would think they were in a buffalo stampede. There was no doubt, on the part of Danbury, that Sam Logan would know everything that the other casinos knew before Danbury even entered the doors of "his" casino.

Not assuming he could just walk up to the casino pit and have Logan available, Lt. Danbury called ahead for an appointment to assure his availability. It also served to help assure Logan that the inquiry was strictly routine. Both men knew each other, however casual in nature. Over the years Steve Berkich's security officers had arrested slot machine cheats, players trying to smuggle loaded dice on a crap table, dishonest employees, pickpockets and assorted customers who had caused criminal problems, and turned them over to the sheriff's department. When an arrest affected the casino, Sam Logan *made* an appearance. Danbury had never been comfortable with Logan. He always felt Logan, no matter how outwardly polite, had a condescending attitude, and talked to him as a minor underling, or just another governmental bureaucrat. He did not expect anything different today. If it turned out that Logan was involved in Willie's murder, it would not just make Danbury's day, it would make his whole year. Nothing would please him more than to bring down the arrogant old man.

151

Like Mannerheim, he also knew Logan well enough not to underestimate him.

Lt. Danbury no sooner walked through the door of the casino when he spotted Sam Logan standing in the crap pit talking to one of his supervisors. As Danbury maneuvered his way through the crowds, Logan looked up, saw him and immediately flashed a smile, as his hand rose in greeting.

"Good morning, Robert. Its been a while since you've dropped by. How about if we talk over coffee. Better yet, have you had breakfast? My treat."

"Coffee will be fine."

As they walked the twenty feet over to the restaurant, located just off the casino floor, he could not help but predict the results. The thought quickly passed through Danbury's mind that this whole discussion was going to be one big futile waste of time. Mannerheim's skepticism of even meeting with Logan was coming back to Danbury as they walked. Danbury was so used to playing mind games with petty criminals that he just assumed he could apply those same tactics on Logan. By the time they approached the entrance to the restaurant it fully occurred to Danbury that Logan had more practice at mind games than he did, and against a better class of minds. Based upon his previous observations of Logan, Danbury was sure, if the need arose, Logan was more than able, and willing to charm or coerce the waitress out of her tip. Still, there was always a chance of a slip of the tongue.

Danbury was brief and routine when he summarized his investigation of Willie Grant's murder. He omitted any references to possible witnesses that would have ever placed Willie in Logan's casino, curious as to whether Logan would volunteer the information. All the while Logan looked straight at him, absorbing every word. Finally Logan was handed a mug shot, taken two years ago by the Reno Police when Willie was last arrested on a minor charge.

"Robert, I've got to tell you the truth. I come into contact with several thousand players a year. Year after year. This guy could have played here, but I couldn't swear to it in court. I used to pride himself on my memory, but I'm beginning to think old age is starting to catch up to me. Tell you what I can do for you. My Shift Supervisors have more day-to-day contact with the players than I do anymore, being the second floor politics are absorbing more of my time these days. I can bounce this picture off my supervisors and see if they can recall anything that will be useful. Or maybe you would want to talk to them directly?"

"No, I am sure you'll be able to stress the importance of the inquiry to them as well as I could. Just remember, he was killed late in the afternoon or early evening, Thanksgiving day. So if anyone can recall seeing him, or anyone with him, on or shortly prior to that time, I would be most appreciative."

"Consider it done. And if there's anything else I can do for you don't hesitate to give me a call. Say, Willie Nelson is playing in the showroom next month." He casually glanced down to notice a wedding ring on Danbury's third finger.

"Can I send you and your wife some tickets? Center booth, of course. Would you prefer a Friday or Saturday night?" Not waiting for an answer to his first question.

"Saturday, if it's convenient."

Might as well confirm his view that everyone can be bought.

"Again, consider it done."

Danbury walked away wondering if it had all been worth the effort, other than making his wife happy.

*

It was almost five o'clock in the afternoon when Mannerheim completed his meeting with the Hotel Manager of the Golden Palace. It took almost two hours to discuss the details of preparing for the accommodations for Yarbrough and his party, as well as space large enough for what was sure to be prolonged meetings over the next few weeks. Mannerheim wanted to go over the preparations, and examine the actual rooms. It also served to stress the confidentiality of the meetings. Mannerheim told their Hotel Manager the purpose of meetings was to discuss the possible sale of Aaron's eight hundred acre ranch along the foothills. He claimed Aaron wanted to spend more time in Palm Springs, as well as Hawaii. Besides, the profit margin of the ranch, as a ranch, was marginal anyway. Mannerheim told him that if word got out that a sale of the ranch was pending, it could cast suspicions that Aaron was hurting for funds. The story was believable enough to satisfy the Hotel Manager as to the need for confidentiality.

Mannerheim was walking down the stairs from the Golden Palace's second floor, noted that it was his normal quitting time, and decided he would have a drink in one of their bars. Mannerheim opted against having a drink for nothing just two hundred feet away and decided he wanted a change of scenery. He also wanted some peace and quiet more than he wanted to talk shop with anyone he might run into at the Lakeside Room. Mannerheim remembered the Golden Palace had a quiet little bar named the Pine Cone Room. He headed for it.

The bar was quieter and smaller, but also darker than the average casino bar. As he stood there waiting for his eyes to adjust to the lesser amount of lighting, he heard a voice ask him, "Can I buy you a drink, Mr. Mannerheim?"

It took a second for Mannerheim to focus on, and recognize, the speaker. It was Scott Sherman.

"Sure."

Mannerheim settled into the empty seat of the two-seat table that Sherman was occupying. The sole barmaid who worked the little station came over. Mannerheim ordered a red wine. Sherman was still lingering over a white wine.

"Almost surprised you would join me, Mr. Mannerheim."

"Call me Paul. Unlike the majority of people in this racket, I try not to take everything too personal. But I would suggest you not bother to extend a similar offer to Elliott."

"Somehow I think you might be right... Paul."

"The truth of the matter is that I was almost entertained by your performance in Desmond's office. And I'm not too proud to acknowledge when an opponent has done their homework, and succeeded in their cause. In case word hasn't gotten back to you, your side has succeeded in their goal. We'll probably sell out to your boss."

"I have no idea what you may be talking about."

"Right." It was worth a try.

"How are you enjoying your stay at Tahoe?" Changing the subject.

"Facilities are excellent, but similar to a thousand other places. The scenery is what sets it apart from the pack. It's a much better setting than Las Vegas. Everything seems a little more relaxed here. There are even fewer hookers walking the street."

"Oh, if they walked the street here they would need a parka for a good chunk of the time. It does diminish their ability to engage in effective advertising. But to be honest, we probably have our share of hookers, but they're far less obvious. Our Casino Host sure seems to know where to find them."

Mannerheim paused to see if his reference to Vic would generate some reaction. Scott just reached for his wine, patiently waiting for Mannerheim to continue.

"I know what you mean about Vegas. Most of us refer to it as 'plastic town.' At least people feel more comfortable here, as we take their money. Your wife enjoying Tahoe?"

"No wife, just an ex. Too much of a rolling stone to suit her. She was right. Especially when our daughter came along, who's now a senior at Stanford. Seems I just couldn't change direction. How about you? You married?"

"Not me, I only look stupid."

Mannerheim was a percentage player. After looking at the broken marriages, bloody divorces, and resulting alimony payments associated with almost every friend he ever had, he determined marriage was too high-risk for him. He could get better odds playing roulette. Even his combat experience demonstrated better survival statistics. He feared the conflict that he saw in most marriages. His occupation provided enough of that. Besides, he was fast approaching a point in his life where he was getting too independent, as well as were all the women he met over the last ten years.

"I once came close to marriage, I was even engaged. Fortunately we planned a long engagement. In the end our relationship degenerated down to the point where she wanted to remove 'trust and obey' from our wedding vows, and I was all for substituting them with 'heel and fetch'. We both finally gave up the idea before the fateful day arrived."

"At least that realization came before the wedding. Divorces can be messy."

Aside from an attempt at small talk, Mannerheim knew Sherman was not married. Hamilton provided a background report on Scott Sherman several days before. It provided some interesting reading.

"Knowing your background, I must admit I was a little surprised with your involvement with Yarbrough. It doesn't fit your typical operating procedure."

"Who?" This time Sherman said it with a grin.

Mannerheim also smiled.

"Let's just say your partners." Worth another try. "I thought you worked alone. What got you into this?"

"What gets any of us into anything? Money, of course." Answering his own question. "It's what turns the world."

"Yes, as with us all. We all end up selling the minutes of our lives for money. Well, it would appear the wheels of time are passing both of us by. Events have been marching ahead in the last few days. I don't know about you, but I think of myself as just an interested spectator. The outcome is in the hands of others at this point."

Unknown to Sherman, Mannerheim was thinking about both the marker rip-off by Logan, as well as the sale of the property to Yarbrough.

"I would agree. My part is done. The play is set. Either a comedy or tragedy, depending on your point of view."

"Tell me, Scott, is it the outcome you anticipated?"

"Oh, I anticipated a far different outcome to events thirty years ago. I can't complain about the lifestyle, just the priorities that one establishes in life."

Mannerheim had to agree. When he was twenty-five years younger he also carried the different outcomes for his life. He never thought he would cure cancer, or be President of the United States, but he always thought he could look back on a life that would leave the world a little better than he found it. It was not working out that way.

"Yeah, I know what you mean. My first real job was to look down from the night sky, find targets and adjust artillery on them... much to their regret. Now I basically counted money for what amounted to nothing more than a large, but legal, bookie operation."

He now realized he would probably leave the world a little more worse off than he found it.

Everyone envisions the high roller, arriving in his Learjet, a blond on each arm, rolling the dice on the crap table. No real harm done. In reality, Mannerheim knew who loses most in casinos... people who can least afford it, people on unemployment, people on social security, people on welfare. Desperate people who take what little they have and try to turn it into a little more, and end up losing the little they started with. Every morning the previous day's revenue numbers went over his desk. They represented numbers of despair, numbers of hopelessness. Mannerheim always tried to look at himself as just a curious spectator on the sidelines. Lately he was forced to admit he was a direct participant in the human tragedy around him. Mannerheim had heard various politicians promote the establishment of gambling in their respective states on the basis that it was "entertainment." Mannerheim thought a similar agreement could be made if you could tax the money paid by junkies for their drugs. After all, it is just another piece of the pie for the continuation of their entertainment. He suddenly remembered the eyes of the child he saw last week. He realized he was drifting into another state of melancholy. It must be the effect of wine. Maybe he better switch to beer.

"Scott, why do I get the feeling you're an idealist?"

"It comes and goes."

Scott's mind was back in Oklahoma, and the ideals his father lived by.

"I'll make an appointment with my doctor next week and get a shot for it. How about you?"

"Me! I'm a total realist. My emotions are bullet-proof. I build my walls high and thick enough to keep them that way."

Sherman held up his wine glass. "To bigger and better walls."

"Scott, I understand you came from Oklahoma originally. I remember going through there when I was in the army. As I remember, it was flat, treeless, cold and windy. Imagine you're glad to be out of there."

"If all you saw was the scenery, I guess you could say that. But I remember the people. I remember my father. He was a good man, sometimes I think a much better man than I have become. I have gained much in material possessions, but sometimes I think I lost my foundation...my better character."

This was turning far more sober than Sherman anticipated. But if you were to do some soul searching, perhaps a stranger was the best person.

"Yes. At times I think my talent got me this far, but that's just vanity. There's plenty of talent around. I was just born the right time, the right place. I was born male, born white, born American. That's about a fifty to one shot at birth, and it all provided me with a tremendous advantage that I sure didn't earn. So it boils down to more luck than talent. That, and good parents who believed in the work ethic. They believed in other ethics too, but sometimes I think that's the only one I kept."

"My father's work ethic only helped to put him in the ground he plowed."

Feeling this discussion was only plowing up sad memories, Scott decided to change the subject. For the first time in his life, Scott was looking at the frightening prospect of regular employment. It occurred to him he knew little about it.

"Tell me Paul, you enjoy working in casinos?"

"Yeah, they're interesting. Surroundings are beautiful. The pay is decent, and the work is comparatively easy."

"Compared to what?"

"Well, as we said, I wouldn't want to work in Vegas, and New Jersey is out."

"I understand they have some really nice casinos there. Don't like the East?"

"It's not that. I enjoyed the East during the few times I've been back there. I just don't like the activity... too busy. When Atlantic City opened their first casino in 1978, it was mobbed. Thousands of people poured into the place. They're required, by the State of New Jersey, to close their doors at four in the morning. I understand they announced closing time every five minutes for a half hour before four o'clock. Even then their security had to physically pull the arms of little old ladies off the handles of the slot machines. They wouldn't even leave when they turned off the power to the machines. Security had to form a V-wedge line and move through the casino in order to clear it out. They opened again six hours later, at ten. The crowds got so large at their entrance they announced that there would be no running, for fear people in back would crush the slower ones in the front when the doors were opened."

"It was that busy?"

"There were so many people waiting for a chair at their blackjack tables that if someone got up, they would lose their place. The stools were wearing out every six months, only because people would urinate where they sat rather than lose their place to go to the bathroom."

"Jersey must be better now. They've built a bunch of new casinos since then."

"They have, but the stories we heard of those first few years reinforced my image that there are just too many crowds back there for my taste."

"Human nature being what it is, your customers couldn't be any better."

"True. Working in these places has made me a true cynic, but things happen that still amaze me. Couple months ago, an eighty-year-old woman passed out on the floor. Security gave her oxygen, but had to work around another old woman playing the slot machine next to her. She wouldn't leave. She even stepped over the old woman's body, as she lay there dying, and took the nickels that were still in her machine's tray."

"Amazing. Customer theft a big problem for you?"

"Not really. Daily we get customers who try to pull some petty scam on us. They bring in a bug so they can deposit it on a salad and get a comp meal. They complain they discovered a hair in their room, then want us to comp the room because it's dirty. But to answer your question, I worry more about employee theft. We've had employees hide chips in their cowboy boots, under their tongues and who-knows-where-else in order to get them out the door. Still, all things considered, I'll keep Tahoe."

"So if you're planning on staying, are you looking forward to changing employers? Would you find any difficulty switching your loyalties from Aaron Davenport to a new owner after the place is sold?"

"None. Corporate survival rule #4; *There is no such thing as corporate loyalty, only individual loyalty.* With rare exception, there's no loyalty from the employer to the employee, or from the employee to the employer. It all just boils down to the numbers. It has been my experience that most top management is more concerned about its numbers than even its own accountants. By comparison, Japanese companies take a long-term view. They make decisions that promote the financial strength of the company and generate profits far down the road. In America we just seem to react. Too often management makes decisions so the quarterly earnings numbers look better to the stock analysts on Wall Street. They're too concerned with the market price of their stock and its effect on their pending stock options, as opposed with solid business decisions. We've become too short-term to have long-term loyalty to employees, and the employees know that and react accordingly. That's the sad truth in America. I didn't make the rules, I'm just trying to survive the system."

"I've never met him, but I have it on good authority that Yarbrough's good at keeping his word. Think he'll be any different?"

Mannerheim had to smile at that remark.

"I'll keep an open mind, but the odds are slim. I've seen a lot of business deals and none involved honor."

That evoked a comment by Scott.

"Honor! I've seen a lot of clashes stem from people's sense of honor."

"When it comes to honor I'm not talking about a husband who attacks some guy that glances at his good-looking wife. That's pride, and there's plenty of that around. Honor is rare. Usually you see a person's true character when things involve money. People trend to hold their wallets close to their hearts. Keeping your word when you do not benefit... or knowing it will cost you... there lies honor, and I've seen little, if any, in my observations."

"You planning on changing the world?"

"Don't get me wrong. I don't claim to be a model of nobility myself. Just trust me when I tell you not to trust anyone on faith... get everything in writing."

Scott could see the truth in the answer and returned the smile with his reply.

"I'll remember that. In case I find myself working in the corporate environment, I hope I can count on you to help me learn the other corporate survival rules."

"It will be my pleasure. Maybe with enough trust the system will change. Maybe we can even change for the better."

This time Mannerheim held up his glass. "To change." As the glasses touched.

As guarded as the conversation started, it evolved into more candid discussion of life, goals, triumphs and failures. Maybe it was the wine. Maybe the lack of need to hide much at this point. In another time they could see themselves as friends. If things worked out maybe they would soon be on the same side. But not now, not quite yet. About eleven they realized it was time to depart back to their respective camps. Like two soldiers from opposite sides, sharing common shelter in the middle of a battlefield, they left.

*

Tuesday, December 6

Todd McDonald was taking some unscheduled time off, always on weekdays. Mannerheim started to observe that McDonald was not in the pit during his usual shift. There were only four Casino Shift Managers, and all were well known. Any changes in their work schedule did not go unnoticed. Mannerheim's call to Hamilton was not needed. Hamilton was already aware McDonald was not at work. Ben Weaver informed him that he could not locate McDonald at his home, and could not pick him up at the casino.

Not trusting Ben Weaver, Hamilton took it upon himself to find out what he was up to. Based upon McDonald's routine of disappearing on Tuesdays and Thursdays, Hamilton camped out at four o'clock in the morning outside of McDonald's home and followed him as he left at six o'clock.

Hamilton managed to trail him as he headed west into California, always managing to buffer his car and McDonald's with two or three other vehicles. All went well until they reached the traffic of San Francisco. He was not used to maintaining a four-foot gap between himself and the car ahead of him. Every time Hamilton permitted an empty car length to develop in front of him, somebody from the adjacent lane forced themselves into the opening. A frustrated Hamilton quickly lost sight of McDonald's car in the big city's unbelievable traffic. He thought it amounted to false advertising when the local authorities referred to those routes as "freeways". "Snailways" would have been a more accurate description.

Once Hamilton inched his way off the freeway, he took surface streets for the next two hours until he managed to locate an obscure little shop known only to the small community of private investigators. There he rented a hi-tech, high-cost little gadget that transmits a signal to a receiver in his car. It enabled him to determine the direction of McDonald's car, once the transmitter was attached under his bumper. Hamilton drove back to Tahoe to try again.

McDonald arrived back at work on Wednesday, as scheduled. McDonald's engine was still cooling down as Hamilton was crawling under the car in the employees' parking lot.

*

Thursday, December 8
6:03 a.m.

As predicted, McDonald again headed west, with a more confident Hamilton in pursuit. Again McDonald quickly managed to disappear in rush-hour traffic. Rush hour started at six in the morning and ended sometime after midnight. Even with his new toy, it took Hamilton a full hour to locate McDonald's car, which was sitting on the third floor of a parking structure located next to the business district in downtown San Francisco. Direction was helpful. A lack of one-way streets, traffic lights and road construction would have been more helpful.

Once he found the car he could do nothing more than wait for McDonald to return. After three hours McDonald finally appeared. Locating him at that point only served to provide Hamilton with something to look at as McDonald lead the way back to Nevada.

*

The next time Hamilton arrived at the same parking structure ahead of McDonald and waited for him. Another wasted effort. McDonald parked in a different structure a mile away.

This happened twice more before Hamilton admitted defeat, realizing his small town surveillance techniques had difficulty working in a much larger, stranger city, with endless gridlock.

CHAPTER 23

Monday, December 19
10:32 a.m.

It had been almost two weeks since negotiations with Yarbrough and his team had begun. Mannerheim knew he disliked attorneys before this, but now he was even taking a dislike to his own profession. In addition to Yarbrough's tax experts from Price Waterhouse, Mannerheim had to call in tax accountants from their outside auditing firm of Coopers & Lybrand. Elliott also had several corporate attorneys from a high-priced San Francisco firm. A total of fifteen people sparred between the two camps. These experts were almost always separated into smaller groups, depending on their area of expertise. With each hour that ticked by, the combined cost to the two sides was almost five thousand dollars.

Mannerheim kept in daily contact with Aaron by phone. Allan's Bear Camp closed for the winter shortly after Elliott's visit, but Aaron decided to stay over in Anchorage to play tourist. Seems he wanted to check out Mount McKinley, by air due to his age, and each of the ten thousand glaciers, located in every bay in Alaska. He did monitor the progress with scheduled phone calls, and a fax machine. Despite several attempts by Mannerheim to talk him into coming back and to participate in the debate, Aaron was becoming more convinced that he did not want to get involved with grunting out the details. He did concede that he would be heading back to his ranch shortly, to await the final settlement. Mannerheim understood his desire not to get bogged down with fast talking attorneys and accountants. Plain talk totally disappeared. Legal jargon and tax buzz words now replaced English.

Mannerheim had anticipated a lengthy period of negotiations, but this was dragging on and on and on, with no end in sight. It was agreed that any sale would be formally postponed till the coming year in order to defer the taxable gain one additional year. Now Mannerheim was wondering if January was even a realistic goal. Considering they were selling a business that built nothing, created nothing (except money), held no patents, or no intangible assets, Mannerheim had hoped it would help expedite the analysis, but that was not to be the case.

Even though both sides accepted an "offer in principal," it was contingent on confirmation of the basic underlying value. This requirement was due to

Yarbrough's need for third-party financing. His bankers, like all bankers, required seeing something on paper, written by people calling themselves experts. It appeared bankers liked the large profits generated by wheeler-dealers, but always wanted to check the numbers before going into the deal.

Each side was to select its own independent appraiser. Then the two appraisers were to jointly select a third appraiser. The final appraised value would be an average of the three. From there they would still haggle, but it at least formed a basis for discussion. It sounded good on paper, but Mannerheim was having trouble getting his own appraiser to concede that a favorable selling price would not compromise his "professional ethics." He thought accountants were conservative, but since the Savings & Loan disaster it seemed all appraisers thought their best protection from possible lawsuit was to lowball their report. If Yarbrough did not need to provide his financial backers with an appraised value, Mannerheim was tempted to try to omit the need for any appraisal at all.

The only point that proceeded with any speed was the mineral rights issue. As anticipated, Yarbrough dismissed the whole issue. He assured Aaron that the purchase would be made as is, with a related statement in the selling agreement that he was fully aware of the mineral rights issue. Not surprisingly, one of Yarbrough's team members was a lawyer named John Stremel, the previously unknown third person on the signature card of the Nevada Silver Shaft Mining Corporation's checking account located at the Tahoe Bank and Trust. It was now considered ancient history, and Mannerheim saw no reason to make an issue of it at this point.

Rumors were flying thick and fast among the employees. Within three hours of Yarbrough's arrival it seemed everyone knew about it. Based upon the assumption that new management would logically terminate the lower ten percent of the employees, employee theft seemed to be running rampant. Everyone automatically assumed they qualified to be included in those marginal employees who represented the ten percent.

A bartender was discovered to have taken several hundred dollars from his register. In order to offset the missing cash, he inflated his beverage charges and transferred the difference to a hotel "comp" billing belonging to a high-roller. It was only discovered because of poor luck on his part. He made the mistake of charging a hotel RFB (for complimentary Room, Food & Beverage) billing that belonged to one of the outside auditors, and not a high-roller. A high-roller would not have even wasted his time looking at the total as he signed out, because he did not have to pay for it, he could care less, which was what the bartender expected. However, the Coopers & Lybrand auditor, who spent two days doing an interim review of inventory procedures prior to the year-end audit, did not want his manager to think he was on a constant drunk during his stay. He, therefore, did review the billing and reported the inflated bar charge as a discrepancy to Fitz before heading back to Vegas.

Similar employee thefts were up five fold. Considering they probably caught less than half the actual number of thefts performed, Mannerheim was hoping the employees would leave the furniture in place before he had a chance to sell it to Yarbrough.

Whenever a Casino Manager dies, retires or was replaced, the Casino Shift Managers and supervisors quickly become casualties shortly after the new Casino Manager arrives. Since their job promotions and security rested on individual loyalty to their boss, the new boss found it easier to guarantee that loyalty by bringing in his old Shift Managers and supervisors from the departed casino. Not trusting in the remote chance that Logan would be retained, or one of them would be promoted from within, telephone usage doubled to casinos all over the state, as well as casinos in New Jersey, various Indian reservations, and even a few in the Caribbean. Shortly thereafter, resumes from the pit started clogging the local post office. Besides the pit, almost all second floor executives were hedging their bets as they quickly contacted their sources in search of better job security.

Mannerheim moved into a suite at the Golden Palace in order to be close to the negotiations and away from the rumor mill. He seldom went to his office. With near panic among the executive staff, it was now more of a combat zone than a refuge. Between one location or another, he found peace an elusive commodity.

As hectic as it was with Mannerheim, it was the exact opposite with Sam Logan. He did get back to Danbury and reported that one of his Shift Supervisors thought Willie had played blackjack there from time-to-time, but nothing approaching a regular basis. Both Lt. Danbury and Hamilton had been digging into Logan's financial and personal history. Claiming to be everything from insurance adjusters to disgruntled players, they talked by phone to hundreds of people, but as yet they were unable to come up with a smoking gun. By all appearances Logan was playing it cool. He seemed almost unconcerned with the possible sale of "his" casino, or the pending murder investigation.

Mannerheim checked in with his secretary three times a day. Betty was otherwise instructed not to page him unless it was deemed an emergency. At ten minutes to eleven his pager went off. Mannerheim looked down to see which of his two pagers were calling him. It was Betty. He was in the middle of checking over some obscure tax code reference and welcomed the interruption. He returned the page. Betty informed him that Susie Parsons inquired as to the possibility of him to joining her for lunch. It did not seem to fit the definition of an emergency, but Mannerheim could think of nothing better or more urgent to his sanity than a pleasant escape from his current frustrations. He told Betty to get back to Susie and tell her that he would meet her in one hour, at an out-of-the-way restaurant, located about three miles away.

On the way to the restaurant Mannerheim was beginning to regret his choice of locations. The road still had ice on it from the previous night's snow storm. Fortunately, his four-wheel drive Bronco was under him. He finally arrived at the restaurant about ten minutes late, but still ahead of Susie. Due to the road conditions, the restaurant was almost empty, which was fine with Mannerheim. Five minutes later Susie walked in. She found Mannerheim enjoying a hot cup of coffee at a corner table.

"Hello, stranger. Long time no see."

"Just a slave to my job. Good to see you. Have a seat."

"You've been a busy little boy. How does it feel to be in the hub of all the activity?"

"I'm just at the mercy of the prevailing current. Everything is spinning by with little or no regard for my wishes. If fact, I don't think anyone has even noticed my absence. How are things going at the zoo?"

"There's a marked increase in meat-eaters in the jungle."

"How so?"

"Let me ask you. How are you and Elliott getting along?"

"The guy is cooler than the weather outside. He has been the biggest anchor in this whole process. He tries to throw on the brakes every time some minor problem comes up. Twice I've had to go over his head to Aaron in order to get him to back off. We had a cordial relationship before, but now I would classify it as adversarial, and we're supposed to be on the same side. It's like there are three different parties involved instead of two. Yarbrough is really getting frustrated with us because of him. Why do you ask?"

"You may not be on the winning side if you think Yarbrough is going to come out ahead. There is more in this poker game than just the two hands."

"Who else? Aaron already agreed in principal to sell to Yarbrough. It's only a matter of time, and that time would come a lot faster if Elliott would get out of the way."

"But he won't. He still wants to buy out Aaron and take control himself. He has the backing of enough money brokers and wealthy supporters."

"Even if Elliott has some financial support, he hasn't got the support of Aaron. In fact, Aaron doesn't even like the guy."

"Paul, trust me when I tell you, he doesn't need Aaron's support."

"Exactly what are you telling me? Give me the short version."

"You could be a major asset right now and be rewarded in the end. Or, you could lose out if you back the wrong horse. Let Elliott slow up this process!"

"Why? I need more than what you're telling me."

"Remember when Elliott came back from Alaska and informed you about Aaron's decision to sell?"

"Yeah, I remember. One of the briefest, one-sided meetings I've ever had."

"That's because he had a much longer meeting with Desmond and me right after his meeting with you. He has a plan. Elliott has just been waiting to firm up his financing. That has been finalized as of late yesterday. He's now going to make his move for control."

"But *again*, Aaron won't go for it."

"It will be out of Aaron's hands shortly. By the time we finish lunch Elliott will file a petition, with family consent, to have the court declare Aaron legally incompetent, and have the property placed in the hands of Carl Desmond, our noble president, and Aaron's long suffering son-in-law. Remember, Carl Desmond may be just an in-law, but he's Aaron's closest relative, and the father of Aaron's only grandchild. He knows Aaron just tolerates him. Elliott has convinced him not to trust the assumption that Aaron will remember him in his will. He should try to take what's 'his' now. Desmond is the one who must, and did, initiate the petition."

"No way! On what grounds could he support that? Aaron is as competent as you or me, and while I may have my doubts about you sometimes, there is nothing Elliott can use to make a claim like that against Aaron."

"Nothing but the fact that Aaron seems totally disinterested in running his multi-million dollar operation. He's gone ninety percent of the time. Even when its about ready to be sold, he still doesn't appear to show enough interest to come back from a hunting trip. Desmond can claim he needs to file this petition in order to head off a financial disaster for the family, as well as for the ultimate benefit of Aaron himself. To protect him from himself. The case can be made that senility has set in. He is almost eighty and has lost touch with reality."

"He won't be able to prove that."

"Elliott doesn't have to prove anything. He's a big attorney from the small town of Reno. He knows all the judges in town, and now has a big pile of money on his side. He can bring in an endless supply of psychiatrists. He can get an injunction against any possible sale of the property by Aaron. If Aaron wasn't crazy before that, he will be after Elliott and Desmond get through with him. They could tie Aaron up in court until the old boy dies. But it won't take that long. You know Aaron. He will take the obvious way out before that happens, and so should you. Paul, stop and smell the dandelions. Elliott can do it."

"Why are you telling me all this?"

"We need you on our side. You could be the difference between a hostile takeover or a faster, easier takeover. But either way, the result will be the same. Look to your future. Shortly after Elliott takes over he intends to go public. You could end up with a big salary and a bunch of stock options."

"The benefit of blackmail."

"Call it anything you want. Just remember what I said... whether or not you are with us or against us, it won't matter when the dust settles. This is your wake-up call. Besides, I'd really like to see you stay around. Just give the word and that long-term contract is yours. But if you oppose us, he *will* crush you."

"What do you think of all this? You sleeping well at night?"

"We all do what we have to do to get along in this world. I like Aaron, but I've got to think of my future. Aaron is bailing out. We'll all be left to fend for ourselves."

Just then the waitress arrived with two orders of lasagna and a basket of fresh bread. They both ate in silence. Mannerheim just considered his options. The lunch ended with Mannerheim acknowledging he would consider her proposal.

Mannerheim returned to the Golden Palace to continue his role in the stalemate. As he was walking past the lounge, he heard some performer sing Cher's old hit, '*Gypsies, Tramps and Thieves*'. Mannerheim could not help but wonder if she was advertising the name of some law firm.

CHAPTER 24

Tuesday, December 20
10:34 a.m.

Lt. Danbury met with Steve Berkich to review some surveillance tapes made by the overhead cameras. Normally the tape machine recycles and tapes over anything older than forty-eight hours. As a result, most of the video was long gone, but Berkich did manage to pull out and save the tape of Willie Grant receiving a marker, on the night Hamilton was waiting for him.

Most surveillance camera angles are set up to aim directly down on the table activity. They were examining one of the few camera angles that just rotated across the length of the casino floor. It panned an area of several hundred feet. Due to the distances involved, Danbury was having trouble making out the grainy images on the tape. Despite the fact it was of marginal quality, he could still make out the image of Willie Grant receiving a marker from Todd McDonald and Sam Logan. Both Berkich and Danbury bent over the tape machine as they intently examined the images.

"Well Berkich, I hope your eyesight is better than mine."

"I can enlarge any frame you're interested in."

"You're beginning to sound like my wife. Lately, every morning she hands me a magnifying glass so I can read the paper."

"Well, when you're old, you're old. Just be glad we have the technology to enlarge this stuff. When I first came here we didn't even have surveillance cameras. Just a dirty catwalk in the attic above the casino floor. One-way glass next to the planks which the 'eye-in-the-sky' stood on. At that time they used binoculars to watch the tables below. No cameras, no monitors, no tape."

"Yeah. Everyone keeps telling me of the benefits of technology, but over the last ten years I've felt like I spend more time studying than I did when I was in school. Even then, last week our greenest rookie had to explain to me how the computerized data display in my police car worked. Imagine, now we have computers in the cars."

"You think they're worth the cost?"

"Must admit they come in handy when we need to run a license plate. Last year we recovered almost forty stolen cars. But they can sure be a pain to understand, or figure out how they work. How about you, ever wish for the old days again?"

"Every time I see a good looking blond rolling dice on a crap table."

"Come again?"

"About eight years ago, when I first started working here, I saw this gorgeous looking blond rolling dice. Her low-cut dress barely covered her... chest. She was on a real winning streak. The more excited she got, the more she forgot, as Mannerheim would say, to cover her assets. The crowd got so thick around that crap table I had trouble keeping her in view. So I headed for the stairs, went up the catwalk and used those binoculars for a beautiful birds-eye view."

"Why you dirty old man!"

"Yeah, that's what Mannerheim had been telling me lately. But that old simple system is history. Look what replaced it."

Berkich motioned around at a roomful of surveillance monitors.

"Now it should be called the 'lens-in-the-sky'. Everything is out of this sterile control room. Besides the gaming areas, we have cameras covering the bars, restaurants, cage, even in the elevators. More money for more toys. But unlike your police computers, I sometimes doubt if it's worth the cost."

"How do you mean?"

"Notice we're the only ones in this room. Back when all we had was a catwalk, we had one guy looking through those binoculars. Let's say there's fifty games in action at any given time. Even when the surveillance guy was on duty he could only watch one game at a time. That's only two percent of the total tables under surveillance at a time. Also we should factor another variable into the equation. One employee can only work five shifts, but there are three shifts a day, or twenty-one shifts a week. All things being equal, that results in him looking at *possible* dishonest dealers or players less than a quarter of the total time. So we end up with two percent *table* coverage, with the twenty-five percent *shift* coverage, which results in a table being observed by the 'eye-in-the-sky' only about one-half of one percent of the time, less coffee breaks."

"But you must have more than just one employee in surveillance now?"

"Sure. Now we have a whole department that consists of three employees. Wally Lowe, a supervisor who drinks a lot of coffee, and two people who actually look at these monitors. So the coverage climbs to a full *one* percent coverage."

"And I thought we were spread thin."

"Boils down to basic economics. Being the dealers and players can't see through the black bubble holding the camera, built into the casino ceiling, they don't know if they are being monitored or not. So the whole system provides more of a *psychological* deterrent, as opposed to any real threat to a criminal.

Mannerheim once explained to me that if we had anything approaching total coverage it would be just too expensive. He used the term... 'cost prohibitive'. Turns out it would be cheaper to let the players and dealers steal from us. It's like hiring a security guard to follow around each employee. All it does is double your payroll. It's not cost effective at that point."

"I *guess* that makes sense."

Both looked at the world from the viewpoint that there should be no cost limit for security. The economic argument may have been logical, but it was not totally convincing for either one of them.

"I tried to buy some of the one-way glass when they took it out, but it was sold in bulk to some small casino in eastern Nevada. Thought of some creative ways I could put it to use."

"I see the dirty old man in you again."

"Still, all this new equipment does provide us with an advantage. Just because nobody's monitoring them, doesn't mean these cameras don't keep recording their pictures. If we know something happened, we can always go back and examine it later, as long as it's before it tapes over itself. Which gets us back to why we're here. What do you want to do with this tape of Willie receiving the marker from Logan and McDonald? It proves Logan lied to you. They did meet before."

"Unfortunately, that's all it proves. Logan made sure to mention to me that he *could* have met him. I show him this tape and he will just tell me again about his failing memory. Even my sergeant has the same problem. Patrick is sure he knows Willie from somewhere, but can't remember the situation."

"You're probably right, but for what's its worth, if you want, you can have the tape for your case file."

"Sure. You never know how it will tie into something else down the road. But I don't have to tell you that. Hamilton told me you were also once a police officer with the Reno department."

"Ancient history now. It seems like another life. I've got to tell you, I don't regret not being face-to-face, on a daily basis, with vermin like Willie Grant. From his car to his character, everything about him was repulsive. I have to admire your dedication to even pursue a murder case with this kind of victim. I think I would be tempted to just file it away, knowing society would be better served with him no longer in a position to harm any more innocent lives."

"Yeah. The first day I read the rap sheet on him I had that same thought. But I just hate to think someone could murder anyone, even someone like Willie, and get away with it."

"How about letting us buy you lunch. I guess I can stand to be around someone as noble as you for another hour."

"Sounds good. I've got the time. My next trip is the morgue, and that subject isn't in any hurry."

"Don't tell me you have another murder on your hands?"

"No. Our murder quota is only one a year. This one is a suicide. I've just got to clear up some paperwork before we bury the body. It will sure wait until after lunch."

"Who's the deceased?"

"Nobody you'd know. Just an old part-time maintenance man called Sarge."

*

Washoe County Morgue.
12:47 p.m.

Danbury was finishing up the required paperwork associated with Sarge's suicide, when his pager went off. It was from his sergeant, Patrick Miller.

"Hi Pat, what's up?"

"My memory finally kicked in. Now I know why Willie's picture has been haunting me. Remember me telling you about that case with the dishonest blackjack dealer? The one who palmed aces, then dealt them back to his partner, posing as a player?"

"Yeah, I also remember the case was later dropped."

"That's the one! We could never locate the dealer's partner to make the case. But I went back in the file and pulled the photo made from the surveillance tape. It was Willie! That must have been how Logan first made contact with Willie. He spotted him from that scam and used him in his own marker scam."

"Makes sense. But..."

"What's the matter Bob? It helps tie Logan closer to Willie."

"Contract the Reno PD. I need to know something else."

*

2:45 p.m.

Mannerheim pondered the possibilities and probabilities.

With the threat of prolonged legal battles facing him, Aaron would probably

172

succumb to Elliott and Desmond. Without a quick and definitive conclusion, which was not likely, Aaron would face years of protracted and useless court battles. To be at the mercy of a merciless system. Mainly because of the differences in their ages, their varied backgrounds and the lack of day-to-day contact, Mannerheim never felt very close to his employer. It was hard to build a rapport with a telephone, or a fax machine, and most of the contact Mannerheim had ever had with Aaron was on a long-distance basis. The concept of changing employers did not even concern Mannerheim, up to this point. Regardless, he did like, or at least felt he understood Aaron, and did not like the idea that he would end his days being pulled around the legal system with his name dragged through the papers. He knew Aaron to be a proud man. Too proud to have his sanity questioned, especially for the whole world to observe. Newspapers have a tendency to grab on to soap opera like stories and run them to increase sales. The Reno and Tahoe papers were no different. Win or lose, Aaron's chances of avoiding damage to his name and spirit were slim. In time, Aaron would die a broken man with a lifetime of other achievements overshadowed by innuendo.

Mannerheim enjoyed money, and the things it could buy, as much or more than most. And he certainly did not consider himself naive. Still, it surprised him what an individual did to gain money and power. As a student of history, he saw the darker side of human nature reveal itself when those elements were involved. Now he observed it, with more clarity, in the workplace around him. Sometimes Mannerheim wondered if he had been in the system long enough to be corrupted himself. He hoped not. But, before that happened, Mannerheim told himself he must try to stop Elliott, before he turned into somebody like him.

Mannerheim did not know what to do, or how to do it. But he at least knew enough to combine forces with "kindred spirits," or at least those with the same vested interests. He would have to bring Vic Welles and Scott Sherman into any scenario to try and save the deal with Yarbrough. They already had their futures tied to Yarbrough. Paul needed them as useful allies against Elliott. He also realized he had to take a chance and try to separate Susie from Elliott. He needed to arrange a meeting to determine any common ground and hopefully a plan of attack.

*

Tuesday, December 20

Vic and Scott arrived at room number 1204 of the Golden Palace at 7:10

p.m. As long as the sun went down, Vic could be counted on to appear within a reasonable amount of time. At Mannerheim's request for an additional meeting to discussion alternative possibilities, a very reluctant Susie Parsons finally knocked on the door at 7:30.

During the twenty minute delay Mannerheim found out from Vic that he had never seen Susie. Due to different hours and much different working environments, Susie and Vic knew of each other but, surprisingly, had never met. Mannerheim answered the door and was about to make the introductions when things were taken out of his hands. Vic, upon seeing Susie, came to full attention. He was like a well trained Golden Retriever observing the first pheasant of the season dropping from the sky.

"Hello beautiful! I just have three questions for you. Are you married? Do you want to get married? And what are you doing a week from Tuesday?"

"What!"

Susie was totally unprepared for anyone like Vic, and could not think of anything else to say.

"Then how about a cheap physical relationship?"

Vic was about as subtle as a chain saw. Despite the notion that women liked sensitive men, the case could be argued that opposites *did* attract. Vic also thought he could get away with anything, basically because he always had. Mannerheim came to the conclusion long ago that Southern boys, along with dirty old men, said things that he could never get away with. It reminded him of the phase "Country Folks." Seems that President Johnson, himself a Texan, said, *"As soon as anyone told me they were just 'Country Folks', the first thing I did was put my hand firmly on my wallet."* Not bad advice. However, if Vic's unique style of southern charm was going to kick in, it had better hurry.

"That's four questions! How did you get so obnoxious?"

"It's a gift."

"Typical pit attitude, and their view of women. Just useful for bedding down and raising kids. You probably regret we ever got the right to vote?"

"Oh no, not at all. But I do question why we ever gave you driver's licenses, but we can go into that later. How about at least going boating with me?"

This was not going according to plan. Mannerheim took a couple steps in order to get between them before Susie drew blood, but thought better of it. If this unholy alliance was going to fall apart, it was better that it happened now.

"Do you even own a boat?"

"Me! No pretty lady, I don't even believe in boats."

"Then what do you believe in?"

"Oh, I believe in friends who own boats... and I believe in you."

Vic probably got that line from some old country & western song, but it seemed to work. It managed to bring a small smile to Susie's face. Mannerheim breathed an audible sigh of relief.

All this time Scott Sherman was standing off to the side like a poor relative. As Susie was strolling around the room, Scott finally came into Vic's line of sight.

"Susie, my girl, I'd like to introduce you to my good old buddy, Scott Sherman. He doesn't have near my style, charm, or winning ways, but you will still find him the model of a Southern gentleman."

"Well, at least there's one in the room." Said in tones milder than the words implied.

"Thanks a lot," responded Mannerheim.

"Okay, two then."

Mannerheim decided he better get things on track before the bubble broke again.

"Now that we're all buddies...

CHAPTER 25

Wednesday, December 21
6:10 a.m.

The phone rang at Elliott's home twenty minutes before his alarm.

"Yes... who is it?"

"Tom, it's me, Susie. Sorry to be calling this hour of the morning, but we've got to talk. I found out last night that there is a plot against you. I don't want to say anymore over the phone. Can you meet me for breakfast at the Yankee Diner? Say in about an hour?"

"Yeah... I'll be there."

*

Yankee Diner
7:00 a.m.

Both were early and met each other as the doors of the restaurant opened. At Elliott's request the hostess seated them in the rear of the restaurant. A ten-dollar tip from Elliott insured them some privacy. The hostess pocketed the bribe and agreed to seat future parties well away from their table, at least for the next thirty minutes.

After they received coffee, and the waitress left, Susie started the discussion.

"Thanks for meeting with me on such short notice."

"Based upon your opening comment, how could I not. So now that we're here, what's the situation?"

"I attended a meeting set up by Mannerheim last night. First the good news. Paul has seen the light and has agreed to join us. He's a realist and knows Aaron will lose out in a protracted legal battle. The old boy just doesn't have the time, or the will, to be dragged around the legal system during his remaining years. Besides, Paul certainly doesn't have any loyalty to Yarbrough. He does want a solid contract for a minimum of five years, and an annual salary of one hundred twenty thousand dollars."

"No problem with that. But tell me about this threat."

"As a sign of good faith Paul wanted to warn me that Sam Logan is fully aware you're forcing Aaron out. The man has spies over the entire property. Nothing escapes him. Logan also has the temperament of a junk yard dog.

177

Nothing is beyond him. After thirty years in the casino business, Paul assures me he has even meaner contacts to the mob. He can be extremely dangerous."

"I've always thought so, but what has that to do with me? I've only seen Logan seven or eight times during those silly Thursday executive meetings and have spoken less than a dozen words to him. He was always a little cool, but I just figured he doesn't like lawyers. So what does he have against me?"

"According to Paul, Logan is known for only one ethical trait, and that's loyalty. Don't you see? You attacked Aaron, his old friend. You've threatened to embarrass him by having him declared legally incompetent. The man who has provided Logan with protection and support over all these years. Taking you out will be an act of honor in his eyes."

"How did Mannerheim become aware of that information? Logan and Mannerheim aren't known for being all that tight themselves."

"True. He didn't know until yesterday, but Vic Welles, the Casino Host, did. He was also at the meeting. Paul wanted him to tell me directly. Vic is the only casino guy with close ties to Logan, but still young enough, and smart enough not to tie his horse to Logan's wagon. By the way, the only reason Vic came over to our side and volunteered this information was that Paul assured him we would protect him after the takeover. I also had to guarantee him a solid five-year contract at one-hundred fifty thousand a year."

"Great! That's cheap at twice the price. I've been thinking about ways we could keep him on board anyway. As mediocre as most of the players are at this casino, I don't want to lose the best players when they leave with Vic, as he walks out the door moments after we dispose of Logan. Just didn't know how or when to approach him."

"Yeah, I didn't even know Vic myself till last night. That's another thing we can thank Paul for providing us. But I've saved the best news till last. We've figured out how we can take care of Logan. We need to meet with Mannerheim so he can tell you about it..."

*

Wednesday, December 21
10:54 a.m.

At this time of day neither Sam Logan nor Vic Welles were at work. Logan shifted his hours depending on the day of the week, and its related activity occurring on the casino floor and on the second floor. As for Vic, nobody ever remember seeing him in the casino before noon. At least no male could ever remember.

Logan was at his home, preparing to leave for the casino, when the phone rang.

"Hello."

"Sam, Vic here."

Logan looked at his watch before responding.

"Vic, something wrong? You okay?"

"Oh, I'm fine, but your well-being is in major doubt, old buddy. We've got to talk. How about meeting me at that pretty little cove, near that golf course you belong to. Can that four tons of Detroit iron get you there by eleven thirty?"

"I'll be there."

*

South Lake Tahoe Beach
11:30 a.m.

Logan arrived at the location on time. It was a beautiful, sandy beach along the southern end of Lake Tahoe. The golf course was right next door. Four months earlier its shore was jammed with summer swimmers. Shielded by several huge rock outcroppings, the beach was protected from nearby golfers who hooked their shots off the fourth fairway. But during this time of the year, both the golf course and the beach were almost deserted. Much to Logan's surprise, Vic was waiting for him.

"Vic, what is going on?"

"Just wanted to keep away from curious eyes and ears."

"You needn't worry. My office is as secure as the Oval Office. I control all the little hidden eyes and ears, which let me know what's going on. But being you got me out here, what's the big emergency?"

"If you know all that, then you must already know...Elliott is out to get you."

"What! I know that miserable little weasel is trying to gain control of the property. He and that female scorpion in Personnel. But why would Elliott target me? I'm not standing in his way. From what I hear, he should be going after Mannerheim. As far as I'm concerned, they can have at each other."

"If you know Elliott plans to take over, then you must know he plans to eliminate you and your entire pit."

"No big deal. I've been toying with the idea of retiring anyway."

"He's also going to get Aaron declared legally nuts."

"I know about that, too. I feel for Aaron, but he's got lawyers to protect him."

"Being you are known for your loyalty, he figures he has to take you out to protect his backside. From what I understand he's also saying there is something wrong with your paperwork. I hear he plans a full look see into your players, and some large unpaid markers."

"Markers! Where did you hear this?" ·

"From the love of my life, Susie Parsons."

"The scorpion!"

"Sam, you take everything too personal. She wants to protect me. I'm the big John Wayne in her life. She's concerned for my happiness and well-being. Between the sheets, she told me what to avoid, namely... you."

"What else did she tell you about me?"

"Nothing that makes any sense. Just mumbled a few names in her sleep."

"Such as?"

"Something about the Singapore National Bank...and the Bahamas?"

"Enough said. You've got my interest... Okay, you called me here. You must have something in mind, let's hear it."

"Don't say I don't take care of my friends. I've figured out how we can take care of Elliott. Let me tell you about it..."

*

Wednesday, December 21
7:11 p.m.

Elliott, Mannerheim and Susie Parsons met in hotel room number 1126. Elliott and Mannerheim eyed each other with caution. In an effort to establish a more casual tone, Susie asked Mannerheim to brief Elliott.

"Okay, here's the situation. I believe Logan is in the process of ripping off the casino by pulling a marker scam."

Not comfortable being a listener, Elliott immediately interrupted Mannerheim.

"I think I know, but tell me again what is a marker?."

Mannerheim almost went into shock. To think this man felt he could take over a hotel/casino operation.

"A marker is credit, or a loan granted to players by the casino, based upon their prior experience with us, or other casinos. It's like a bank loan, except made by a casino. But if the bank makes a loan and doesn't *intend* to collect it, not that that would happen, it ceases to be a loan and instead becomes a gift. In the case of a casino, it's called theft."

"*If* you could prove that intent."

"True. Anyway, the use of markers, in theory, is simple. The casino shouldn't bury the player in debt that they can't repay. Nor should they deny credit to a good player, and restrict him to just the cash he happens to bring with him. That would give him less to play with, and result in less win for the casino. Here's the process of the scam. I believe he granted markers to a bogus player. Later Logan received our negotiable chips back from that player, which Logan must be converting into cash, which I think he will take out of the country, leaving us with those worthless markers on our books."

"The term 'marker' may be the name on the paper, but I know about credit. You make it sound like you run a bank down there. Aaron told me about being stiffed by players when the casino gives out credit. Seems it happens all the time. He mentioned a player didn't pay him forty thousand just last year."

"Based on that dollar amount, I'd say that was probably a player named Bob Snyder, who got hooked and was in the process of self-destructing. If we hadn't taken his money, then another club would have in our place. Sure, we got stuck with his final forty thousand marker, but Aaron failed to tell you that we got two hundred thousand from him before he hit bottom."

"Well, so much for the banking theory."

Even though Mannerheim expected it, he was still getting frustrated. Lawyers! Always wanting to attack. Besides that, they couldn't keep their mouths shut. Especially coming from Elliott, who seemed to be lecturing him about the moral tone of gambling, considering his track record on ethics.

"The markers I'm talking about are different. No prior experience, no Central Credit information... just Logan's word for *paper* players."

"Okay, let's just say you're right about these particular markers. How much do you think he took?"

"As I was about to say, it looks somewhere between three to four million dollars. We can't tell for certain. The bogus markers are mixed in with our normal, valid marker activity. It could take up to a year before we find which ones become paid, and were therefore valid, and which ones are totally bogus. Unfortunately, we can't wait that long."

"Why is that?"

"I hired a private investigator. He followed Logan to the Bahamas. There he discovered Logan established a bank account."

"Then he has already deposited those millions in a foreign account?"

"No. He just established the account. He opened the account with just a few thousand dollars. We think he will move the funds out of the country after he converts it from cash and chips, and into something more transferable. Our currency has become too easy to locate since they put those counterfeiting strips in the bills. By the way, Logan has also established a new identity. He's using the name of Henry Hopkins."

"I'm impressed. You managed to find out a lot. Even though my specialty is not in criminal law, I can tell you as an attorney that you haven't got enough to arrest him."

"We know that, but time is running out. He could disappear to the Bahamas any minute, along with the money. Especially considering the pending sale to either you, or Yarbrough."

"With the prospect of having Aaron declared legally incompetent, Yarbrough has ceased to be a factor. And with your help in persuading Aaron how hopeless his situation is, he will cave in and sell out to me within days."

"Tom, there's one more thing you should know about Logan. We also think he murdered a minor accomplice by the name of Willie Grant. The guy was found dead about a month ago. You may remember a short article, with his picture, in the local paper. We have surveillance pictures showing him with both Logan and McDonald. They don't prove Logan murdered the guy, but they do confirm they knew each other."

For the first time Elliott was at a loss for words. Mannerheim decided to let the moment settle in on Elliott, so he waited for Elliott to finally say something.

"Why would Logan kill a member of his own gang?"

"We think he was the guy who accepted the markers on the players' side of the table. Logan issued markers under the names of numerous players, but probably used only one real person, which we think was Willie Grant. No reason for Logan to expand that circle of people when one will do. Just needed a warm body for the sake of appearances, and somebody who wouldn't think for himself too much. So when I started to ask about those strange markers, Logan must have thought it was time to wrap up his scam. Willie just outlived his usefulness. We haven't had any similar markers, from any players, since Willie came up *dead*."

Mannerheim wanted to use the word "dead" as many times as he could for

Elliott's benefit. As Mannerheim recalled, during Elliott's handling of the union dispute, the lawyer was ruthless in his own environment. In the court room he knew how to attack like an angry pit bull going after a kitten. However, that did not necessarily equate to bravery. Many "talkers" fell apart when faced with the possibility of physical injury. Mannerheim wanted to develop that *possibility* to the point where it was a *certainty* in Elliott's mind, and in his every waking thought.

"You really think Logan will come after me?"

"From what Vic tells us, Logan is furious with you. Considering you attacked his big brother figure, Aaron, he wants to take you out before he leaves for the Bahamas. He knows insurance will cover Aaron's losses, but eliminating you will placate his conscience. Sort of an offset for his marker theft."

"Just because I'm having Aaron declared legally incompetent?"

"How would you feel if someone wanted to ruin your 'brother', and have him declared legally incompetent. But even without Aaron in the picture, Logan has no reason to think kindly of you. He knows you will remove him as soon as you take over."

"Okay, okay... I accept the fact that Logan can kill, and has cause to go after me, at least in his own mind. So how can we prevent him from killing me? Susie said you have a plan to take Logan out."

"Yes. I think we can use Logan's own plan against him. In time, his marker scam can be documented and used against him in court. But considering we don't have the luxury of time on our side, I suggest we accelerate the whole process and get him arrested now."

"How?"

"We establish our own bogus player. I can create a player as well as Logan can. I'll make him a Canadian. Let's say... a wealthy car dealer down from Vancouver, British Columbia. I will generate a picture perfect credit report from Central Credit, or at least Logan will think the paperwork came from Central Credit. I'll give him a great background. A high-roller the pit will greet with open arms. Our timing couldn't be better. The casino has a flood of players on the floor due to the Christmas holidays. One more will fit right into the mix."

"Then what?"

"We have our player apply for credit. After he's issued a marker he asks to meet the Casino Manager. That's not at all unusual. Casino executives want to know the players, and players want the top management to know them. The higher the casino rapport, the better the treatment, the better the perks. Then our player repays his marker directly to Logan."

"Paul, do you really think Logan will steal the money instead of turning it in? He's already sitting on millions. He wouldn't do something that stupid."

"I don't think he will either. I'm assuming he will take the player over to the cage and have the marker paid off there. But here's the key to the plan. We don't record the payment. Remember, I control the cage. Instead we wire the funds directly to Logan's Bahamas bank account. We accept wire transfers all the time from players who are paying off their markers. The system also permits us to wire transfers out to banks. We can transfer it through our on-line computer system, by a modem, to a Miami bank with instructions to make the final transfer to the Bahamas. We have a documented theft, tied right to Logan. With money in a bank account that we can prove he established. The Bahamas Government will not let United States authorities go on a fishing trip into its banking records, but it will open them up if we can tie a specific account to a specific crime. We will have that smoking gun. Logan then gets arrested for marker theft. That will cause the Gaming Control Board to pull his gaming license."

"But Paul, wouldn't the Miami bank *verify* the propriety of the wire transfer by requiring an established individual code?"

"Sure they do, but who do you think briefed Logan on wire transfers, and taught him how to use the computer system? He was amused by the process. Logan thought it was just another hi-tech toy. I don't believe he has ever used the system, but he felt he should know *everything*. He probably doesn't even remember the *individual* code we established for him, but I do."

"But even if it works, he could still go after me, even from jail."

"True, but by then you will be in charge of the whole operation. You could work a deal. You're an attorney. You've probably negotiated deals for clients hundreds of times before. This time you have more of a vested interest because it will be for yourself. Tell him you will get the charges reduced or dropped if he returns the money and disappears, leaving you alone."

"Okay, I'm beginning to think this could work, but who are you going to use as our bogus player?"

"I can use that private investigator who is already working for me. Nobody in the pit knows his face. In fact, I've already put him on notice. If you give the word, I could have him in the casino within minutes. It's already busy down there. He'll fit right into the crowd. I've advanced him a few thousand to throw around and establish an image. He'll need some time to make Logan feel comfortable. Right after he gets and repays the marker, then we wire the funds directly into Logan's account."

"So how long do we have to wait?"

"Probably about four or five hours. We just wait for the call from my Cage Manager, so I can wire transfer the *exact* amount. Our player will ask for a hundred thousand dollars, but considering it's his first exposure to Logan, my guess is that Logan will approve a lesser amount for a first-time player, no matter what kind of report he gets from Central Credit. We won't know till Logan authorizes the marker."

"Sounds great. Paul, I can't tell you how much I appreciate this. Just wait until I take over and I'll show you my gratitude."

"Fine, we can discuss that after you take over. I don't think much of the tactics you used during this takeover bid, but we can set that aside for now."

"Well, try not to hold that against me. It was just a case of doing what has to be done in order to obtain what you want. In the end it looks like nobody will get hurt... nobody except Logan, who deserves it. Aaron will have a peaceful, and profitable retirement. I'll gain control of the operation, and the two of you will increase your income and positions under my leadership."

"I guess you're right. Okay, but for now, just relax. Just give the word and within a few hours your problems with Logan will be over."

"Yes! Do it."

With that Mannerheim picked up the phone. Within seconds it was answered. Mannerheim told the person on the other end of the phone a single word.

"Go!"

CHAPTER 26

Wednesday, December 21
11:34 p.m.

The pressure was rapidly building. It was fast approaching the Christmas weekend, soon to be followed by the New Years' weekend. In the spirit of the holidays, the whole casino was adorned in white, snow-like, winter-like decorations that added to the surreal atmosphere. For the next two weeks, the casino would be enjoying a higher level of activity. More high-limit players were arriving each day, and the casino was at its busiest since last summer. Most of the players were from the casino's "A" list, and the rest were up-and-comers from their "B" list. Both gourmet restaurants were fully staffed and providing their best service. The casino reserved more than a third of the showroom's best seats for this night, and every night, until after the holidays. The casino even had to quickly reserve a couple of the better suites at the Golden Palace for some high-rollers who arrived without making reservations.

Tonight there was a especially high level of excitement. Over the last five hours, C-2, a high-limit crap game attracted some heavy action. Normally it was staffed by two dealers and a boxman, but the level of play demanded an extra dealer. There were at least forty players going in and out of the game during the evening. The two other crap tables, "C-1" and "C-3", were available and near "C-2", but both were generating much less activity. Earlier in the evening, Logan established lower limits on those tables, practically insuring most of the top players would stick to "C-2".

As Casino Shift Manager, Todd McDonald was patrolling the crap pit with as much concern as an expectant father outside a maternity ward. During his current pass through the area, Frank Shaw, the boxman, saw him and broke away from the high-limit crap game.

"Todd. My table is way too crowded. Give the word. Raise the limit on the other two tables."

"No can do Frank. Logan wants to maintain the fever pitch of the game. Thinks they will all encourage each other to raise the level of activity, like a feeding frenzy. But if you need another dealer, I'll swing an extra one over."

"You kidding? I couldn't even make room for anyone else around that table!"

With that said, the boxman made his way back to his crap table.

In the middle of a player's third roll of the dice, a man dressed in dark blue overalls suddenly came through the crowd and approached the crap table. The overalls were the normal uniform of someone belonging to the hotel's maintenance department. Before Frank could say anything, the man bent down and started to crawl underneath the crap table.

Frank Shaw looked under the table and yelled in a voice high enough to be heard over the activity around him, "What the hell you think you're doing? Can't you see we have a game in action!"

The repairman got up and announced,

"I've got a workorder to adjust your drop box. The brackets holding the drop box to the underside of the table have a few loose screws."

He was holding a screwdriver.

"Can't you do it later?"

"If you don't want me to adjust it, then that's just fine with me. They pay me around here whether I do anything or not. Just don't blame me if your drop box falls off the underside of the table and spreads money and chips all over your casino floor."

To an already insane night this minor complication was beyond Shaw's belief.

"How long will it take?"

"A couple of minutes," came the reply.

McDonald came over when he saw the man first approach the table and was listening to the brief conversation. Shaw looked in his direction for guidance. McDonald gave a shrug of his shoulders, followed by a nod of his head. Shaw turned back to the repairman.

"Okay, but be quick about it."

"You got it. Be out of here before you know it."

True to his word, the repairman crawled back under the table, finished his work and left the area within five minutes, much to the relief of Frank Shaw.

*

Thursday, December 22
12:08 a.m.

The procession moved quickly from table to table. The small group was composed of two uniformed security guards and a security supervisor, dressed in an inexpensive suit and tie. One by one, the security guards were unlocking the drop boxes from each table and swinging them on to a large metal cart which they pushed in front of them. When the box left the underside of the table, a spring was automatically released; as it left the brackets holding the box to the table, the opening toward the table top was closed and the box was sealed. The guards then pulled an empty box off the cart and attached it on the underside of the table, relocking it before moving on to the next table. Each box was painted with its corresponding table number and type of game. Immediately in front of the table number a letter indicated the type of game: "C" for craps, "BJ" for blackjack. The only physical difference between the two boxes were being exchanged was that the removed drop box had a large "S", for swing shift printed above the table number, while the new drop box had a "G", for graveyard shift. This procedure was performed after each of the three shifts, seven days a week, whether a table had any action during the shift or not.

After they left "BJ-23", the miniature parade approached "C-2". Shaw stopped the game, and his dealers stepped back to allow the security guard room to "pull" the drop box. A security guard unlocked the box from the table and removed it. Just then thirty-eight pairs of eyes focused in on the drop box. One side of the drop box was cut along three sides and bent up, sort of like a can of sardines with the wrong side pried open. As the drop box was being suspended in the air by the security guard, a couple chips and a few loose bills fluttered out and dropped to the floor.

*

Outside the building two men approached each other in the dark parking lot. Both anticipated the excitement occurring back in the crap pit, but they were more preoccupied with the next phase of the operation. They disappeared into a windowless van parked in the northernmost corner of the parking lot. It took half an hour of counting and sorting before they emerged.

They then walked over to a red Mercedes-Benz 500 SL parked a short distance away. As the shorter man surveyed the parking lot, the taller man pulled a tool from his jacket and played around with the trunk lock of the sports car. Within a minute the trunk flew open, a blue bundle was carefully placed inside, then the trunk slammed shut. With that both men slowly walked away. One went to bed, the other went in search of a telephone.

12:21 a.m.

Inside the casino, "C-2" was shut down. The players were collectively moved to "C-3", replaced at the first table by security guards and pit bosses. Steve Berkich had arrived on the scene and immediately instructed his supervisor to take down the names and addresses of all the players around the table, as well as the names of all nearby pit employees. In addition, he notified the Douglas County Sheriff's Department for immediate assistance.

Logan also arrived in the pit and was pulling a John Madden imitation in front of Todd McDonald and Frank Shaw. Berkich was at least twenty feet away, but could still hear Logan over the numerous other discussions near him. He almost felt sorry for the two, but immediately dismissed the impulse.

About six minutes later a large, overweight deputy arrived from the Sheriff's Department and headed for the crap pit. Berkich gave him a condensed version of the robbery and pointed to the broken drop box lying on the floor next to "C-2", just where the dumbfounded security guard had dropped it. Earlier, Berkich complimented the guard on putting the drop box down so quickly, avoiding any additional handling of the key evidence. The security guard accepted the praise and said nothing to indicate any other motive.

It was ten additional minutes before a security guard arrived from the cage with the preliminary estimate of the loss. Based on corresponding copies of fill and credit slips, marker issuances and payment slips, the figure roughly amounted to one hundred twenty thousand dollars. Upon hearing the amount of the loss, the deputy quickly reached for his portable radio and requested his dispatcher contact Lt. Danbury at home.

*

1:35 a.m.

For Danbury, the drive to the casino involved waking up his sleepy mind and deciding on a course of action. In all his years on the force he never heard of a case like this. Already two of his patrol cars had established a road block on the highway heading north, while the South Lake Tahoe Police set up their road block on the same highway heading south into California. His remaining available patrol car was heading to the crime scene to back up his deputy. Three additional cars were moving up the mountain road from Minden to provide additional support. Based on the anticipated press coverage this crime would generate, Danbury instructed his dispatcher to call the Sheriff and see if he wanted to make a personal appearance for the cameras.

Berkich's Security Shift Supervisor was the first to see Lt. Danbury enter the area. He quickly explained that Berkich was in the process of interviewing the crap dealers. The two nearest offices, Berkich's for the dealers and Logan's for Shaw and McDonald, were being used to interrogate all concerned. He explained Berkich wanted to interview the key witnesses as soon as possible before memories faded. Danbury agreed. The Security Supervisor handed Berkich's initial investigation notes to the detective and went to inform his boss of Lt. Danbury's presence. Danbury examined the written list of what was collected. Berkich's prior police experience was apparent. Berkich's approach to the case matched Danbury's. The major items on the list were well organized and the course of action similar to his own. However sound the approach, the results were limited to a scant few bits of useful information.

Until Berkich arrived, Danbury decided to check with his deputy who had just finished talking to the majority of the players. The sight of Lt. Danbury provided the overwhelmed deputy a tangible sense of relief. He updated his superior concerning his end of the investigation. It seemed that the majority of the players took little, if any notice of the thief, other than general agreement that the man wore dark overalls. Some thought they were dark blue, others said black, gray came up several times and red was mentioned twice. After that, consensus quickly disintegrated. A few said the man was of medium height, most said he was short, and three remembered him as a midget. The fact that the man was bending down as he went under the crap table, did little to help their memories. Nobody could get past the dark overalls to give any description of the man's face. Like everyone who sees an anonymous uniform in front of him, that is all they seem to remember.

Danbury's deputy proudly announced his only "solid" finding:

"The players did manage to give a more accurate estimate of their actual cash losses. Even allowing for some exaggeration, looks like they collectively lost more than the initial pit estimate. It's now about one hundred and thirty-five thousand dollars."

"This just keeps getting better and better."

Danbury glanced over at the crowd of players. To add to his problems he quickly realized that, of the vast number of people around the table, only a handful were even close to being sober. A few were even asleep on the floor. Of those with their eyes open, almost all had a glazed-over look that Danbury had seen too often at crime scenes. To further depress his condition, a cocktail waitress was entering the area and serving another round of drinks to the players.

Danbury quickly turned to his deputy. With fire in his eyes, he announced, "Did it ever occur to you to cut our witnesses off from any more booze?"

The poor deputy just stood there until Danbury finally said, "Get over there and get that cocktail waitress out of here."

As the deputy quickly ran back to the crap table to enforce his superior's instructions, Lt. Danbury was trying to mull over his options. He took some comfort in the fact that the theft took place in the middle of a casino. That comfort rested on one fact: a casino was always covered by a massive network of overhead surveillance cameras. He could at least count on the cameras being sober.

Just as he was looking around for Steve Berkich, he saw the Head of Security pass under the yellow police ribbon circling the twenty feet around "C-2."

Berkich was the first to speak.

"Am I glad to see you. I can't believe this. When it rains, it pours. Let's get out of the center of the floor and talk in my office."

Unknown to either of them, they were walking into a situation that provided even less confidentiality than the open floor of the casino, thanks to a new bug recently installed by Wally Lowe, head of the surveillance department.

"Sure."

On the way Danbury was already expressing his frustration.

"Steve, I've never seen so many witnesses at a crime scene come up with so little in the way of descriptions. I bet your players can't even remember what the cocktail waitress looked like. And, judging by how much most of them consumed, they must have been looking at her half the evening."

"Well, the dealers were of absolutely no help either. Their eyes were glued to the chips and activity on the top of the crap table, as per their job description. It seems only Todd McDonald and Frank Shaw got a good look at the man. They are waiting for you in Logan's office. But be prepared... they can't remember what the guy looked like."

Danbury was amazed.

"Tell me you're joking. These clowns are in a business where they're suppose to remember people."

"True, but remember, we pay them to remember important people. Which they define as people with large amounts of money. They can both remember the faces of every decent player in our files, but it seems they have trouble remembering the non-important people. Just try asking them to describe the waitress who served them dinner a couple hours ago. I doubt if they ever make eye contact with servants. Both of them do agree the man was of medium height."

Danbury clapped his hand to his forehead.

"Wonderful! That manages to narrow down the list of suspects to a mere seventy-five million people. Tell me some good news. Have you seen the surveillance tapes yet?"

"Yeah, I'm afraid so. They are not much help. I've got them ready for your inspection, but they don't show much."

"What do you mean? How could they not?"

Steve shrugged his shoulders.

"They show the guy wore a baseball cap. That alone blocked any decent view from the overhead camera located directly above the table."

"What about the other cameras? Didn't they get a side view from another vantage point?"

"Robert, you've got to remember how we set up our camera system. It's to protect our money, which is not locked away in some vault like a bank, it's sitting on the tables. As I said a couple days ago, we do have some cameras scanning our open areas... looking at the hotel lobby, bars, restaurants, and parking lot. But they're just 'fixed-focus' cameras for property security. Our state-of-the-art, 'pan-'n-tilt', zoom lens cameras are the ones that look directly down on the tables for signs of player or dealer theft. Their field of vision takes in only the immediate circle of players around the table. Despite that, we did pick up some distance shots from a couple of cameras that were scanning between nearby tables. Unfortunately, we couldn't see much more than a medium sized guy, dressed in dark blue overalls with his collar up, a baseball cap, dark rimmed glasses and a mustache. Put that outfit on you or me, and a jury wouldn't know the difference."

"Great! Just great!"

Just a month ago Danbury's major concern were kids spray painting the side of the local video store. Now he seemed to have a major crime wave on his hands.

CHAPTER 27

Thursday, December 22
4:38 a.m.

Again the phone rang at Logan's home. After his late-night performance at the crap table, Logan had only been asleep an hour when he was awaken.

"Yes... What is it?"

"Sam, do you recognize my voice?"

It was the voice of the head of the surveillance department, Wally Lowe.

"I do."

"Looks like you've been set up. Danbury thinks you're involved in the crap table theft and is coming after you. Turns out half the missing money turned up in your Bahamas bank account. Somebody told him Elliott is your partner. Danbury figures he has the other half of the money. Unless you feel you're in a position to defend yourself... you better take off."

"Damn!"

With that comment, Logan hung up and started moving.

*

7:27 a.m.

Elliott awoke to a totally different morning. Now on the road back to the hotel/casino, he felt the effects of just four hours of sleep. The last twenty-four hours were busy, but worth it. He made great progress toward his goal. He was full of confidence, only a last few obstacles remained. And their removal was assured. The unfolding plan was sound. Aaron would be history within days and Logan within hours, if not already.

Thanks to Susie, he now knew everything Mannerheim knew about Logan, and that was more than enough to seal Logan's fate. Using Logan's own marker rip-off against him was a great move. Logan was even nice enough to establish an off-shore bank account in the Bahamas, in a false but traceable name. What lingered in Elliott's mind was the fact that Logan had probably killed a minor accomplice who outlived his usefulness. That point alone convinced Elliott of the need to remove Logan, and as soon as possible, before the old goat took him out.

Anyway, from a basic business point of view, Logan should be taken out of the picture. Leaving him in charge of the casino over the next few months would insure there would be nothing left to take over. He would pollute the casino's relationship with every decent player. It could take years to mend fences and reestablish a strong player list. He would have no incentive to do otherwise. His peculiar loyalty to Aaron aside, Logan certainly knew his days were numbered the moment Elliott assumed control.

Elliott also reconciled in his mind that he would have to get rid of Mannerheim right after he took over. Mannerheim's position required him to make a hundred decisions a day. All Elliott had to do was wait for a questionable call and then use it against the controller. Elliott was considered one of Nevada's top labor attorneys. He'd find something in Mannerheim's employment contract to justify his termination. It will not be a problem. But for now, Mannerheim would come in handy in convincing Aaron to give up any possible legal battle and accept Elliott's takeover. After that, he could not trust Paul on an ongoing basis. Better to replace him with someone who knew less of Elliott's ways of dealing with people. Elliott did consider it a shame to lose such a devious person. However, a basic truth in business prevailed: *If you hire someone, you can demand their loyalty. If you inherit them, their loyalty is always in doubt.* Unfortunately the same was true of Susie. She knew him too well. There would always be the chance she would use that knowledge against him down the road. But her removal must be given a great deal more thought. For now, Elliott had other matters on his mind. There was time to take care of those details after the takeover.

The call to Mannerheim, from his Cage Manager, came about 12:30 in the morning. Within minutes, sixty-five thousand dollars were wire transferred into Logan's account, using Logan's own password. Elliott then left it up to Mannerheim to notify his suspicions to the local Sheriff's Department and have Logan picked up, his fate sealed.

As those thoughts was going through Elliott's mind he looked in his rear view mirror and saw red and blue flashing lights. He immediately checked his speed; but he was under the speed limit. He again looked in his mirror. They were not going around him. He pulled over.

From out of the police car stepped Lt. Danbury, a deputy and Jeff Meyers. Danbury walked up to the side of Elliott's red Mercedes-Benz 500 SL. The deputy stayed a few feet to the rear, on the driver's side, while Meyers stood behind the open passenger side door of the police car.

"Mr. Elliott, could you please step out of the car?"

"Is there a problem, officer?"

"We have a court order to search your home, office and vehicle."

"I'd like to see that court order."

Lt. Danbury politely asked Elliott to move away from the car as he handed him the search warrant. Elliott examined the paperwork as Danbury began looking under his seats. By this time, a second police vehicle arrived to back them up. After Danbury searched the inside of the car he asked Elliott for his car keys so he could examine the trunk. Elliott, hiding his irritation, accepted the situation and handed over the keys. The trunk was visibly empty except for the spare tire. Only after Danbury pulled out the tire was the blue bundle revealed. As Danbury unwrapped the blue overalls out spilled table copies of fill slips, credit slips, marker issuances, payment slips, chips and a lot of currency. All the slips of paper were time stamped and indicated they originated from the swing shift, table "C-2," December 21st.

Elliott just stood there, mouth open, and for the first time in his life, utterly unable to think of anything to say.

*

7:36 a.m.

Sergeant Patrick Miller and three deputies gave a shout of identification and a quick knock on Logan's door, right before using a battering ram to get through the rapidly disintegrating door. With guns drawn, they moved quickly from room to room. Within ninety seconds they realized their search would not yield their prey. Logan was long gone.

*

9:35 a.m.

Berkich and Mannerheim were waiting for events to unfold in Mannerheim's office when Betty announced that Matt Hamilton was on line three.

Paul snatched up the phone. "Matt, talk to me."

"Just got a call from Danbury. Elliott's in custody. He's confident he can tie Elliott to Logan's marker rip-off as the previously unknown partner. Believes they both tried to pull one last marker scam prior to leaving the country. Blamed it on sheer arrogance on their part. Danbury also sends his thanks to you for alerting him to Elliott's possible involvement."

197

Paul heaved a sigh of relief.

"Perfect! That will take Elliott out of consideration for a gaming license. The Gaming Control Board will make sure of that. And, without a gaming license, you can't run a casino. When that makes the newspapers, his backers will pull out of his takeover attempt within minutes."

"From what I hear, Elliott is yelling he was set up. That's the beauty of the situation. He can't really tell anyone how he was set up without also disclosing he was trying to frame Logan in the process. Elliott did describe Logan's marker scam in detail. Danbury then told him *we* already brought the details of the scam to him weeks ago. All it did was convince Danbury that Elliott was trying to sell his partner out. But, what if Elliott tells Danbury that you set him up, instead of Logan?"

Mannerheim was not worried.

"Even if he tells Danbury about some wild plot to set up Logan, which was turned against him, the paperwork won't support him. He will find out that not only the marker *payment*, from some unknown car dealer in Canada, was never recorded, but the pit never even *issued* a marker for sixty-five thousand in the first place. Because we never used you as our bogus player, having Elliott mention that won't get him anywhere. His side of the story won't be credible. Do you think Danbury is satisfied?"

"Satisfied! He's thrilled. He has solved his crime wave in less than a day. Combining that sixty-five thousand you transferred to Logan's foreign bank account with the other sixty-five thousand I put in Elliott's trunk, Danbury is satisfied the entire amount from the robbery is fully accounted for."

"So tell me about Logan, what's up with him?"

"Skipped out of town. Somehow Logan became aware Danbury was coming after him and just disappeared. Danbury has an all-points bulletin out on him. Looks like the case is closed, except for finding Logan."

"It's disappointing he's still loose, but at least he's not in our way anymore. Logan's involvement was my major worry in this whole plot. Just glad Vic talked Logan into shifting all the high-rollers onto one game and got McDonald to approve Scott Sherman working on that drop box."

"Yeah, that provided enough circumstantial evidence to convince Danbury to look in Logan's direction. The money transfer was the icing on the cake. Like to have seen Logan's face when he realized the scam was on him, as well as Elliott."

"I've seen that look before, be glad you didn't. Looks like everything worked out. The hardest part on my end was waiting for you and Scott to count the money in the van. My main concern was keeping Elliott busy with our little ploy so we could keep his car available and in the parking lot. After you gave me the funds, I used it to balance the cage and offset the transfer into Logan's account. You two did a great job. How'd you like working with Scott Sherman?"

"I don't know where you found him, but he's one cool character under pressure."

"He's had plenty of practice."

"Paul... one thing. I enjoyed participating in your little plot because I had no direct exposure. All I did was count the money and hand it off to you after the phone call. But that alone would jeopardize my police pension and I have a family to protect. Even though I'm comfortable that we took out the bad guys, and nobody can tie me into anything, remember... you assured me that Elliott will not go to prison, and will be cleared soon after his deep-pocket brokers drop out and Aaron closes his deal with Yarbrough."

"You have my word on it. I just needed Elliott out of the picture so I can kill the competency case. Next week, events will reveal circumstances that will help Elliott prove his innocence and your involvement will never come to light. There would be no harm, no foul."

"Sounds good. I don't know what you have in mind, but you're the one with the most exposure so I'll leave it up to you."

"Trust me Matt, it will work out. Keep me informed and I'll talk to you soon."

*

Desmond canceled the usual Thursday executive luncheon. There were two undeclared reasons for the cancellation. Without Elliott or Logan attending the meeting, the numbers of major players decreased to a point it would merely serve as a social gathering. That alone posed no problem, as Desmond was at his best attending social gatherings. However, without Elliott, Desmond was directionless. He bet everything and lost. Without the financial backing from Elliott's money brokers, the lawsuit to get his father-in-law declared legally incompetent was doomed. Shortly after that failure, he would find himself without his position, title or prospects of any future inheritance. No need to face a roomful of gloaters while he was feeling so confused and depressed.

As Desmond was looking through his office window he was comparing his future to the dark storm clouds marching over the western side of the Sierras. Just then his nervous secretary let him know Paul Mannerheim was outside his office, and insisted on seeing him. He just nodded as he continued to observe the weather.

Mannerheim entered and noticed Desmond's face.

"Carl, don't look so down. I come as a friend."

"Friend? The last person I trusted as a friend did me in."

"True, but let's see if we can make the best of a bad situation. I've talked to Aaron and I think we can work something out."

"What do you mean?" he asked as he turned away from the window and looked at Mannerheim.

"We suggest the following. First, you immediately drop your legal competency lawsuit. I can have Aaron's attorney here within an hour with the necessary forms for you to sign. In return, Aaron will provide you with an immediate five million dollar settlement. In addition, another five million goes into a trust fund for Adam. Fifty thousand dollars will be available to him each year after his eighteenth birthday, as long as he goes to college. Ten thousand dollars a year if he doesn't. The balance of the trust becomes available when he turns thirty. Agreed?"

Desmond said nothing, but he gave a weak nod.

"Also, this will eliminate any possibility you will be named in his will for anything more than an additional dollar. Aaron also wanted me to tell you your position as company president will be terminated, effective as of today. But I wouldn't let that bother you too much. You knew that was going to happen when Yarbrough took over anyway. All in all, it's not a bad deal."

"I guess."

Conversation seemed to dry up and after a couple of empty minutes, Mannerheim just gave a quick wave and left the office.

*

On the way back to his own office Mannerheim went by to see Susie. Earlier, she phoned Mannerheim's office, only to find out from Betty that he was in the meeting with Carl Desmond. Not wanting to wait for the preliminaries, she immediately jumped to the primary question,

"So how did it go with Carl?"

"Fine. It's all worked out, Madam President."

"Say again?"

"The future you were expecting has arrived sooner than planned. I had a conference call with Aaron and Yarbrough this morning. I recommended you as our new company president. Aaron agreed and will make it effective tomorrow."

"Aaron agreed?"

"Sure! Don't take this personally, but he would have agreed to the janitor becoming president of the place as long as he was clear of his legal problems and could finally close the deal with Yarbrough. At this point, Aaron just wants to take his money and run. He's already booking his cabin for the Inland Passage cruise back to Alaska. Mentioned something about moving up there. In fact, he..."

By now Susie figured out Mannerheim was toying with her so she cut him off.

"Okay, okay! What about Yarbrough? Did he agree to this?"

"Relax, your position is secure. Yarbrough will confirm and continue your new position when he takes over next month."

"I'm in shock. I thought you would move up to be president."

"It was a choice between two radical options. Either a woman in charge of a hotel/casino, or an accountant. Both would be unique, but I'm comfortable as the Controller. Besides, it should be more entertaining with you as boss. Yarbrough still contends he will maintain a hands-off position concerning the day-to-day operations of the place, but he needs to fill two other positions himself. Vic will become the new Casino Manager and Scott Sherman will fill the position of Casino Host."

"Vic as Casino Manager?"

"He'll be fine. He is a little sneaky. Just watch your back."

"I'm more concerned with various other parts of my anatomy."

"Well I trust you can handle yourself."

"Thanks Paul, you can count on that. I don't know what to say. Except one thing. I'm curious, what would you have done if Elliott won out?"

"Oh, I had a backup option."

"Which was?"

"Can't say. May still use it some day. There's always tomorrow."

CHAPTER 28

Friday, December 23
9:35 a.m.

It was coming up on one of the three biggest weekends of casino activity during the year, the Christmas holiday. New Years and the Fourth of July weekends were the other two. Judging by the level of activity that had been building through the week, this weekend should exceed all predictions.

It always amazed Mannerheim that people would go to a casino to celebrate Christmas. Before he began his casino career, he just assumed everyone would travel back to Kansas, or wherever they came from, to eat turkey and open their presents with the old folks and young children. However, for tens of thousands of people that was not the case. They seemed to prefer the company of slot machines, either by their circumstances or desires.

Normal weekend activity required Mannerheim to shift about two million dollars from their commercial paper activity (savings) into checking, then into cash, which provided the casino with the extra working capital needed during the weekend. For this holiday the transfer would have to be somewhat larger. Due to the fact Aaron and Desmond had a policy of spreading goodwill, and their influence in the local community, twelve different savings accounts were scattered among the local banks. Each of these accounts represented the largest account for that individual bank. The account balances, depending upon commercial paper fluctuations, were between one and three million dollars. An account each banker cherished. Every banker was also very aware of the procedure and patiently expected his turn to supply cash. Each Friday, the bank selected for transfer would prepare the funds, with the gleeful anticipation of larger funds being returned on Monday morning, factoring in a sizable profit from the weekend activity. Each bank strove to make its transfer go smoothly whenever its turn arrived. None wanted the wrath of Mannerheim, or Logan, if the specified funds were not properly delivered. Due to the special holiday, a special emphasis was present.

Mannerheim dialed his first number. It was the phone number to Tahoe Bank and Trust. He gave his name and asked for the Branch Manager, Richard Becklund. Whoever answered the phone recognized the name and quickly alerted the manager. Within seconds Richard Becklund was on the phone, full of professional good cheer.

"Mr. Mannerheim, I've been expecting your call. When you initially alerted me earlier this week I made all the appropriate preparations. We're ready for transport whenever you give the word."

"Fine, Richard. I understand the security people will be there about noon. The armored transport from Reno ran into mechanical problems, so our own security people will make the pickup. I'm going to accompany them. I need to place some papers in our safety deposit box."

"Excellent. Does that mean you may be available for lunch?"

"Tempting offer, but I just don't have the time. Maybe next week."
Even for an accountant, having lunch with a banker did not rank as a high point among Mannerheim's weekly activities.

"Of course. I'll look forward to your arrival."

Mannerheim put down the phone momentarily as he reached for his phone directory, but before he could dial the next number Betty buzzed in. "Mr. Hamilton is on line two."

"Matt, what's up?"

"Do you still have the monitoring device on your phone?"

"Yes, but its been clean since you found that bug."

"Great. I'm surprised you're in your office. When you didn't answer your pager, I thought I would give your office a try but I really expected you to be buried in those negotiations you're having with Yarbrough's group."

"I was, but they went back to New Orleans to spend Christmas with their families. We will start again next week. In the meantime, I have to make some preparations for the Christmas weekend. It's one of our major periods of activity and we still have customers to think of. Sorry about the pager, but I figured after yesterday things at your end would be quiet, so I forgot to wear it. What's up?"

"Just got a call from Lt. Danbury. Since we informed him of Logan's trip to the Bahamas, he has been monitoring the airlines and travel agencies. Late last evening a one-way reservation to Miami was made under the name of Henry Hopkins, Sam Logan's alter ego."

"What about Todd McDonald, did he also make a reservation?"

"Don't know. Unfortunately, we were never able to find his new alias. However, if Logan is leaving you can bet the farm McDonald will be with him. Danbury is also betting that Logan is leaving with the money. It will provide enough evidence of the marker theft. Besides, after the table rip-off, he now has enough to hold him. Danbury's confident he can make the murder case. He also knows this is probably his last chance to catch him. Logan will be long gone if he misses him now. Lt. Danbury has even given us, including Berkich, the opportunity to witness the arrest. The only condition is that we view it with his people, which means out of sight. Are you interested?"

"Definitely. When?"

"This afternoon. His flight is scheduled to leave about three o'clock, but we meet at one o'clock in the office of airport security. He wants us there early so we don't accidentally bump into Logan and blow the arrest. This is a rare opportunity. It's only because of our assistance in the case that he's permitting us this chance. Frankly, I wouldn't do it if it were my case, but I didn't tell him that."

"One o'clock?"

"Don't tell me you have something more important scheduled?"

"No, not after all we've been through. I'll be there."

"Okay, and I'll phone Berkich and let him know. See you at the airport."

Again the phone rested in its cradle for only a moment before Mannerheim was calling Steve Berkich.

"Steve, I will be moving some important papers between several banks for a couple of hours today. Could I borrow a couple of your security people?"

*

Tahoe Bank and Trust
12:05 p.m.

Berkich provided Mannerheim with two security guards, which seemed to Berkich to be an overkill. No matter how important the papers were, they were still just paper. Berkich assumed they were probably the latest revisions of Aaron's will, but did not inquire into the boring details. If Mannerheim wanted four security guards to transport a roll of nickels to the bank, Berkich still would have provided them without question.

Once outside the bank Mannerheim gave his instructions to the security guards.

"A large metal box needs to be relocated from the bank to our warehouse locker. It pertains to the prior year's accounting records that will soon be replaced by current year records. They are just not the priority now where we need to pay premium fees to the bank for their storage. We stored them here because we are required by the auditors to keep them off-site from the hotel, in case of a disaster like a fire or major earthquake. From here they will be relocated to cheaper, less

205

secured storage facilities. Just wait until I give you the signal, then load it into the back of my vehicle. Any questions?"

There were no questions from either man. In fact, neither of the guards was concentrating enough to hear much more than "any questions?". Both worked the day shift and enjoyed a chance to get out of the casino into the open and smell some fresh air. Their minds were focused on a unique cloud formation just appearing over Mannerheim's shoulder. Both were also very junior in the security department and correctly surmised they were there only as window dressing.

"One other thing. We're shifting some payroll data between several banks. Therefore, I thought we could take care of these paperwork requirements all at one time, so I need you to escort me through several stops today. Okay?"

Both just nodded. Neither of the young security guards was going to question the company Controller on anything he wanted to do or anywhere he wanted to go. They considered the trip a milk run, but also knew Mannerheim was high up on the corporate ladder. Neither wanted to go back and face Berkich if they were the source of any problems.

With that established, Mannerheim went into the bank and made his way to the desk of Richard Becklund, Branch Manager, as the two security guards waited by the front door.

"Good afternoon, Mr. Mannerheim. Glad you could make it."

"My pleasure, Richard. I'm a little pressed for time but thought I'd keep an eye on the security guards since I was going in this direction anyway. At first it bothered me that the armored transport broke down. But, perhaps it's better this way. A more casual transfer will draw a lot less attention. Everything ready for transport?"

"Just need a signature authorizing the release of funds."

"These security guards come and go so fast. Most of them don't even have readable penmanship. I'll sign it being I'm here. Makes it more official."

Becklund quickly handed over the release form and received a key in return. Within a minute he was signaling over his administrative assistant to open the vault, while Mannerheim signaled the two security guards to step forward. Mannerheim then disappeared into the safety deposit vault and emerged almost immediately, just as his two security guards were picking up a metal box, the size of a large microwave oven, and hauling it out to Mannerheim's vehicle. Neither of the guards questioned the need of a lock on a box that housed some accounting records.

Within five minutes two vehicles, one containing Mannerheim, followed by the other containing the two security guards, were off to the next bank.

CHAPTER 29

Friday, December 23
Reno Airport
2:45 p.m.

Mannerheim was rushing through the airport when Hamilton saw him on the surveillance monitors located in the airport security office. Paul was heading in the wrong direction. Matt raced for the door. He caught up with Mannerheim only because he was stuck in a long line waiting to get through airport security's metal detector.

"Paul, where you been? Don't you know the time?"

"Sorry, but I had some loose ends to tie up. I just couldn't get away."

"Trouble finding your way after the airport remodeling?"

"Yeah. Everything looks so different since I was here last. Just got turned around."

"But at least you made it. Let's go. Danbury spotted Logan and McDonald checking in several packages about twenty minutes ago. He has a search warrant to inspect anything they may have. We'll know in a few minutes what they found. Follow me and we'll go the back way up to the security office."

It took about eight minutes of maneuvering as they quickly wove their way through the back hallways of the airport building. Mannerheim figured whoever designed the facility did so with the arrival gates in mind. As an afterthought they must have thrown the offices into the leftover center space. Without Hamilton leading the way, Mannerheim would have been totally lost. Finally, they emerged at the top of a stairwell and went through the door of Airport Security. In the room there were three airport security employees, Lt. Danbury, along with two Douglas County deputies, Captain Pete Jansen, along with his two Reno Police officers, and Steve Berkich. All were looking out the one-way window onto the floor below. Lt. Danbury turned and noticed Hamilton and Mannerheim enter the room.

"Nice of you to join us."

"Sorry."

Danbury wanted to continue the discussion, but at the moment other things required his attention. One floor below, Sam Logan and Todd McDonald were walking up to check in at Gate 17. Danbury managed to arrange for the airline to shift gate assignments in order to obtain the better vantage point for their observation. Both Logan and McDonald appeared nervous while they waited for their flight to announce the boarding instructions.

Suddenly the security office's phone rang. Danbury picked it up, stated his last name and silently listened to the caller. Within twenty seconds he put down the receiver and announced,

"They found false bottoms in three of their suitcases. They contained bundles of high-denomination foreign currency, mainly five-hundred and one-thousand dollar Canadian bills, along with a lot of Swiss and German denominations. Now we know what McDonald was doing during those trips to San Francisco. Probably went through some third-party broker in order to avoid the ten-thousand dollar transaction reporting requirement that banks have to make to the government. We can sort that out later, but for now, I'd say we have them with their hands in the cookie jar."

With that news he again picked up the phone and dialed the number for the phone next to the gate attendant. In actuality the gate attendant was one of his own, Sergeant Patrick Miller of the Douglas County Sheriff's Department. Danbury spoke quietly but clearly.

"It's a go. Make the arrest."

With a nod by Sergeant Miller, four officers went into action and converged on Sam Logan and Todd McDonald. Both looked shocked. After a quick frisk the officers led the two away in order not draw any more attention to the situation then they already had. Everything went as planned.

To put it all in conclusion, Hamilton announced, "Well, that's it!"

Lt. Danbury turned to address Hamilton. "Not quite." He then looked right at Steve Berkich.

"I arrest you for the murder of Willie Grant. I'm sure you know your rights. You've probably said those rights to a couple hundred people you've arrested, but we have to go through the formality." As he was giving Berkich his Miranda rights Mannerheim and Hamilton were both standing there with their mouths open. "Do you understand these rights as I have explained them to you?"

Berkich had a strange, blank expression. "Yes" was his only response.

Mannerheim finally managed to said, "Steve, tell me it's not true."

Berkich ignored Mannerheim. Instead he turned to Danbury.

"What makes you think I'm the guy?"

"Combination of several things. Remember, while we were looking over the surveillance tapes, your comment about the deplorable state of Willie's car? Besides a handful of us, nobody knew much about Willie's car... other than the person who drove it from Tahoe to the Reno airport. That started my doubts about you. Those doubts mounted when my desk sergeant saw photos of Willie Grant on the top of my desk. He finally remembered the surveillance tape from the dealer scam. I wasn't involved in the case of your dealer and Willie, but he was, and you were. You were the person trying to track down that missing partner. When I found out you knew Willie from that previous case, and didn't tell me about it, my suspicions were really high."

An oversight that never occurred to Berkich. Part in anger and part in frustration with himself, Berkich whispered to himself,

"Just my luck. The curse of working with a small police department. In any other city, a petty unsolved theft would never cross paths with a murder case."

"Based upon that, I made another call to the Reno PD, and their ballistics department. This time I asked them to check any case where you may have fired his weapon. Remember the time you had to wound the rapist in '87? The bullet was still in the archives of the Ballistics Department. They located it and managed to match it with the slug that killed Willie. Lucky for us, you haven't fired it much since you left the force, which would have marred the rifling pattern enough to make the match difficult. You should never have bought back your old 9mm service weapon when you left the department."

Like a good attorney, Danbury choose not to say anything more. Instead he let the moment hang in the air. After a full minute, Berkich finally broke the silence, convinced in his own mind that Danbury presented a solid case.

"Yeah, I forgot that old ballistics report was still on file. That I should have remembered. Stupid mistake."

"Your mistake was killing Willie. In the end you would have defeated Logan. Instead you went for the money. Now you will end up in the cell next to him."

Mannerheim again wanted a reason.

"When did it all go wrong, Steve?"

"Remember the night Hamilton first spotted Willie, and took the pictures of him with McDonald? I didn't say anything, but I knew Willie as soon as I saw his picture. I recognized him from previous surveillance tapes. Remember the case of the dishonest dealer and his missing partner? The guy I gave chase, but lost in the crowds. Willie was also the missing partner of the dealer."

Hamilton interrupted Berkich with the observation,

"So that scam must have been how Logan first came into contact with Willie!"

"Probably. My guess is Logan also recognized Willie. Instead of turning him in, he found him and cut him into his marker scam. Instead of going to jail,

Willie stood to make thousands. He must've thought he won the lottery. Anyway, after I saw Hamilton's photo I went back to the jail and visited the dealer. I told him I'd get his charges dropped if he would tell me were I could find Willie. Remember when I told you the District Attorney insisted we drop the charges? Well, it was me, not him, who insisted on that. That favor got the petty little dirtball to roll over on his partner within five minutes. Real honor among thieves. He told me exactly where Willie lived. Turned out he lived in a small, miserable, rusted-out trailer. Even then it took me several weeks to find Willie. Seems his new found income kept him so busy he seldom came home."

Feeling no sense of urgency, Berkich helped himself to some water from a nearby cooler before continuing.

"I could tell you I was looking for information to help solve the case, but at this point it doesn't make any difference. The truth is... I was just trying to get some of that marker money for myself. All that stood in my was a dirtball with a bad attitude."

"But you couldn't have needed the money that bad."

Berkich looked at Mannerheim like he was a stranger who lived on another planet. Despite all their previous conversations, he now found it necessary to explain his basic financial problems to an accountant who should have known better. It amazed Berkich that his friend seemed so totally removed from the circumstances surrounding his plight.

"Oh yeah! You can say that. No matter how things turned out, you can take your education and experience and move on to another big income position. You know how difficult it is moving into a another Security Chief position? Money is tight at my level of management. My slot doesn't pay enough to begin with, and everyone wants a piece of me. You think a police retirement and my salary with Aaron should have been enough? Is that what you're thinking? My police retirement doesn't fully kick in until I'm fifty-five. You seem to have forgotten alimony payments to two ex-wives and three child support payments each and every month. Mix that with a high cost of living in this area and the result is poverty dressed up in a suit."

Mannerheim realized he knew the various pieces, but failed to see the total picture of his friend's desperation. Building desperation that lead to such a conclusion.

"Enough to murder him?"

"Sure. I could sit here and tell you my conscience bothered me. But in truth... it doesn't. I considered it a public service. I couldn't leave him as a witness. I followed Willie as he made his final appearance posing as Logan's bogus player. When he pulled off the road I knew it had to be their meeting place. Figured I had to act before McDonald arrived to pick up the marker money."

Since Berkich was so talkative, and he already acknowledged his legal rights, Danbury thought he would join the discussion to strengthen his case. He had already activated a small recorder he carried for just such an occasion.

"Care to tell us about the actual murder?"

Berkich knew from his experience as an ex-cop he could easily cut a deal with the district attorney. Berkich already knew he would offer them a clean guilty plea in exchange for a shorter stay at a medium security prison, in a cell away from the general prison population because of his background. Considering the victim, he figured a seven-year sentence. He would be out in three.

"Why not. It was so easy. His back was to me so I didn't even see his face. My first concern was getting rid of Willie's car. I just took enough time to pull the body out of sight and cover it with some branches. I figuring I'd do a better job when I returned. Just as I was pulling out and driving north to the Reno airport, I saw McDonald's Cadillac in the rear view mirror. He was turning into the look-out point. When I got down to Reno I parked that piece of junk in the lot, then I took an airport shuttle back to the Hyatt Hotel in Incline Village. Had a couple drinks in their bar before I headed back."

Berkich then phased again, recollected this thoughts, and went on.

"It was totally dark by then. Moon wasn't even out. It took me hours to hike back to the Forest Service fire access road, where I hid my own car. The only thing I forgot was a shovel. The tire iron from my car wasn't the proper tool to dig a deep enough, or big enough grave. After I went a foot down, the damn ground became nothing more than unworkable thick mud, mixed with tree roots. It was also freezing, and I was exhausted from the hike. Figured it was good enough... Nobody would ever find it. I was right... nobody did... just never figured on a dog sniffing it out. Anyway, I left with the fifty thousand dollars in chips I took off Willie's body. Until he heard of Danbury's investigation of Willie's murder, Logan probably figured his missing partner just took off with the money."

"That the reason you just rented a safety deposit box at Tahoe Savings?"

Another example of Danbury's recent homework.

Suddenly Berkich showed more surprise then he exhibited when Danbury first arrested him. He just nodded. Within a minute Berkich was handcuffed and led away by two deputies. Before Lt. Danbury left, he again thanked both Mannerheim and Hamilton for their assistance.

Both just stood in the empty office for a few seconds until Hamilton spoke,

"Mixed blessing. Logan comes up dirty, but Berkich was the one who pulled the trigger. I'd have never thought it."

"Nor me. Well, if you will excuse me, I have to check on something."

"What's your hurry? I was thinking I'd let you buy me a drink."

"Not right now. If things turned out a little differently I would be leading the celebration. How about if you check with me on Tuesday?"

"You got it. Merry Christmas Paul."

"Thanks, Matt. I'm sure it will be."

CHAPTER 30

When a man reaches his mid-forties, or maybe early fifties, a light suddenly flashes that there are fewer years ahead of him than are in back of him. And those years are more unpleasant than what he has already experienced. The thought of one's seventies, eighties and possibly nineties becomes more disagreeable with the image of each passing decade. There becomes so few precious years left. Years to establish whatever dignity one may be able to salvage. Dignity at least in the form of an adequate lifestyle, to offset the loss of other memories... lost youth, fading appearance, diminished sexual prowess, among many others. Those real, those imagined, those enlarged through time in one's memory. To be replaced, at best, with a comfortable existence. Preferably an affluent existence. Possibly even an extravagant existence. Over one's life, which started with boundless confidence, which then turns to stark reality, which then becomes fear. You no longer consider yourself bullet-proof. Your mortality has firmly established itself in your conscience. In the end, fear is possibly the most persuasive motivator. And so it was with Paul Mannerheim. One step at a time his feet of clay were taking him to gate 11.

Mannerheim found his way down the airport stairs and in front of gate 11 where Reno Air flight 442 awaited. As he approached the gate he handed the woman behind the counter his ticket, and asked her to check on the status of several trunks he left in their cargo department when he first arrived. She punched a few keys and examined her computer monitor.

"Yes, Mr. Finn. They have both been loaded onto the flight."

"Fine. Have you announced the boarding instructions yet?"

"Yes, sir. You can board anytime. Your seat is 4 D. The flight is on schedule and should depart in about twenty minutes. Arrival time in Seattle will be about 5:10. Have a good flight."

*

Mannerheim/Finn settled into his seat and fastened his seatbelt. Because the banks would be closed on Monday for Christmas, it would be at least Tuesday afternoon before all the bankers started to question why their funds were not received back from Aaron Davenport's casino. Of the five banks that prepared cash transfers, only one of them actually had its funds arrive at the casino. The funds from the other four, which amounted to ten million dollars, were actually in two large trunks now occupying space below in the luggage compartment of Reno Air Flight 442. The whole process also left a nice paper trail for the insurance companies. There would be no confusion on their part when they had to determine the amount of the check needed to reimburse Aaron Davenport.

Seated next to Finn was a man in his early fifties. He rummaged through the magazine pouch attached to the back of the seat in front of him, but found nothing of interest, so he turned to Mannerheim and asked,

"First time in Reno, Mr...?"

"Finn. No in fact, until recently, I used to live at Lake Tahoe."

"Beautiful area. So you're relocating?"

"Yeah, no job security in the corporate structure."

"Isn't that the truth. I'm going back to Seattle, but I'm worried what I'll find on my return. This vacation may have been my last hurrah. I'm a Boeing engineer, and the company is talking about laying off another couple thousand workers. There is just no job security anymore."

"I know what you mean." Finn's eyes shifted to the panel of knobs and lights above his head. "I worked seven years with people I could seldom, if ever, trust. You occupy an office you will never own. Even the chair you are sitting in belongs to people you can not trust. Outside the door is a name plate that just slides out, while a new one with a different name, slides in. It all provides nothing more than the substance of smoke. Temporary positions of power, then a shuffling of faces, followed by new positions of power. Just to be repeated every few years. No benefit to man or humanity. Just feelings of ego gratification for those in positions of power. In the end it all means nothing. Just memories of smoke." He then turned back to the Boeing engineer. "Yeah, I know what you mean."

"I hope they at least provided you with a good severance package."

"Adequate... very adequate."

Did you enjoy the book?
Know an Accountant? Know a Gambler?
Or just someone who enjoys a good Mystery?
Send them a gift of the book with the enclosed order form.

Mystery Book Publishers Inc.
P.O. Box 52761 · Bellevue, WA. 98015-2761

Customer: _____

Address: _____

Suite: _____ Apt. # _____
City: _____ State: _____
Country: _____ Zip: _____

Ship to:
_____
(If different from Customer address)

Address: _____

Suite: _____ Apt. # _____
City: _____ State: _____
Country: _____ Zip: _____

Book Title	Quantity	Price	Total
Murder in Tahoe (Large Tradeback Softcover Edition)	_____	x $ 13.95 U.S. (or $19.95 Canadian)	$ _____

(Includes Shipping & Handling)

Sales Tax *if* Washington State Resident (8.2%)   1.14 *Per Book*   _____

Make check payable to: Mystery Book Publishers Inc.   **Total** $ _____

Did you enjoy the book?
Know an Accountant? Know a Gambler?
Or just someone who enjoys a good Mystery?
Send them a gift of the book with the enclosed order form.

Mystery Book Publishers Inc.
P.O. Box 52761 · Bellevue, WA. 98015-2761

Customer: _____

Address: _____

Suite: _____ Apt. # _____
City: _____ State: _____
Country: _____ Zip: _____

Ship to:
(If different from Customer address)

Address: _____

Suite: _____ Apt. # _____
City: _____ State: _____
Country: _____ Zip: _____

Book Title	Quantity	Price	Total
Murder in Tahoe (Large Tradeback Softcover Edition)	_____	x $ 13.95 U.S. (or $19.95 Canadian) (Includes Shipping & Handling)	$ _____
		Sales Tax *if* Washington State Resident (8.2%)	**1.14** *Per Book*
		Make check payable to: Mystery Book Publishers Inc. **Total**	$ _____